JOHN SOLOMON, INCOGNITO AND
THE WISDOM OF SOLOMON:
THE ADVENTURES OF
JOHN SOLOMON, VOLUME 10

H. BEDFORD-JONES

JOHN SOLOMON, INCOGNITO

AND

THE WISDOM OF SOLOMON

THE ADVENTURES OF JOHN SOLOMON, VOLUME 10

H. BEDFORD-JONES

COVER BY
JOHN COUGHLIN

STEEGER BOOKS • 2023

JOHN SOLOMON, INCOGNITO

PROLOGUE

THE HUNTED MAN
AND HIS HUNTER

MY FRIEND Abe has a store in San Francisco. It is not a shop; it is literally a store, a *magasin*. There you may find Chinese cloisonne marked "Ta Ming" and hailing from the clever factory in Kobe; or other cloisonne, unmarked, hailing from the Palace of Heaven in Peking. You may even find a *sang-de-boeuf* vase finer than that in the British Museum.

When Abe showed me the yellow sceptre, among other things, he told me:

"This is a sceptre of good luck, or Ju-i. The word means 'as you desire.' This came from Chinatown—one of our buyers saw it in a window there. As the inscription shows, it dates from the time of Wan Li, who came to the throne in 1522."

I quoted Laufer to the effect that no specimen of the Ju-i in existence antedates K'ien-lung, and that inscriptions are highly suspicious; whereat Abe fell into troubled thought. However, it was a very beautiful piece of yellow *deng-ho,* the rare soapstone which the Chinese value by the ounce. The relief carvings were exquisite. An imperial piece, beyond a doubt.

Passing on to other treasures, I temporarily forgot the yellow sceptre. Some weeks later I mentioned it while talking to Jim Debray, the revenue man. Jim nibbed his specs uneasily and gave me a look, as though to say that he could tell things if he would.

"From what I figure," he said, "there's a lot of blood on that sceptre. Sure, I know something about it—or rather, I can guess.

Ever hear of Cap'n Wrexham and his schooner? Well, he's the only one who knows the whole story."

Jim showed me newspaper clippings about Wrexham, which I copied into a notebook. A year afterward I became well acquainted with Captain Wrexham; this was in Martinique, after Wrexham had left Louisiana. He had John Coffee with him—but that is another story. I must stick to the sceptre.

"May you have your heart's desire!" This is the symbolic meaning of the Ju-i when used as a gift. And here is the story of that yellow sceptre which Wrexham once owned.

II

WHEN WREXHAM struck San Francisco he became a three-day hero along the waterfront. A pilot brought in the beautiful little schooner. One lonely Kanaka, dying as he stood, was perched in the bow. Beside the pilot stood Wrexham, the only other left aboard; he had been at the wheel three days and nights, was staggering on his feet, but appeared as spruce as ever.

He was a rough man in ways and speech, yet with good blood behind him: Canadian, out of Devon originally. Ptomaine poisoning had wiped out his crew save for the lone Kanaka, who died as the anchor went down, and Wrexham himself was not untouched. However, after a bit of sleep, he went ashore to get a crew.

His story was straight as a string. He was owner and master of the *Nautilus,* a rarely beautiful craft, a schooner in miniature. She was more private yacht than trader, and was just now in ballast. More than one shrewd speculator along the waterfront spat into the tide and hinted darkly that there were tales of this craft where *he* had come from; but no man ventured more.

The schooner was glistening from keelson to truck, tended like a yacht. So was her master. Bluff features, square-trimmed brown beard that curled about his strong lips, well-tailored clothes of semi-uniform cut, and a glory of a black pearl blazing

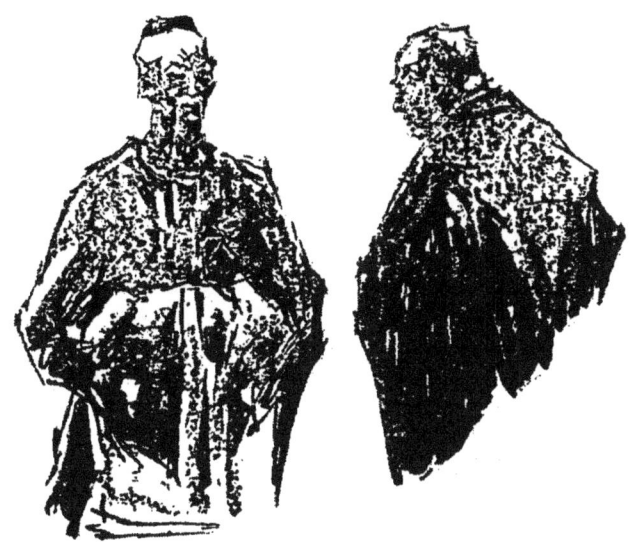

in his white cravat—this was Wrexham. However, as aforesaid, he was not gentle in his ways.

He wanted a crew instantly; five men at least, since he was bound for the big ditch and the Atlantic. Queerly enough, he could pick up no hands. An official of the Seamen's Union told him bluntly that no honest man would ship with him; so Wrexham knocked the official sprawling, paid a ten-dollar fine for assault, and went his ways.

As a matter of fact, there were whispers out, and Wrexham had no lack of money—a bad sign. Nothing straightforward, you understand; whispers only. Whence these whispers emanated, no man would or could declare. Perhaps a Chinese comprador in lower Washington Street might have told, had he so desired.

At all events, Wrexham had a sorrowful day of it. He was desperate for a crew, but the blacklist was out against him and he was absolutely helpless. This did not improve his temper in the least.

"This here's a rum go, and no mistake!" he swore heatedly. "Down me, will they? I'll beat 'em! Curse their rotten laws—if this was some place I know, I'd have a crew in jig time. And I'll get 'em, too; get 'em, if I have to sign on yellow men or black! Tom Wrexham ain't beat yet, by a good deal."

The uneasy light in his eyes belied his bluff words. No man knew better than Tom Wrexham what lay behind him—what evils, what blood dotting the past, what iron-hearted incidents of life lurking in the background. With all this, one could not help liking the man. There was no weakness in him.

He tried hard. He offered bribes, he hinted at crimps and old-fashioned methods, he laid French gold over the counter. All in vain. At length he stormed away and for a space hid himself in the great city, still seeking.

Evening found him in Chinatown, in the restaurant of Thousand Blessings and Good Auguries. He sat at a marble-topped table of imitation teak and scowled at the brilliant room. His eyes bit at the weirdly banging orchestra. No waiter came to him. At length he rose, strode to the desk of the cashier, put out one arm and took the startled yellow man by the neck.

"Listen!" he said. "You say 'no savvy' again and I'll wring your blasted neck, savvy that? There's my order. Fill it, and fill it shipshape—or I'll turn this place into a bleedin' wreck!"

He let the half strangled man drop and went back to his table, raging blindly against the world. Presently a waiter arrived with the food he had ordered. Captain Wrexham flung gold on the table, but the waiter did not pick it up; instead, departed in silence.

"Oh—ho!" Wrexham whistled to himself. "So that's the lay, is it? What've these beggars got against me, anyhow? Hm! I wonder, now—they didn't have a hand in blacklistin' me? No. There's no blasted reason for it. Still, I was a reg'lar fool to come to Chinatown. Why didn't I stop in the city?"

He ate, and ate heartily, then drew some Dutch cheroots from his pocket, bit at one, and began to smoke, sipping at his tea from time to time.

A bareheaded yellow man wearing thick spectacles and the unostentatious lounge suit of a business man, appeared in the ornately decorated room. The waiters spoke to him very respect-fully, as well they might. He made his way straight to the table of Wrexham, blinked at the skipper, and bowed.

"You are Captain Wrexham," he said quietly, his voice smooth as silk. "I am Li Toy, the humble owner of this place, which is unworthy to be graced by your presence. May I speak with you?"

Wrexham nodded and motioned to the chair opposite. Li Toy sat down, lighted a cigarette, and the two men eyed each other. Wrexham instinctively sensed a battle and stiffened. In this, as it proved, he was not quite correct.

"Well?" he demanded aggressively. His somewhat protruding eyes fastened themselves upon the slender yellow man. "Well?"

"Pardon my boldness," said Li Toy gently. "I read of you in the papers this morning. I have heard rumours that you desire to obtain a few men to serve as crew on your schooner. Several men of my business society would be very glad to reach New Orleans in this way."

Captain Wrexham took the cheroot from his lips, staring at his *vis-à-vis*. "Here's a rum go!" he ejaculated in astonishment. "Know me, do you! Is this here a restaurant, or a crimp's parlour?"

Li Toy smiled and puffed at his cigarette. "I can provide six men," he stated briefly. "To-morrow night. Naturally, I would wish a trifling compensation."

"Oh!" said Wrexham. His tone was significant. "Oh! So that's the game! How much?"

"Not money," was the reply, accompanied by a gesture of deprecation. "Not money—no. A present. Cumshaw. Some-where aboard your ship is a yellow soapstone sceptre of good luck, and if you will give me this I will set the men aboard."

A slight start shook the square shouldered frame of Wrex-ham. "Oh!" he said again. "How d'you know what's aboard my craft?"

Li Toy merely shrugged and made no other response.

"All right," answered Wrexham heavily. "All right. It's a bargain. I'll have the papers ready and we'll slip out after dark.

Put the men aboard at seven. I s'pose they want to slip away from the police, eh? Put 'em aboard at six bells. I'll give you the yellow stone Ju-i then."

Li Toy rose, bowed, and departed. After a moment Captain Wrexham also rose, took up his hat, and strode from the place, shoulders back. He went down the stairs to the street, and went down the narrow street to Grant Avenue. There, amid the honk of automobiles and the buzz of passing crowds, his shoulders sagged suddenly.

The man, for a moment, went to pieces as though he had received a mortal blow. He slowly went ahead, and came to a halt by the railing which surrounds the church lot of the Paulist fathers. He clutched at this railing with one hand, and stood there for a space, motionless.

"So that's it!" he muttered, licking his lips with his tongue. "So that's it! Goin' to murder me, are they? Blast 'em! That's the reason for everything—that cursed junk we looted under Palembang Island!"

He understood that he was a doomed man.

Back in the dim distance, back months and years in the Dutch seas, he visualized again that clash with the Chinese trading junk at Palembang. The junk, he knew, belonged to the rich trader, Chuen Ying, of Macassar; a powerful man, no son of Han, but a Manchu prince who was earning his bread at trade. Wrexham's thoughts reached backward unpleasantly. He had almost forgotten about Chuen Ying and that junk.

Wrexham had done the work; no doubt about it! That junk had been looted and burned. The loot had been fabulous; much of it still reposed aboard the Nautilus. Among that loot was a magnificently carved sceptre of the yellow *deng-ho*, the priceless golden soapstone.

The inferences were frightfully plain. This chap, Li Toy, knew about the yellow sceptre. Therefore, he knew where that sceptre had come from. Therefore, he knew that Tom Wrexham had looted and burned the junk under Palembang Island. Therefore, the trader, Chuen Ying, of Macassar, had a world-wide net outspread to catch Captain Tom Wrexham—and Wrexham was in the net!

"Ah!" The word was wrenched from him like a groan. "If I had those Kanakas back now, it'd be a bit of all right, what? Dammit! He'll put those chinks aboard me, and we'll go. Then they'll do for me, six of 'em, and bring the craft into San Pedro wi' some lying story. And what can I do?"

He could do one thing—back out of his bargain. But Captain Tom Wrexham had never backed out of anything in his life. The thought drew him erect, sent his shoulders back once more, sent his jaw swinging forward under the square brown beard.

"Results!" he muttered. "Cause an' effect—consequences— retribution—aye, that's the proper word, now. Retribution! But if anybody's going to bring retribution home to Tom Wrexham, it ain't any yellow-crawed chink—no, sir! And he didn't care a whoop if I guessed his object; that's the worst of it. Just calmly eliminated me. Wonder if Chuen Ying is here in Frisco? Wish he'd come aboard me, just once! I'd show him!"

Wrexham strode to the corner and watched a blinking, yellow-eyed cable car go lurching up the hill. A uniform, seldom seen in Chinatown, came swinging easily along the street—a policeman, dangling his stick and whistling.

From his pocket the seaman produced cheroots. He bit at one and lighted it. As the officer came past, he turned and extended one.

"Smoke with you. See here, I want to hire some niggers, and I'm a stranger in the city. Tell me where the black quarter is, if there is one! Or else, where I'd be apt to pick up two or three blacks. Blacker the better."

The officer sniffed the thin cheroot appreciatively, eyed Wrexham, caught the note of authority in the voice, and nodded.

"Sure, sor," he responded, and gave the required information.

III

THE TINY beautiful schooner of Captain Wrexham
was moored in the fairway, at considerable distance from
shore.

As arranged, the pilot came aboard slightly before six bells.
A light fog was floating in, and the pilot was distinctly irritated
to find Wrexham alone on the craft.

"Goin' to navigate her single-handed?" he queried.

"Not me." Wrexham chuckled and swept an arm toward
shore. "There's a launch comin' out now with my crew. You'll not
mind a wait while they sign articles?"

"Better not wait," returned the pilot. "You'll need all the tide
there is—hardly a breeze stirrin' until you get outside the gate."

"Ho!" Wrexham chuckled. "You don't know this here craft,
mister! Put me at sea with this breeze, and we'll mark down
seven knots. Still, as you say, we'll not delay. Yonder's my crew,
eh?"

His crew it was, sure enough. The pilot spat disgustedly as six
yellow men filed over the side, followed by another who shook
hands warmly with Captain Wrexham. The latter produced a
long parcel, which Li Toy accepted without examination.

"Better look at it," said Wrexham dryly.

"You have a reputation, cap'n," returned the other. "Your word
is good. May all luck attend you."

"Same to you," and Wrexham grinned.

Li Toy returned to his launch, which puttered away. Captain
Wrexham surveyed his crew of six.

"You savvy capstan?" he inquired. "Then hop to it! I don't want
any tug pulling me between the heads."

The pilot grunted again, spat again, swore again. Presently
he went to the wheel and uttered a low word of amazement as
he found how the schooner responded to canvas and helm. The
yellow men swarmed on the lines handily as Wrexham barked
his orders; she gathered way and began to crawl through the

mist. The yellow men sought the fo'c'sle and stowed away their dunnage.

"No mate?" asked the pilot.

Wrexham grunted. "Mate? Not much. Only one boss on this craft—that's my motto. You keep your eye on those ferry craft, and never bother your brain about my business."

"Sociable brute, ain't you?" retorted the pilot, and said no more.

The evening merged into night, and slowly the schooner slipped toward the Golden Gate, and through. Captain Wrexham was so glad to be gone that he even let the pilot gaff him pretty heavily—not a usual thing with the skipper, by any means. He was trying to get rid of the man, when there came a sudden rush of figures from the companionway.

"Hey, boss!" cried a voice. "Ah craves to git me ashoah right quick!"

"What the devil!" The pilot surveyed five black men who were crowding around him, all of them frantic with terror and green with sickness. The heave of the open sea had done the work.

Wrexham cursed into his beard and eyed the yellow men in the bow. They had drawn together in a clump, watching. He could sense them there in the darkness.

"What's this story they tell?" the pilot turned to Wrexham. "They haven't signed articles—you hired 'em to go along—"

"Listen here, my man!" Wrexham took the pilot's arm and faced him about sharply. "If you want to run this craft, you just say so; I'll act accordin'. If you don't, then pile into that boat o' yours and be on your way."

"Man, you can't take 'em unless they signed on!" exclaimed the pilot. Around him crowded the black men, violently ill, imploring him with a babel of cries to take them ashore. "It's against the law—"

"The law be damned!" said Wrexham, calmly. "I'm on the high seas, and you know it. Shall I throw you into your boat?"

Wrexham put his hand into his pocket and shoved out a gun.

The blacks uttered yells of terror as he booted them from the quarterdeck. He approached the pilot, and the latter jumped in all haste.

"You'll hear from this later!" was his parting threat. Wrexham only laughed.

For a moment Wrexham stood at the wheel, eyeing grimly the moaning blacks. Then his voice bit sharply into the darkness. In response, six yellow men silently came to him, and obeyed his orders. They threw the five black men into the hold and clapped on the hatch again.

"That way," reflected Wrexham with a sigh, "I'll have a crew—if I get clear. If not, why worry?"

He divided the crew into watches, sent the off watch below, picked a man for the wheel and made sure the Celestial could follow a course. Then, shoving his gun into his coat pocket, with just a trifle of ostentation he went below to his cabin. The skylight directly above him was open, and he left it open. One of the yellow men, a cook, was already busy with things in the galley.

In his cabin, Captain Wrexham took off his coat, standing beneath the open skylight as he did so, and carelessly tossed the garment on a chair.

"The cursed blacks!" he said softly. "I slipped up badly there—might have known they'd go under when they hit the swell. Oh, lord! It's a rum go, sure enough. My only chance is to catch 'em now, while it's dark. I know every inch of the deck, every seam and nail—and they don't."

He laughed silently at himself. What had been the use of hiring those black thugs, after all? None. They were down below, groaning their black hearts out. They might come in useful later on, if—*if!* The word bulked large.

Leaving his coat where he had flung it, so that the yellow men above might see it through the skylight, Wrexham donned a peajacket that concealed his white shirted shape, and went on deck again, silent as a cat.

He stood there in the dark eddies of mist, and imagination worked strong within him, fermenting. He could imagine terrible things of those six yellow men. Wrexham really knew little about the Chinese, individually or collectively, but he could imagine a good deal—and did.

Now, as he stood here, tragedy dogged his shadow, unseen. All his life it had been the same story; a dogged fighter, making many mistakes, careless of life or death, only holding fast with grim resolve to the faith of his word. Wrexham never broke his word. There lay tragedy, also, in the past. Keeping his word to worse men had led him into more than one pitfall, more than one deed which troubled his sleep o' nights. A lonely man, he could not sense what was wrong within him; but he believed in surviving through invariably getting home the first blow. Well, Tom Wrexham had survived; but at some expense to his peace of mind.

As he stood motionless, a dark spot in the mist, he sensed a shadowy movement behind him. He gripped the automatic in his pocket and waited. It was the yellow cook, coming from the galley, a glitter of steel in his hand. The figure came close to that of Wrexham, and the hand flashed up.

Wrexham whirled and pistoled the man on the spot.

No sooner had he done so, than a horrible wave of realization held him petrified. The cook had been going to the rail with a pan of potato parings—that was all. But, as Wrexham stared, a lantern flashed on him, a shrill yell leaped at him, and pattering of bare feet wakened him.

An angry scream, and a shot. The bullet whipped Wrexham's beard. He answered it, and a man fell. More shrill yells—yells of terror, of amazement, of fear and wild rage. The four remaining yellow men came pouring on Wrexham. One had a pistol, and used it; the others, knives.

Desperate, maddened by his own precipitate action, yet cool to face the peril, Tom Wrexham justified his reputation in this moment. He knew every inch of the deck—every line, every rack at the rail, every crack in the seams underfoot puttied against the tropic sun. The darkness and mist covered the schooner, cloaked everything except the spat-spat of red as the pistols jetted flame. The one lantern fell and guttered out in blood.

Something ran up the rigging, and a knife sang down at Wrexham. It reached him, but he fired up. A scream trailed out and was gone alongside. Blood gushing down his left arm. Wrexham pulled the knife from his shoulder and went on about his business. Presently another shot and a choking cough—that was all.

Into the dim light of the binnacle came Wrexham. He reached out a reddened hand to the wheel, peered forward at the course, and nodded.

"Lucky I hired that outfit of niggers!" he muttered. "I'll knock 'em up presently."

I V

A T   T H I S   same hour, two men sat in a private room of the restaurant of Thousand Blessings and Good Auguries. One of these men was Li Toy. The other was a tall, severe-featured Manchu, who bore himself like a prince.

Upon the table between the two men lay the yellow sceptre of good luck.

"I will tell you this," said the Manchu gravely. "I came here to this city because I was apprised that this man, this Captain Wrexham, was on his way here. I came to meet him and to get this Ju-i from him. Why? Because it was once the property of the Son of Heaven, and his hands are unworthy to touch it; also, because he stole it from me in other days, and I like to get my property back from thieves. Now I shall take the money which its honourable sale will fetch, and I will go whence I came—to New Orleans. You are certain the six men will obey instructions?"

"Certain, honourable sir," humbly responded Li Toy. "They will mail letters to me at each port. They have sworn to guard the life of this white man at all costs, and to bring him safely to the country of Louisiana. But," he added plaintively, "I am sure I do not understand your honorable wishes! I think that I should have ordered those men to kill Wrexham at once."

"Very likely," said the Manchu dryly. "Very likely! But I wish him brought alive and well into my hands. Here, I can do nothing except kill him. There, in Louisiana, I have friends—and I shall enjoy myself at my leisure."

Li Toy assented, in slow comprehension.

That is why the yellow sceptre finally found its way to Post Street. And that, too, is why Li Toy never received any letters from the six men he had put aboard the *Nautilus*. All because Captain Tom Wrexham had an uneasy conscience!

Wrexham, however, sailed on south with his five black men for crew, and felt easier in his mind than for many a long day. That was one of the tragical ironies of his life.

BOOK I — THE STEWARD

CHAPTER I

"EVEN A MANCHU CAN
MAKE MISTAKES"

IN THE old French quarter of New Orleans, there stands a house built by the great Marigny, who once owned all this portion of the town. This house has sheltered princes. Men, numbering their slaves by the thousand, have sat beneath its tapestries and sconces. Now, it is a ruinous hovel. A musty bookstall huddles under its lordly *porte-cochère;* the bare brick walls echo to voices of foreigners. Against the bookstall snuggles a dingy restaurant, a café where one may buy Turkish or Chinese or Greek dishes, where the tables are filthy and unwashed.

At one of these tables sat two men, under the broken-faced clock on the wall.

One was a Chinaman, or passed for such. In reality, he was a Manchu who made his living by distilling illegal spirits down on the Gulf Coast. Once he had borne princely titles.

Now he was old, weary, disease-smitten. Two things out of his past remained unchanged, being things of the spirit. One was the keen black eye, the other was the firm, resonant voice.

The second man was pudgy, cheaply dressed, small of stature. His hair was grey. His eyes were of clear china-blue, set in a face absolutely devoid of expression. He seemed an inoffensive and cringing clerk, outworn and feeble. His voice held a Cockney whine.

"So me old friend Adrien Lavergne is dead!" he said. "I might 'ave knowed it. I'm growin' old, just like that. So Lavergne is gone to 'is long 'ome! And 'e left a daughter?"

The Manchu assented. He was a man of severe dignity.

"He died very suddenly last winter," he responded in flawless English. "Fortunately, his daughter Aline has attained her majority."

"Oh!" said the pudgy little man. "Fortunately? And why so?"

"Because she has an uncle, David Macarty, and a distant cousin, his son Felix. Her uncle is a rapacious wolf. Her cousin is a vulture. And she believes evil of no man."

The white man digested this information slowly. He produced a plug of black tobacco, from which he whittled particles into a vile old clay pipe. At length he lighted this pipe and sighed wheezily.

"You are a werry observing man, Mr. Ah Lee—by the way, 'ow did it 'appen as you went and took that 'ere name?"

The other shrugged lightly. "One name serves as well as another. My own I do not wish to use, as you know. This name satisfies white men, and those of my own race—"

"Ain't askin' questions. I see." The little Cockney nodded. "As I was a-goin' to say, you're a werry observing man, just like that. But even a Manchu can make mistakes."

Ah Lee started slightly. He bent upon his companion a regard which was keen, stern, sharp, and swift as a sword-stroke. One gained the distinct impression that he held the dictum of this pudgy blank-faced man in the highest respect.

"It is written," he replied almost humbly, "that the superior man does not disdain whatever advice may come to his ears."

The white man sighed wheezily.

"Adwice," he observed, "is all werry well in its place, I says, but I ain't got none to give, Mr. Ah Lee. Adrien Lavergne was me friend, just like that! I knowed 'im well. And 'is daughter ain't no fool. She ain't one to be mistook about that 'ere Macarty."

Ah Lee frowned over this for a moment. Then, when he spoke, his voice was soft.

"I have met her often. We have talked much together. She is a flower whose petals have not been touched by any harsh wind. I would do much to save her, Mr. Solomon."

The blue eyes of Solomon dwelt upon him in unruffled calm.

"And what 'as she got to be saved from, sir?"

"I am not sure." The Manchu leaned forward. He dipped his finger in the dregs of his tea, and upon the dirty tablecloth drew a faint outline.

"Here is Cypremort island, on the bayou. The larger portion, so, is the Lavergne plantation. This thin strip, across the bayou, is the Macarty plantation. During the War, David Macarty made much money. Whenever Miss Lavergne comes to New Orleans, she comes in the Macarty steam yacht, with David or Felix Macarty as escort. She would believe no ill of them. Yet they have ruined her, and hold her in a net from which she cannot escape."

Solomon scraped out his pipe, carefully, and refilled it.

"And 'ow is that?" he inquired.

Ah Lee made it clear that he was speaking largely from hearsay. Most of his time was spent in the back bayous and canebrakes. There, in his business of making and selling arrack and rice wine, he was in constant touch with the numbers of outlaws who had refuge in the brakes; with the fishermen, white and brown and yellow, with the negroes and the Cajuns. Thus, what Ah Lee knew was only the gossip of the bayous.

"There is a man named Philbrick, John Philbrick," he said, "who is the overseer of the Lavergne plantation. He is an old fool and a drunkard. None the less, he would give his life for Miss Lavergne! Since the death of her father, Adrien Lavergne, who made some very foolish contracts, this Philbrick has been fighting a losing battle. At the same time, he has been trying to keep the girl in ignorance of her financial condition. He has taken the entire load upon his shoulders in the effort to save her trouble and worry.

"Miss Lavergne leaves all business to him. With him, the Macartys have had dealings. Now they are trying to get rid of him at all costs. Felix Macarty is down there now. I expect to hear any day that Philbrick has been poisoned or arrested or in some way got rid of, so that Felix may take over the place of overseer."

Solomon sucked at his pipe, then asked a wheezy question.

"And what's 'e after? Is 'e in love with 'er?"

"Undoubtedly. All men are," replied the Manchu simply. It was a plain statement of fact. "But this is not the ulterior objective. The Macartys want possession of the whole island, either by marriage or otherwise. Their reason, I do not know. It is a mystery."

Again there ensued a slight silence.

"So she is up 'ere with 'er blessed uncle, is she?" asked Solomon.

"Yes, for a week of the opera, I understand. David Macarty is her great-uncle, I believe; at least, the relationship is not close. It is a great pity that the girl is so dependent on John Philbrick. That man is weak—a weak stick on which to lean. He means well, and he is sincere. However, he is not equal to his task; he is not equal to fighting the Macartys. They have great influence. I imagine that the girl was brought here for a time so that Felix Macarty, who remained at the island, might remove Philbrick.

The old fool is a dreamer, is drunk most of the time, and is terribly afraid of the Macartys. Yet he fights!"

The expressionless face of Solomon showed a faint trace of a smile.

"Even a Manchu can make mistakes!" he said again. "A dreamer—afraid—and yet 'e fights! That 'ere Philbrick ain't such a bad sort."

Disquiet flitted across the wrinkled features of Ah Lee.

This phrase on the lips of Solomon, so obviously a gentle rebuke, seemed to render him uneasy. He leaned back in his chair, brought forth a cigarette-case, and lighted a cigarette. His black eyes searched the once more expressionless face of Solomon.

"While I'm a-thinkin' about it, Mr. Ah Lee," and the blue eyes struck up suddenly, "I suppose you ain't been an' found anything o' that 'ere man you've been wantin' to find a mortal long while? That 'ere Cap'n Wrexham?"

Something moved in the face of the Manchu—rather, underneath the face. It was as though the name of Wrexham provoked, deep inside of him, some terrible convulsion.

"Yes," he answered quietly. "Yes. We shall come together before long. I may wait a long time to pay my debts, but ultimately they are paid."

"Yes," commented Solomon, "I feel sorry for this 'ere Cap'n Wrexham. 'E must be a mortal bad sort o' man, a regular bad 'un!"

The Manchu laughed harshly. "Do you know the last thing he did in the coral seas? Somewhere in the Philippines, it was. He deliberately betrayed two men and a woman who trusted him. Betrayed them to death and shame! I heard of it recently through friends."

The blue eyes rested reflectively upon that wrinkled, powerful face.

"You 'ave friends all about the world, Mr. Ah Lee?"

"You also have," retorted the Manchu, with a smile. "I have not known you long, yet I have known of you for a long time."

Solomon chuckled wheezily. "Well, now, what about this 'ere Dawid Macarty? What's the name of 'is blessed craft?"

"She is called the *Watersprite*. A small motor cruiser—"

"Does she 'ave a steward?" interjected Solomon.

"Yes."

Again a space of silence. These two singular men regarded each other and smoked for a long while. What thoughts were passing behind that wrinkled saffron mask, behind that blank and pudgy countenance, remained a mystery. At length Solomon tapped his pipe empty and broke the silence.

"If so be as I might ask a bit of 'elp from you, sir—"

"My friend," said the Manchu earnestly, "I am at your service, with all that I have! Especially if it is a question of helping Miss Lavergne."

"That's it," assented Solomon. "I want this 'ere steward took off Macarty's craft, and I want it done mortal quick. This werry day! I want 'im to up an' disappear, just like that. It'll cost some money; 'ere's a thousand dollars—"

The Manchu dignifiedly pushed back the roll of bills which Solomon produced.

"Let no money pass between us. This is a matter of our friendship, and of Miss Lavergne. Am I a poor man? Nonsense! Soon I shall be dead, and I wish to see her in safety."

"Werry good," said Solomon placidly. "But if you and me is a-goin' into partnership on this 'ere deal, it's likely to cost you more'n money."

"What do you mean?" The Manchu gave Solomon a quick sharp glance.

"I don't rightly know." Solomon remained impassive. "But I 'ave a notion that Prowidence is a-workin' things out, Mr. Ah Lee. Sometimes Prowidence don't like to see a man payin' of 'is own debts. If so be as you want to draw out—"

"My word is never taken back," said the cold Manchu. "That steward shall vanish to-day."

"Werry good, sir. Does Macarty or 'is skipper 'ire 'is crew?"

"Macarty is his own skipper. It is his hobby."

"So much the better. And where's 'e stoppin' at?"

"At the 'St. Charles,' with Miss Lavergne. Some engine work is being done on the yacht."

Solomon pushed back his chair. "And 'ow long are you a-goin' to be in town?"

"Only a day or so. I am arranging to market a consignment of arrack. Those two Arabs you sent me are good men; I owe you thanks for them. They know the work. By the way, I think that on this trip Miss Lavergne is arranging to mortgage some property of hers in Latouche. Macarty's game may be to force her to marry his son, or to sell him the plantation. I have discovered nothing of it."

Solomon nodded with his complacent air.

"Werry good. I'll 'ave me eye on things, thankin' you kindly."

The two men left the restaurant and separated. Solomon, who walked a bit stiffly, made his way back to Canal Street and hailed an empty taxicab. He handed the driver a large bill.

"Motor up an' down," he ordered the astonished driver. "Anywheres you like. I want to think, just like that!"

He popped into the cab and lighted his pipe. For a space he sat motionless, while the car took the route out to Metairie, then he removed his shabby cap and shook his head.

"Dang it, there ain't no sense to this 'ere thing!" he muttered. "Except for that there Ah Lee, I'll 'ave to play me own 'and. I'm a-gettin' old, and I ain't what I used to be. Just because 'er father was a werry good friend o' mine is no reason for me makin' a bloody fool of myself! But that's just what I'm a-doin' of this blessed minute."

He puffed in reflective silence. Then he spoke again.

"I'll 'ave to depend on Providence, just like that! Providence ain't never yet failed to make good, I says, and ain't likely to start in bein' a failure at this late date. Yes, sir! Just you trust in Prowidence an' do your mortal best to be 'appy, as the old gent said when 'e buried 'is third.

"So I'll go ahead with me plan. That there Ah Lee is a werry good man in 'is own way, too. But even a Manchu can make mistakes. An' 'e went an' made two this blessed day—first about Miss Lavergne, and next about that 'ere Philbrick."

The taxicab drove on.

At five-thirty that evening, Mr. John Solomon called at the "St. Charles" and sent up his card to Mr. David Macarty. With it, he sent word that he wished to apply for the position of steward aboard the yacht *Watersprite*.

At five-fifty, David Macarty had engaged his new steward.

CHAPTER II

HOW AN ANGEL MAY PROVE
TO BE A CLIENT

WHEN THE knock of destiny sounded at his door, Jack Fortier was discharging his typist.

"It's no use, Miss Smith—have to tell you the truth!" he said cheerfully. "Six months without a paying client has busted me. I'll have to take down my shingle and get a job in somebody's office."

The typist took the proffered cheque with some embarrassment. She liked this husky young lawyer from the back districts. She was sorry to see him acknowledge failure.

"Perhaps," she faltered, "perhaps a week or so—I could do without—"

"Bless your soul!" exclaimed Fortier heartily. "Nothing doing that way, my dear girl! I wouldn't have it. I thank you, in any case; I appreciate your offer—"

At this instant came the rap at the door of the inner office. Both Fortier and Miss Smith started.

"No chance! It's somebody with a bill I'd forgotten. But you might see who—"

Miss Smith opened the door.

"Is Mr. Fortier here?" inquired a voice. "There was no one in the outer office—"

"Come right in, please," said the typist. "Very well, Mr. Fortier, I'll get out those letters immediately." The glance she flung Fortier was roguish. She disappeared.

Fortier held a chair for his visitor. He felt helpless, disconcerted, before this vision. Perhaps she, on her part, felt a bit disconcerted over the youthful appearance of the lawyer. He was rather square of feature—those odd angles of the face that show a new generation in the city, a generation not worn down into the mould of citied life and form.

"I am at your service, madame," he said formally, and dropped into his swinging chair.

"You are not the Mr. Fortier I expected to see," she said quietly. "They told me at the bank that you were an elderly man."

Fortier glanced at her. Perhaps a slight compression of the lip showed his inner disappointment. He rose.

"The error has happened many times, madame," he said. "The other Fortier has offices on the floor above this. May I conduct you?"

"No," she said, leaning back in her chair. "No. Sit down, please. I—I must think a moment. I believe that I could trust you."

Jack Fortier sat down again. He was tremendously astonished, even agitated—that last sentence of her speech had held a remarkable simplicity. He perceived that he was dealing with no ordinary person, no woman who concealed her thoughts deftly. This girl was very frank. The grey eyes which she had bent upon him were startling in their clarity. It seemed to him that she must be reading into his heart.

"Excuse me," he said, "but—but I cannot take advantage of a mistake—"

"Please be quiet for a moment," she said calmly. "It is I who am taking advantage of it."

Fortier leaned back in his chair and endured her scrutiny.

He gave her look for look—who could help it? And it speaks well for him that, under his steady regard, the girl felt no twinge of evil. Women feel such things strongly from the eyes of men.

Fortier knew that his own strong-willed aloofness was reeling under the very shock of her presence. He had never seen another such person in New Orleans. A girl indeed, yet matured beyond her years by Southland suns frail and delicate as finest steel, a fair flower crowned by waves of brownish hair and lighted by eyes of golden grey.

It was, for Jack Fortier, a moment of destiny. With her presence, he became aware that a sudden peace and sweetness had descended upon this office of his, this bare room. You have seen the Chinese magnolia, that slender tree, and you know how it perfumes a whole garden with the richest, most rare and subtle of all scents! So Aline Lavergne sat there, and from her exquisite spirit came a poised richness into all his world.

So strong was her personality that, silent, she still dominated. Even then, in this first moment, Fortier sensed how she was going to startle and confound him, and leave him aching with the hurt of loving her; and not him alone, but all who came into contact with the calm peace of her level eyes.

"I should like to know," her voice wakened him, "who you are and where you come from, Mr. Fortier. I am very uncertain whom I can safely trust. You will pardon me—"

Fortier's air made this seem quite the usual thing from client to attorney.

"It is simply told," he said, smiling a little. "I have done my reading in the back country—in the office of Judge Saizon, in St. Landry Parish. Six months ago I was admitted to the Bar and came to New Orleans. I have been here six months. I know nobody. I have not had a client, except in a few charity cases. I have had little experience. If you need a very capable attorney, I should suggest that you see the other Fortier—"

"That's enough," she said, and smiled suddenly. "I need an honest man before I need an attorney—and you are one, Mr. Fortier. My need is for advice and help, not for legal trickery."

Fortier inclined his head gravely. "I am at your service, madame."

He could never afterward think of this first meeting with Aline Lavergne and not lapse into an extravagance of ideas. She was so perfectly poised that one thought her a woman of the world, yet she was pure of the world, aloof from it. Aline was no untutored ninny, no ignorant slip who thought that children were left in the cabbage patch. Yet, Fortier understood that she had been all her life in a retired corner of the State, down on the Gulf Coast. About the girl was something untouched and infinitely sweet—a quiet force of character. Later, perhaps, you will more clearly understand what is so difficult to reach with words.

She told him of herself and of her family. This was why she had been afraid. David Macarty was concerned in many lines of business, was in touch with many men; she had been in fear lest her present errand become known to him. She told Fortier about Cypremort island, the greater part of which was her property, and about Philbrick her overseer.

"I have just learned, through an accident," she went on, "that instead of being wealthy I am poor—and shall probably be poorer. I am convinced that my uncle and my cousin are in some way trying to keep me under their control, trying to impoverish me. I have no proofs of this. They are very kind and ostensibly my best friends. But they hate Philbrick, who dislikes them in turn. The antagonism has always been open there."

Fortier nodded, astonished by her perfect poise. Somehow, too, it heartened him—made him see most clearly that this girl had nothing to fear. There are some people to whom no evil can come from within. There are still fewer people to whom no evil can penetrate from without—whose hearts are absolutely immune to the touch or circumstance of evil's corroding finger.

Of this latter class was Aline. The sheer wonder of her held Fortier silent, awed. Two or three times in a life, perhaps, one encounters such a person, and one is liable to the thought that they are too good for this world, moving through life like beings set apart from its realities. This is wrong. In such a person the humanity may be hard to awaken. Once roused, it comes into bloom very powerfully, a sweet and marvellous thing.

"I received a letter to-day from Philbrick," she went on. "You must understand him. Here is an enclosure from his letter—he wrote this."

Fortier took the paper she handed him. He was amazed at the lines of verse. The girl had etched Philbrick swiftly as an old man, a heavy drinker. This dissolute old overseer was, then, a poet! The remarkable thing was the very ecstasy of youth which breathed in the lines; not their perfection, but their spirit. Few men retain that first springing exultation of youthful fire; few men in later life but regret in vain the fled divinity.

"He is a wonderful man," affirmed Aline, "when he is understood. That, I believe, applies to most people."

"It does," assented Fortier slowly. "Only—we seldom find other people worth our understanding. That is the trouble with many of us."

"Now you must read his letter." The girl laid another paper on Fortier's desk. "It will amaze you—particularly the last paragraph. It will also help you to understand things better. Unfortunately, I don't understand them all myself."

Here is as much of Philbrick's letter as is important—a letter written by an old drunken overseer of sixty:

DEAR MAGNOLIA FLOWER: The gulf is blue and sparkling, but the land is dark and sombre. Only good seems to blow in from the sea, only evil comes from the bayous—a miasmatic mist of passions.

Much peddling of liquor hereabouts. No honest corn juice, but heathenish abomination. That saffron fiend, Ah Lee, gives the hands rice wine. I have ordered him off the place; he understands I will shoot on sight. I do not like Asia, anyway. Then there is a new man here, came the day after you left, with a wonderful little schooner. A Captain Wrexham. He has brought some good whisky. A queer devil spewed out of some far corner of the world. He tells wonderful stories. He saw the photographs on the mantel, and I think he has fallen in love with you.

I am horribly afraid—of what, I know not. I am afraid by day and night. Your cousin Felix sits all day fishing just off our dock, and watches. His father's dam is going up daily behind. We must install new pumps at once, but there is not quite enough money.

I think that devil Ah Lee has tried to kill me. Two nights ago I got a big black buck in my room—He weighed two hundred. He was putting a white powder into my whisky decanter when I dropped him. I have great regrets for the whisky. The black was a stranger—probably an outlaw. Don't worry, however. Yours in love,

Jno. Philbrick.

Jack Fortier studied this astonishing letter. Behind it, his mind sensed a looming pattern of dark purposes and evil men. He fancied that this overseer must, despite his admitted terror, contain some great qualities of soul. As he read that letter again, he sensed something more in it, some stratum of conflicting forces which he did not understand. He perceived that Philbrick was no fool. Why this mention of the unknown Captain Wrexham and the Chinaman? And what silent fight was waging between Philbrick and Felix Macarty?

"If I'm going into this," said Fortier slowly, "I must understand everything. First, this Ah Lee. Why does Philbrick write to you about him?"

"Because Ah Lee is a friend of mine," said the girl simply. "You see, Philbrick is very opinionated and stubborn. He knows or suspects that Ah Lee makes liquor and sells it to the negroes. Perhaps; I don't know. I have often met Ah Lee, however, and talked with him. He is interesting, a gentleman, an educated man. He is old and wise. But Philbrick thinks it is dangerous— treats me as though I were a child, bless his honest heart!"

She smiled as she said this.

"Very well," said Fortier. "Then, about Felix Macarty. Would your overseer dare say—"

"Listen, please!" Aline spoke earnestly, swiftly. "Philbrick has been with us for many years. He is almost a member of the family, you see? He has always disliked the Macartys, and they him. But we never discuss the matter at home. You must not consider Philbrick as a servant, but as a very dear friend whom I would trust with my life."

Fortier assented. "This final paragraph—do you believe your Chinese friend tried to murder Philbrick?"

A cloud troubled her clear eyes.

"No. No—that is impossible, incredible! Philbrick doubtless believes it, but I cannot. There must be some other explanation which we don't know."

"Very well. Now, Miss Lavergne, this mention of a dam and pumps—"

"Oh, that is the important thing!" cried the girl swiftly. "You see, we've been in the city for a week or more, and shan't return for another week. Uncle David has been getting his franchise from Baton Rouge—"

The lips of Fortier twitched. "Not so fast, please! What franchise?"

She laughed at her own impetuosity, although the shadow lingered in her clear eyes.

"It gives Uncle David the right to dam the bayou behind the island, in order to form some kind of electric power. Now, something I overheard my uncle say in the hotel yesterday gave me the—the idea that this will hurt our plantation and that he doesn't care. An arm of the bayou overflows our rice fields; they must have a lot of water, you see. If he dams the bayou—"

"He wouldn't be allowed to cut off your water," put in Fortier.

"We can't stop it," she said. "I remember, now, that Philbrick has hinted to me about it. Perhaps he was trying to keep me from suspecting the truth—oh, I feel so helpless! But we shall have to put in pumps and machinery. I have always thought that we were quite rich—and I realize now, after I have been to the bank, that we are not.

"You see," she added naively, "I have never bothered with business. Philbrick has done everything. I have just been a silly, useless spender of money. Now, I hope, I have wakened to something better! And I do know that just before he died my father made some rice contracts. Philbrick has not said much about it, so to-day I got some information at the bank. They said they could not advise me, and sent me to you—or to the other Mr. Fortier. They gave me an outline of the contracts—I have it here."

Jack Fortier frowned.

"Miss Lavergne," he said. "I am interested in this matter. None the less, I hesitate to step in. If the bank sent you to Mr. Fortier, it was because they knew him to be well versed in certain kinds of law. For your own sake—"

"For my own sake," and the girl flashed him a smile, "I ask not skill, but honesty. Uncle David's hands reach very far, I assure you! If he were to discover that I have retained a lawyer, he would probably try to buy you off or else—"

"By all means, come into the open and let him discover it, then!" said Fortier. "Now about those rice contracts—did the bank give you any notes on them? Do you know who holds the contracts?"

"I don't know. Yes, here is a memorandum which the bank furnished me—rather reluctantly, I must say; perhaps it will help you. Now, Mr. Fortier, I must be gone—I do not want my uncle to suspect anything. That is, until I am certain of my own suspicions. Here is a cheque for five hundred dollars—no, I insist! And I may stop in tomorrow and clear up whatever I have forgotten or overlooked to-day."

Fortier tapped the cheque in his fingers, frowning slightly.

"Let us say the day after to-morrow. Miss Lavergne—at any hour. I must run up to Baton Rouge to-night. The member from Opelousas is a very good friend of mine, and he can furnish me some information regarding your uncle. Also, that franchise."

"Very well. And thank you!"

Fortier bowed over her hand gravely. There was in him a touch of rural courtesy which is too often lacking in city life.

"Thank you, Miss Lavergne! The opportunity to be of service to you is, I assure you, its own best reward. And I trust that when you return I may have some news for you."

Aline Lavergne departed.

A little later, the typist tapped on the door of the private office, and entered. She found Fortier sitting in his chair, looking from the window, lost in abstraction. A smile touched her lips.

"Is there anything further to-day, Mr. Fortier?"

He glanced up, and flashed her a responsive smile.

"No, Miss Smith. I am glad to say that the office will remain open for a while yet."

"Oh, I am glad, too—for your sake," she answered.

CHAPTER III

HOW A CLIENT MAY PROVE TO BE A ROGUE

WHILE IN Baton Rouge, his friend in the legislature supplied Fortier with abundance of information—and a word of advice.

"Chuck it, Fortier! It's ruin for you to go against David Macarty, as I believe you hinted you are about to do. The man is powerful. So is his son. Both are unscrupulous, and will not hesitate to wipe you out like a fly on the wall. You can't possibly do a thing against them, and will only ruin your own future. Macarty has a finger in a dozen business pies, and he's infernally clever."

"Much obliged," said Fortier quietly. "See you later."

"Stubborn devil!" retorted his friend. "Don't drag me into it."

Returning to New Orleans, Fortier worked hard getting his facts marshalled in order. When he had finished, he was appalled by the results.

Shortly after luncheon, on the day appointed, Aline Lavergne entered the office. As he received her and made ready to impart what he had gathered. Fortier's face gave no indication of the hopelessness which he felt. Just the contrary, in fact. The thought of Macarty and what was being done to this girl, brought steel into his blue eyes and anger into his heart.

"And what have you learned, Mr. Fortier?" she asked, her calm eyes searching him.

"Enough. I'm afraid. It appears that your father made extremely unwise contracts. Financially very favourable, they bound him to unfortunate things. If the rice crop failed due to mismanagement, he was responsible. The sole person to judge of the mismanagement was the other party to the contract. No business man would have signed such a paper, but your father was a gentleman, not a business man."

"And—does my uncle hold those contracts?"

"I don't know. They still have two years to run. I could discover nothing about them. Do you know whether last year's crop was sold to your uncle?"

"Yes! Philbrick mentioned it several times. The price was very good and—" Fortier's mouth hardened.

"Then there is no doubt of it. Macarty holds the contracts. I presume we shall find that Philbrick was helpless to break them, since they bound the estate and not the living planter. You see, they put the estate absolutely in the power of Macarty. If the crop fails, he alone is the judge—he may declare that the failure is the fault of Philbrick, and then collect his damages."

"But that is unjust!" exclaimed Aline, her eyes widening.

"Exactly. The law makes no pretensions to justice, Miss Lavergne. The Code Napoleon sets a standard of laws, to infringe which is wrong. A contract is a sacred thing. Your father signed a contract, which must be adhered to. Now, let us proceed.

"Here is a map of Latouche Parish, showing your property." Fortier spread out the map before the girl. "Under the name of the Cypremort Power Company, your uncle obtained a franchise giving him large theoretical powers down there. But, provided he dams the bayou and erects a power plant, to whom will it give service?"

Aline glanced up. "Why, nobody! We're twenty miles from Latouche, and there's no other town—"

"Exactly." Fortier made a gesture. "You see? That power plant is a blind! It will never be anything except a dam. Now, then, why did your uncle obtain the right to dam that bayou? Because, in so doing, he would check the overflow of water which made the lower portion of Cypremort island the richest bit of rice land in the State!"

The girl nodded. She regarded him gravely, trouble lying deep in her clear eyes.

"Now let us digress a moment," pursued Fortier. "I must pry into your personal affairs, before going on with this theory of the dam. If you were wealthy, the dam could not hurt you. But you told me that you were not. Is your land mortgaged?"

"No," she replied. "Not the plantation. I have just arranged to mortgage some town property in Latouche. But Cypremort is clear."

"Have you any knowledge of why you are not wealthy? Do you suspect anyone of theft?"

A slight tinge of colour came into her cheeks.

"No. Philbrick has always been in full charge. Whenever he needs money, I sign a cheque. You would not insinuate that he would thieve? Why, if he needed money for himself, he could have it and welcome!"

"I suspect nobody," returned Fortier, "and least of all, Philbrick. Perhaps be is a poor manager, a poor overseer. You say last year's crop was good—"

The girl made a weary gesture.

"Perhaps the chief fault has been mine, Mr. Fortier! I have been silly, extravagant, perfectly heedless of money. I never thought of it as hard to get—Since father died, we have spent a great deal on the place itself. The house has needed repairs, and we have put up new quarters for the hands. Whenever I wanted something done. I told Philbrick to get it done—that was all. And then boats! We have many of them. Launches and so on. I think Philbrick said the wharf we built this spring cost two thousand dollars. You see? It is all my fault."

Fortier nodded. He perceived only too well how things had gone.

"Did your uncle encourage this expenditure? Or was he ignorant of it?"

The grey eyes flashed suddenly.

"Oh! That—that is true! I remember now—and it was Felix who spoke about the quarters for the hands! And about that beautiful little launch we bought last month—it was Felix who said he could get it for me at a low price—"

"How much?" queried Fortier dryly.

"Let me see—I think fifteen hundred—"

"Very well. Now I can understand things much better," said Fortier. "Let me show you, now, just what can be done by your uncle. When or before the dam is completed, he will order Philbrick to install an irrigation system. If Philbrick neglects to do it, and the rice crop fails, Macarty can obtain a judgement against you in the courts. I suppose you have no idea what such a system would cost?"

"Yes," said the girl unexpectedly, and drew a card from her pocket-book. "There are the figures. I obtained them yesterday. Pumping system and all."

"Have you sufficient money to install it?"

"Not by half. Unless we mortgage the island."

Fortier made a comprehensive gesture, and leaned back in his chair.

"There is the whole thing in a nutshell, Miss Lavergne. All is perfectly legal. We cannot proceed against your uncle in any way, shape, or fashion. The damage has been done, and there is nothing to do but to pay the piper. That is, on the assumption that my suspicion is correct. If Philbrick is ordered to install an irrigation system—we shall know that the suspicion is true. But we can prove no conspiracy or other wrong."

"I believe that you have diagnosed the whole matter correctly," said the girl calmly. "Surely there must be some way of escape?"

Fortier nodded, drumming on the desk-top with his fingers.

"None. We haven't finished our diagnosis yet, however. Why is your uncle doing this? Let us say, to get control of Cypremort plantation. Then, for what reason? He is wealthy enough. At least, he is comfortably off. Why does he want that island?"

Aline shook her head. "I do not know. He has never said that he wanted it."

"Of course. Is anything there of some great value?"

"The house and its contents, yes. Otherwise, nothing."

The eyes of Fortier searched her face.

"Pardon me, Miss Lavergne—but has your cousin ever proposed marriage?"

The question brought no confusion to her eyes. She nodded quietly.

"Yes, several times. I do not care for him, however. You mean, that if I were to marry him, the whole thing would be solved? Yes, I understand. But that is entirely out of the question, Mr. Fortier!"

"Good!" exclaimed Fortier. Her eyes widened.

"Why do you say that?"

Fortier laughed suddenly, boyishly. "Because I'm pleased, Miss Lavergne! From what I have learned, I do not believe your cousin to be entirely honourable—to be the sort of man for whom you would care. So, for your sake, I'm pleased!"

Now, indeed, a slight tinge of colour crept into the girl's cheeks.

"There is absolutely nothing to be done at present," pursued Fortier quickly. "But I would suggest that you write Philbrick, tell him that you have wakened to the truth, tell him all about your talks with me. If he is served with a notice to irrigate the island, that will mean open war with your uncle.

"In the meantime, I would suggest no open break with the Macartys—at least, not until you get home again. Keep everything pleasant, if possible, at any price. I want to learn everything that I can about David Macarty, here in the city, and about his son. Then I want to go down to Cypremort and make an investigation on the spot."

"To what end?" queried the girl. "You say there is no hope—"

"No, no! I said there was no escape." Fortier laughed. "There is always hope, Miss Lavergne! If I go down there, it will be to fight. I tell you frankly, I see no chance of contesting matters with Macarty in a legal battle—as things now stand. Down there, on the ground, I may find many loopholes."

She regarded him steadily for a moment.

"Shall I give you a note to Philbrick, then?"

Fortier shook his head.

"Let us wait. I shall be busy here for several days, in any case, and there is no immediate hurry. When I shall go to the island is uncertain. One must first go to Latouche?"

"That is the end of the railroad," she assented. "You had better write Philbrick of your coming, so that he can meet you with a launch. But, Mr. Fortier, if you are going to give your time to such an investigation, I wish that you would have some agreed compensation with me. You understand, I am thinking hard about money these days, when I should have been doing it in past months and years!"

Fortier made a negative gesture. His eyes, as he looked at her, were forceful.

"I am not taking this case for money. Miss Lavergne. I accepted your retainer because I needed it—but it is a fee, not a retainer. If I am unable to be of use to you, I shall return that money."

The girl's shoulders went back, but Fortier continued before she could speak.

"Please bear in mind one thing, Miss Lavergne! My name, like yours, is an old one."

She caught the proud unuttered significance of those words. It was true that she had been tempted to think of him as a lawyer, a hireling, one who served for a fee. Now, as she met his steady gaze, her face changed. Her hand went out to him.

"I am glad that you are my friend, Mr. Fortier. Have you any further instructions to give me, now?"

Fortier looked down at her slim hand in his, then let it fall and shook his head.

"Nothing, Miss Lavergne. Write Philbrick at once; tell him to advise me of any other details that he may learn—particularly as to why the Macartys should want to get hold of your land. Let Philbrick understand that I am handling the case for you. If any business matters turn up, refer them to me. Macarty may down us, but we'll give him a fight!"

"Just what kind of a fight?" queried the girl. "A legal one?"

"Any kind he wants," returned Fortier, with frankness. "From what I understand, your uncle will stop at nothing. Well, neither will I stop at anything! I am fighting for you—and, if need be, I shall fight the devil with fire!"

The calm grey eyes of the girl kindled for a moment—kindled into a swift flame that came and went again. Then she turned to the door.

"Very well. Au revoir!"

Fortier showed her out. When the door of the outer office

had closed behind her, he turned and met the gaze of the typist. Miss Smith smiled at him.

"What a beautiful gown!" said the little stenographer.

"Yes?" murmured Fortier. "I didn't observe it."

"A gentleman was here a few moments ago. He refused to give his name or to wait, but said he would be back shortly."

"With a bill to collect?" and Fortier's lips curved whimsically. "Still, I can pay it!"

"No, sir—I think he was a client."

"Impossible! Well, if he comes, bring him in."

Fortier returned to his desk, and forgot the new client.

His thoughts were of Aline Lavergne. Everything in him revolted against the chance of that rare flower being stripped and plundered by the Macartys. Either plot or circumstance had placed her in their power: he could see no logical way of working out her salvation. Yet he knew that somehow, somewhere, he must find a way.

"And what's the motive?" he reflected, puzzled by this point. "They're spending a lot of time and money to work it adroitly— why? Merely to get hold of her plantation? I hardly think so. There must be something behind it all."

Miss Smith knocked and came into the office. She closed the door behind her.

"He's here again!" she exclaimed eagerly. "He had no card. His name is Thompson."

Fortier nodded and gestured assent. Miss Smith showed in the caller.

He was a tall stooping man with mournful eyes and large hands. He was dressed in dark blue, and his yachting cap bore the insignia of some craft.

"You're Mr. Fortier?" he said. "My name's Thompson. I've just heard that a relative of mine has died in San Francisco, leaving me some money. I'm a seaman—second mate on a craft here in harbour—and I'm tied up. Can I hire you to go to Frisco and get my money?"

Fortier shook his head.

"I'm afraid not, Mr. Thompson. I'm quite busy, and can't very well—"

"Oh, there's money in it for you!" interjected Thompson quickly. "Maybe you think I'm poor? But I ain't. I got a thousand in my pocket to advance you—a thousand in cash. Then I'll give you a percentage on the estate. It ain't small pickings, either—about thirty thousand all told. It's worth it to me to have it attended to."

"It's quite impossible," said Fortier curtly. "If you'll step to the office of Gray & Fortier, on the floor above, you'll be able to get your case handled—and you'll not have to pay out so large a fee. Good day."

Thompson, with a growl, departed. The man seemed ill-pleased.

Lighting a cigar, Fortier stood looking out the window over the array of roofs and office buildings opposite. How he would have jumped at this client only a few days ago! How the very thought of a thousand-dollar fee would have made his pulses leap! And here he had turned down the man with scant courtesy. Why?

A tap on the door. Miss Smith, eager in her employer's behalf, entered.

"Was it another client?" she exclaimed.

Fortier turned, removed the cigar from his, lips, and smiled. He knew and appreciated the kindly quality of her curiosity—was aware that it held no impertinence.

"No," he said whimsically. "It was a gentleman who had a bribe in his pocket, Miss Smith. The next caller, I presume, will carry a blackjack."

She stared at him, wide-eyed.

"I don't understand, Mr. Fortier."

"Unfortunately, Miss Smith, I cannot explain. But don't be

alarmed—and don't take my words literally. By the way, I shan't be here until noon to-morrow. And if any other clients show up, turn 'em over to Gray & Fortier, upstairs."

Miss Smith looked horrified.

CHAPTER IV

THE KNIFE AND THE MAN

DURING TWENTY-FOUR hours, Jack Fortier devoted himself to delving into the past of David Macarty and son. With the father this was not difficult. Macarty had been well known in the business world for a score of years, and was something of a politician. With Felix Macarty, however, it was another matter.

The father bore by no means a bad reputation, as the term goes. He was known to be a shrewd man, in many ways a hard man; he was not a big man, either in his operations or his successes. From all he could learn, Fortier concluded that David Macarty had worked in devious ways, in the bypaths of small politics. If not upright, he had at least been very careful of his name. He was connected with a number of normal business enterprises.

With the son it was otherwise. Felix Macarty was a plunger, and one who succeeded. There were dark rumours about him— whispers and shrugs, hints that connected him with the putrid corners of the Vieux Carre. He was a cross, men said, between vulture and fox. Yet he had his share of the carrion, always.

Thus, Jack Fortier really got nowhere in his search for information. He gained no definite knowledge against David Macarty, although he comprehended that Felix was a blackguard to the backbone.

Upon the afternoon following his second interview with Aline Lavergne, Fortier received a call from no less a person than the Honourable Alfred Gray, of the firm of Gray & Fortier. Gray was an elderly man, carefully groomed, prominent in legal circles, with a cold eye and humorous mouth. He was a criminal lawyer, and a good one.

"I am glad to make your acquaintance, Mr. Fortier," he began cordially, when Miss Smith had left the two men alone. "I have heard much of you—the similarity in names, you know, has frequently caused errors!"

"Sure, I know," and Fortier laughed. "Have a cigar?"

"Thank you, no. I dropped in on business. We picked up a bit of business that was not quite in our line, and I thought I might, as it were, retain you to handle it."

"Delighted, Mr. Gray!" returned Fortier, and meant the words.

"It's like this. A very promising concern down on the coast, the Cypremort Power Company, is in need of the services—"

Fortier started slightly. His face changed. Under the steely brightness of his eyes, the other man's words died out.

"You're wasting time here, Mr. Gray," said Fortier coldly.

"But, my dear fellow! You don't understand! Here is the opportunity to solidly build your future—"

"Devil take my future, if it lies with you and your blackleg clients!" roared Fortier, with a sudden burst of temper. "You damned scoundrel, get out of here before I forget myself—get out!"

He advanced on Gray. The latter seized his hat, backed hastily to the door, and fled. Fortier slammed the door after him with a jar that shook the room.

A moment later, Miss Smith tapped and looked into the room.

"Was that the blackjack?" she inquired, a twinkle in her eye.

Fortier broke into a laugh.

"No, Miss Smith, that was the prelude to it."

The typist wisely withdrew and left Fortier to himself.

That evening, Fortier dined as usual at the humble *pension* in the old quarter where he made his home. It was a sweetly romantic old house, very cheap but very clean, kept by a prim old dame who lived largely in the past. Once inside the place, there was the sense of home.

Outside, it was different. The Italian quarter encroached all about. The old houses of Marigny and De Pontalba bricks were fallen into disrepair and ruin. Despite the touch of sunlit romance, this section of the city was become little better than a slum. It was even outside the usual run of tourists.

After dinner, Fortier went forth. He was perplexed and disturbed in mind, unable to obtain any surety of thought. Here inside of two days he had flung away proffers of money and fame. To most men, this would have been the perplexing feature. To Fortier, the uneasy thing was the hidden menace in the background. He realized that he had meddled with forbidden things.

"Twice they've tried bribery—now they'll try something else," he reflected as he strode along. "By George, that girl must have been watched, followed! Or else my friend at Baton Rouge sprung a leak. Well, if it was worth while to buy me off, then there must be some reason for it—that's the very ticket! They're afraid to have me get into the game!"

This thought was consoling. With a new spring in his step, Fortier walked to Canal Street and sought out a moving picture palace, where he invested "two bits" in as many hours of mental relaxation.

None the less, in the back of his mind remained the thought of the Cypremort Power Company. Were they really afraid to have him come down there, to have him in charge of Aline Lavergne's interests? He began to doubt it seriously. After all, he was only a very obscure and young attorney, wholly unknown. Such men as Macarty would not be afraid of his probing. They would be too carefully armoured and guarded.

No, they were hardly afraid of him. He was congratulating himself too soon. More likely, they simply wished to save themselves future annoyance. He was no more than an insect to them.

"I should hear by the end of the week from Philbrick," he reflected, as he walked down Royal Street on his way toward home. "He may have pertinent information. I don't like his attempted poisoning looks bad. Young Macarty must be in league with the canebrake outlaws. Then there's that Chinaman! I can't quite get Aline Lavergne's line-up on the chap."

It never occurred to Fortier that he might have been drawn into a net of fate whose meshes reached across the world. He never dreamed that there might be other factors in this affair—factors as yet dimly sensed, yet very powerful.

Now, when he had turned from Royal Street, he was in a region of poorly-lighted walks, closed shops, dark doorways. He strode along, whistling under his breath, thinking of the problems which faced him.

Here, then, it happened—with a paralysing swiftness.

Behind him, Fortier caught the soft thud of a rubber-soled foot. He glanced over his shoulder, carelessly. He saw a figure leaping at him with upraised hand. Startled, he turned, attempted defence—too late!

The blow fell, striking with a glancing smash, yet with enough power to send Fortier staggering. Dazed, half-stunned, he saw the figure dart in for another blow, saw the slungshot upraised, knew that he was helpless to prevent its fall. Blackjacked!

But the second blow did not fall.

From a dark doorway behind Fortier, a second figure showed itself for a moment. There was a movement, the quick glimmer of steel in air, the soft sound of a thrown knife going home. Fortier's assailant halted in mid-stride, flung out his hands. The slungshot fell to the pavement. The assassin spun around and went down without a cry.

So rapidly had all this passed, that Fortier was slow to comprehend it. He stood gazing down at his fallen assailant, then put a hand to his head and gazed around. Who was it that had saved him?

"I've 'ad me eye on that beggar all night," said a wheezy voice. "And, dang it, I come near bein' too slow! Werry sorry I am, sir, as 'ow 'e got in that 'ere first crack."

Fortier stared at the man who came forward. A rather small, pudgy little man, wiping his face with a bandanna, grey-haired. This was all Fortier could make out in the dim light.

"I seem to be indebted to you," he said quietly. "Was it you who threw that knife?"

"Yes, sir—werry sorry I was to do it, too. But 'e ain't dead, not 'im! Now, sir, if so be as you'd like to 'ave a lesson—"

The pudgy man stooped and picked up his knife. To the amazement of Fortier, he saw that the assassin had not been pierced at all. Gradually he understood—when his rescuer had handed him the knife, had explained his action.

The knife was peculiar. It seemed an ordinary seaman's sheath-knife, yet the handle was large and rounded, and was made of lead. This weapon, thrown butt first, had struck the assassin at the base of the skull, paralysing him instantly.

"A bit 'arder, and 'e'd 'ave been crocked for fair," said the pudgy man reflectively. "Per'aps you'd like to lay information against 'im, sir?"

"No," said Fortier. "You know him?"

"Dang it, sir, I ain't no crook! An honest seaman, that's what I am. Solomon's me name, sir—John Solomon. If so be as you'd like a bit o' grog," he added apologetically, "why, I'd be werry 'appy to stand you a drink, sir! Liquor is a werry bad thing, I says, but even the worst o' things is werry good in their place. And this 'ere, says I, is the place for a bit o' grog."

Fortier laughed. He was amused and astonished by this character.

"Good! Lead on—if you can find a drink. It's hard work, these days."

"You come along o' me, sir."

Fortier followed. He understood that he had been very close to the hospital, and he was not slow to suspect whence the blow had come. The assailant had been an utter stranger to him, as a glance showed—a thinly-bearded evil man dressed in rough corduroys. Fortier, himself accustomed to the bayous and timberland, gained the fleeting impression that this man was not a city dweller. Yet he attached small importance to the passing notion.

"That's what comes," said John Solomon, as he tramped along, "of sending to do 'alf a job. Now, if e 'ad been sent to kill you, sir, chances are you'd be a werry dead man this blessed minute! But no. 'E come to put you in the 'ospital—"

"Eh? How do you know that?" demanded Fortier in sharp astonishment.

"Well, sir, don't it stand to reason?" was the apologetic response. "What for was 'e a-usin' of a slung-shot, except to bust you up a bit?"

"How do you know he was sent to do it? That he was not a mere footpad?"

The pudgy little man chuckled.

"Them as asks questions gets less'n they asks, I says! I don't know, sir, for a fact. I was a-guessin' at it, as the old gent said when 'e kissed the 'ousemaid on the ear. Now, sir, 'ere we be! If you'll be so good as to step inside?"

Unlocking the door of a modest house, three steps above the street, Solomon pushed the door open and stood aside. Fortier perceived a light in the hall, and entered, not without a feeling of astonishment. He guessed at once that this was a *pension* similar to the one which he inhabited. A *pension* in New Orleans is about the last place on earth into which an ordinary seaman could obtain entrance.

Fortier's astonishment increased when he glanced around. The tables in the hall, the tapestries of Gobelin weave, the marvellous rug into which his feet sank, were such treasures as are seldom found even in New Orleans; nor were they relics of some ancient grandeur. Against the wall was hung a suit of armour—that of an officer in the Imperial Guard at Peking. From peacock crest to bow, the thing was a mass of gems and wrought gold. No impoverished creole family would have such a thing.

"This 'ere ain't a boarding 'ouse, so to speak," said Solomon wheezily. "But I 'ave me friends, and I'm welcome to stop 'ere when I'm in these parts. Right 'ere we are, sir."

Fortier stepped into a plain room, unadorned except for a sixteenth-century Ispahan on the floor. It held a plain desk, plain chairs, with a rickety smoking-stand bearing plug tobacco and several clay pipes.

Fortier sat down. His host produced a box of excellent Havanas, then got into an old smoking-jacket and a pair of carpet slippers. Now Fortier perceived that Solomon was rather an old man, with grey hair and a round expressionless face. The eyes, however, were very blue and very innocent.

"A queer customer all around!" reflected Fortier. "Yet he threw that knife like an expert—"

Solomon set out glasses and a bottle of Scotch whose label caused Fortier new astonishment.

" 'Ere's 'ow, sir!" and Solomon lifted his glass with a chuckle. "And to your 'ealth if I may make so bold—"

The pudgy little man proceeded to carve off some tobacco and stuff a clay pipe.

"You're a seaman, you say?" inquired Fortier.

"Yes, sir—ship's steward, sir." The blue eyes were guileless and direct. "The beggar as tried to scrag you—'e's a fair bad 'un, sir! P'tit Jean, they calls 'im—"

Fortier's brows lifted. "I thought you said you didn't know him?"

"Only by sight, sir. 'E was pointed out to me to-night. You see, I was a-settlin' a deal with a ship's chandler o' me acquaintance—a deal in cabin stores, sir. This 'ere chap was pointed out to me as a werry dangerous character; an outlaw, so to speak. So, when I see 'im a-following of you, sir, I made bold to interfere."

"And mightily obliged to you I am," said Fortier heartily. "That first blow of his had me groggy. The skin's not broken, though—" and he felt his skull tenderly. "No. It's all right, thanks to you."

He took out his card-case, and handed Solomon one of his cards.

"If I'm ever in a position to repay your good turn, call upon me," he said. "Sometimes a lawyer comes in mighty handy."

"Werry good, sir. I'll bear it in mind," and Solomon nodded sagely. "I don't suppose as 'ow you 'ave any notion of who might 'ave set 'im on you, sir?"

In those mild blue eyes Fortier read only an interested curiosity.

"Yes," he answered. "Yes, I have a mighty good notion! But there's nothing to be done about it."

"Werry good, sir. If so be as a man knows who 'is enemy is, all well an' good, says I! 'Cause why, then it ain't so 'ard to be careful. Knowin' 'ow to be careful is a mortal 'ard thing to learn, as the old gent said when 'e married 'is third."

Fortier laughed. He liked this pudgy little Cockney.

"What line are you with?" he inquired.

"None at all—private craft. The yacht *Watersprite,* sir. Belongs to a Mr. Macarty, she does. I ain't 'ad me position but a few days, sir."

"Oh!" said Fortier.

He gave no sign of the surprise that shot through him. His alarmed suspicion of a trap was promptly dismissed. It was evident that the old steward spoke in all innocence. That blank face, those guileless eyes, were incapable of dissimulation.

None the less, Fortier rose to his feet, thanked his host, and refused another drink.

Solomon escorted him to the front door, shook hands heartily, and bade him good night. Fortier walked home thoughtfully. Beyond a doubt, some ironical providence had impelled his rescue from Macarty's thug, at the hands of Macarty's petty officer.

"The old chap is above suspicion," thought Fortier. "Queer beggar! But I like him. What would David Macarty say if he knew, eh? Well, I'll have to watch myself after this; he may strike again. Some queer things that old steward said—he certainly saved me from an unpleasant experience. And that Petit Jean never knew what hit him! Clever work."

Fortier retraced his steps to the scene of the assault. As he had expected, however, Petit Jean had vanished. The thug had doubtless come to his senses and had slunk away.

It occurred to Fortier that the old ship's steward was a more formidable person than he appeared to be. The attorney attached little importance to the thought, except to conjecture that Solomon might come in useful at some future occasion.

When he got home, Fortier found a telegram and a telephone call awaiting him. The latter was from Aline Lavergne. The former was from John Philbrick.

CHAPTER V

ONE MUST SOMETIMES
TRUST STRANGE DICE

UPON THE following morning, as indicated in the telephone message, Fortier put in a call for Aline Lavergne at her hotel. He did this as soon as he reached his office. In his pocket was the telegram from Philbrick. He could feel it burning there.

"Good morning!" he said, when the connection was established. "This is Mr. Fortier. You left word for me to call you up?"

"Yes," answered Aline's voice. It sounded oddly disturbed. "Yes. I—my uncle requested me to ask if you would lunch with us to-day, at the 'Louisiane.'"

Her uncle had requested!

"With pleasure," said Fortier quietly. "At what time?"

"About one." Her voice drooped until it was barely audible. "I may call this morning. Good-bye."

Fortier intervened as she was about to ring off.

"One moment! Have you heard from Philbrick?"

"No."

"All right. *Au revoir!*"

Fortier swung from the telephone with blank astonishment and uneasy perplexity in his eyes. He was in a turmoil of emotions.

"What the devil has caused such a change in her, unless she has heard from Philbrick," he muttered. "But she hasn't had his news. She must not have it, either—at least for the present! How did her uncle learn about me! Or rather—why this invitation?"

By degrees his brain cleared. The contents of that astounding telegram were still hammering away at him. He forced himself to forget it temporarily; he must forget it in order to cope with this new situation.

Had there been an open rupture between Aline and her uncle? It was hard to say. At all events, Macarty had shown Aline that he was aware of her having called in an attorney. This must have happened the previous evening. Fortier sat and figured it out slowly.

"No, there was no rupture," he decided. "Macarty expected that I would be landed in hospital to-day, put out of business. So, like the cautious and careful man he is, he took occasion to have a talk with Aline. Perhaps he suggested that she hire a lawyer. Perhaps she admitted having done so already. And Macarty, instead of showing anger, frightened her by suavely commending her good sense and suggesting that she get her attorney to lunch with them to-day.

"Yes, that's about it! His unexpected attitude probably alarmed her horribly. Now it's a question what will happen to-day. Macarty will know that he has failed to bribe me, and that his thug failed to do me up. He wants me out of the way, but he's afraid to act on the spur of the moment. He'll wait, and let his precious Felix attend to me, perhaps. Or else he'll spar for time, write Felix, and get advice."

He remembered that telegram again, with a start. Had David Macarty received the same bit of news that this telegram contained? Very possibly. This would change Macarty's plans, too; would render him cautious, would make him gain time and leave the game in the hands of Felix Macarty.

Instead of receiving a call from Aline in person, however, Fortier answered his telephone an hour later to find her on the wire.

"I am afraid to come to the office," she said quietly. Her voice was cool as ever, and quite undisturbed now. "I want to tell you to please not come to the 'Louisiane.' I shall have to dispense with your help, Mr. Fortier."

He was staggered by this.

"Why, please?" he queried.

"Because—I'm afraid that it will be dangerous for you. It is not right—"

Fortier broke into a laugh of relief.

"Oh! You're not displeased with my work, or disappointed—"

"No, no!" she exclaimed quickly. "It's only that there may be some risk—"

"Nonsense, Miss Lavergne!" he interjected. "Please say no more on that head. I shall be at the restaurant without fail. Several things have happened since I saw you, and I am full of information, enthusiasm, and ability to cope with any danger! So don't you dare worry about me. Please tell me just how this invitation came about. Did your uncle suggest that you get a lawyer?"

"Why, how do you know?" she asked in surprise.

"I don't. I guessed."

"Yes, that was it—last night at dinner. I had to tell about having seen you. He was not a bit surprised, and said that I had acted very well indeed."

Fortier chuckled. "Good for Uncle David! Go on."

"Well, something in his manner frightened me, that's all. After I had telephoned you this morning, he was delighted to know that you would lunch with us. I know that he had a telegram from Felix last night, and it made him very happy. Oh, I can't bear to be so suspicious—but at the same time, I was so afraid!"

"Forget it, Miss Lavergne," said Fortier quickly. "I think I know what was in that wire he received, and perhaps he'll not be so happy later on. Some things seem to have been happening at Cypremort. I'll tell you about it in good time, but not yet. If we can avoid a show-down with your uncle, we must do it, for the present!"

"Very well, Mr. Fortier. Is there anything else you want to know?"

"Has your uncle any reason for wanting to meet me?

"I think not—except his professed interest in my affairs."

"Very well. I don't think you need hesitate to come around to the office in case of need—or telephone me and I'll come to the hotel. I must do that in any case, as I want to have a talk with you before you leave the city. I want to go down the first of the week, myself."

"But what has happened down there? You mentioned—"

"Oh, nothing vital! I had a wire from Philbrick with some news. Perhaps I'll have a chance to show it to you to-day."

"Very well. Good-bye!"

Fortier hung up the receiver and lighted a cigar, feeling well satisfied with himself. He realized that Aline must see that telegram from Philbrick, after all. Its astonishing contents had better reach her from friendly lips than from those of David Macarty.

He astonished Miss Smith that noon by paying her salary two weeks in advance and telling her that he was going away for a few days. As this was a Saturday, he sent her home at noon, with the understanding that she was to remain in charge of the office during his absence.

Fortier started for the "Louisiane", but his way thither was not direct. First he dropped in at police headquarters and indulged in a conversation with the chief of detectives. The latter obtained a dossier containing the information Fortier wished, and retailed it.

"Sure! Here's the whole works, Mr. Fortier. Jean Hennepin, alias Petit Jean, and so on. He broke jail in Latouche while waitin' trial for robbery and murder. Prob'ly slipped into the brakes—there's a heap of outlaws in the back bayous, you know. Up the Atchafalaya likewise. It ain't healthy for officers in them parts—all wild country.

"This here Hennepin done a bit of three years, quite a spell back. He's under suspicion of several crimes. He's got a brother, Michel—both Cajuns. The brother is wanted for a shootin' down to Terrebonne. Got any information on them?"

"Not a bit," said Fortier. "The name merely came up in a case on which I was working. I'm much obliged to you."

He went on to his luncheon engagement, thoughtfully enough.

It was surprising to note how this information bore out the remarks of that queer little chap, John Solomon. The latter had conjectured that Petit Jean was not trying to kill Fortier outright. Nor was it likely that Hennepin would have pulled off such a piece of work in the city itself, unless strongly impelled to it.

"Looks like a sweet gang we're up against!" thought Fortier. "That scoundrel's face was devilish. Hope Philbrick knows what he's doing down there! If he's made a mistake in this man Wrexham, then we're in for trouble."

Realizing that he was late, he hurried on to the "Louisiane". He found Aline Lavergne and her great-uncle already there.

Fortier shook hands with David Macarty, who acknowledged the girl's introduction with hearty warmth and cordiality.

"I'm very, very happy to meet you, Mr. Fortier!" he said. "My niece speaks very highly of you. It gives me great pleasure to believe that she has placed her interests in capable hands."

"I appreciate the implied compliment, Mr. Macarty," and Fortier smiled. "The more so, since your disinterested kindness has been so excellent a guide to her."

"Ah, but I am not a lawyer, my boy! And, to avoid misunder-standings, these financial matters must be kept out of family hands. It is better so. Ah, there is our friend Ferdy! I trust, my dear Aline, that we may leave the ordering in his hands?"

Macarty rose to speak with the proprietor. He was soon back.

In the cool grey eyes of Aline, Fortier read amusement at this first exchange of compliments. For his own part, he was quite on his guard, and was resolved to be just as smooth as was David Macarty.

David Macarty was an affable, distinguished looking, even a handsome, man. He appeared younger than his forties, but his "poke" collar and old-fashioned cravat lent him an air of dignity. He was well groomed; his taste appeared excellent.

One seeking in the man's face for any hint of moral obliquity would have sought in vain. His eyes were frank and humor-ous, his lips a trifle compressed, lending an air of caution. His heavy-lidded eyes betrayed secrecy—not a bad trait at all. Any movie actor, cast to act this part as that of a villain, would expire in blank despair. There was nothing big about Macarty, but neither was there anything big in his operations or successes.

Fortier, indeed, discovered a definite charm in the man. Had it not been for that bump behind his ear, he might have begun to think his suspicions were false. As it was, he had both the bump and the telegram from Philbrick to hold him to his game.

Aline said very little, but she missed nothing.

Macarty betrayed a lively interest in Fortier's ambitions, and it was inevitable that the impoverished state of Cypremort should be touched upon. Macarty mentioned Philbrick's name, then turned to his niece with a smile.

"You don't mind if I am frank, my dear? It would never do, you know, for me to say things behind your back—but I should really feel it my duty to speak a word here!"

Aline gave him a cool glance.

"Oh! I have already told Mr. Fortier that you and Philbrick

don't like each other. We shall only be too glad to have your advice, Uncle David."

"It is most unfortunate," said Macarty to Fortier, "that I have never liked this overseer. I believe he is thoroughly honest, an extremely fine character in many ways! But at times he drinks to excess, and his ability falters. I would suggest, Mr. Fortier, that you look into his management."

"I intend to do so at once," said Fortier, nodding assent. "Your advice seems admirable, sir, and I thank you warmly for offering it. It seems to me that there may be some method of removing the management from Philbrick, without affronting his integrity."

"Quite so, quite so!" agreed Macarty, cordially. "One hesitates to wound an old servant who may be inefficient yet is very faithful. Philbrick, when under the influence of liquor, is liable to the most extraordinary acts! Only a few days ago, I understand, he shot a negro—killed the poor fellow!"

Fortier looked up with a swift frown.

"Really? That sort of thing is bad, sir! Very bad! It cannot be endured for a moment. Is Philbrick under arrest, then?"

Macarty compressed his lips for an instant, as though impelled to say something which he was determined not to utter. Then he waved his hand, glanced around, and leaned forward. He spoke softly.

"For the sake of my niece, Mr. Fortier, you will understand that we must avoid all notoriety, if possible. Therefore, I undertook to keep the matter quiet. I have a little influence in the parish, and I believe that Philbrick will never be molested by the law. Of course, such actions cannot go on for ever."

"I understand," assented Fortier. "Under the circumstances, Mr. Macarty, your kindness speaks volumes for your good heart! Perhaps we can get rid of the man without trouble."

Aline Lavergne heard this conversation with a very slight flush in her cheeks, but her grey eyes flashed. Fortier hastened to give her a hint.

"You will pardon these remarks, Miss Lavergne? I know your attachment to Philbrick, and I would not cause you any unhappiness. I think your uncle will bear me out, however, in the statement that sentiment is a very bad thing in business."

"Exactly, my boy, exactly!" affirmed Macarty at once. "You have the right idea, sir. Handle things like a gentleman, but with a firm rein."

"We shall see," murmured the girl.

The luncheon was nearly over when Macarty suddenly turned to his niece.

"By the way, Aline! You may recall that I had occasion to engage a new steward for the yacht? An odd little Englishman?"

The girl looked up. "Yes. You spoke of him."

"He has proved to be an absolute treasure!" said Macarty with enthusiasm. "Upon my word, the man is a genius! It appears that he knows his business thoroughly, and he made a report this morning that astonished me. That scoundrel who disappeared had been grafting regularly—must have stolen a good sum of money from first to last! This man Solomon handed me a cheque for a hundred dollars, the so-called 'commission' for cabin stores. He actually turned it over to me, as rightfully belonging to me!"

"I suppose you made him a present of it?" asked the girl, a twinkle in her eyes.

"By no means!" stated her uncle. "I made him a present of five dollars. His gratitude was quite touching, I assure you. By the way, Mr. Fortier, when do you go to the island? Aline says that you intend to look over the ground in person."

"I hope to run down next week," said Fortier.

"Then, sir, why not come with us? There is a spare cabin aboard, and we shall get away Monday noon. We would be delighted to have your company, eh, Aline? And it would save you a rather disagreeable trip by train."

"Certainly," said the girl. Her eyes met those of Fortier, and in them he read a sudden warning message that belied her words. It was a message almost of fright. "By all means, Mr. Fortier!"

"Thank you," returned the latter. "I shall be delighted to accept!"

A moment later, Macarty was summoned to the telephone. No sooner had he left, than Fortier took a yellow slip of paper from his pocket.

"I think it is best for me to accept this invitation," he said quietly. "Please let me be the judge! And read this message."

Aline Lavergne spread out the telegram. It read:

J. FORTIER, NEW ORLEANS: They have got me this time. Am leaving plantation in charge of Captain Wrexham. Do not interfere with him. No hurry. Love to Aline.

J. PHILBRICK.

"Don't worry," said Fortier quickly. "A good deal must have happened down there—more than we can guess. Philbrick is no fool."

"I am not worrying," said Aline. Her grey eyes were serene once more. She was still smiling gravely at Fortier when David Macarty rejoined them.

CHAPTER VI

EXPLAINING THE MANUFACTURE
OF CIRCUMSTANTIAL EVIDENCE

IT WAS well past noon on Monday when the *Watersprite* started on her hundred-mile voyage to the Gulf Coast. Fortier had heard nothing further from John Philbrick.

In his younger days an enthusiastic amateur yachtsman, David Macarty was nominally captain of this commodious little cruiser. In reality, his two mates did all the handling of the craft. There was a crew of six white men—one of them a quartermaster, Gros Michel by name. A fat hulking ruffian, this.

On coming aboard with Macarty and Aline, Jack Fortier was introduced to the second officer, Thompson. The latter touched his cap, without apparent recognition, and Fortier chuckled to himself at the sullen features.

Yet this slight incident worried him. David Macarty had undoubtedly sent Thompson to him. Macarty would now know that he must recognize Thompson, yet was unconcerned. Why so? What game was David Macarty playing so genially and affably?

Of his friend, the steward, Fortier saw nothing at all until the city was behind and Solomon served drinks under the after awning. The man's face was blank, expressionless as ever. He was a perfect servitor.

Early in the afternoon, David Macarty retired to his own tiny stateroom for a nap. Before departing, he presented Fortier to the first officer, his actual captain—a fine brisk seaman named Wright. Fortier liked the man, guessed him to be thoroughly reliable. Wright shook hands and departed to the bridge.

"How do you like the boat?" inquired Aline, when she and Fortier were alone beneath the awning. Fortier met her gaze, and found it sweetly poised as ever, yet somewhat probing and questioning. He puffed at his cigar a moment, then removed it from his lips.

"She seems a fine craft," he responded slowly.

"And—her crew?"

Fortier looked into the grey eyes again. A smile curved his lips.

"You have an uncanny fashion of reaching to the heart of things, Miss Lavergne!" he answered. "Is it intuition?"

"I think so," she said quietly.

"H'm! I believe it is. Well, I'll be frank—I don't like the crew! That chap, Thompson, was in my office last week; he had a big fat bribe to induce me to go to San Francisco on a mythical legal errand. He was inspired to it, of course."

"Oh!" she said. "Then there can be no doubt—"

Fortier made a slight gesture, and she fell silent. Two of the crew, hangdog rascals, with Gros Michel, the quartermaster, were approaching. The three men set to work furbishing the brass of the quarter-deck.

"Not a fraction of a doubt," returned Fortier in his usual voice. "By the way, when do we reach your island?"

"Some time to-morrow if all goes well." Aline Lavergne eyed the distant river shores as they slipped past. "We should reach Latouche in the morning, and may stop there for mail and supplies. As a rule, uncle leaves the *Watersprite* there when he is not using her. Latouche is the parish seat, you know."

Fortier nodded.

"By the way," said the girl, after a little silence. "I have with me a number of papers that father had left in his safe-deposit box in the bank in New Orleans. They all seem to be deeds and old papers dealing with the estate. Would it be worth while your looking them over?—I thought we might as well have them at hand, in case it becomes necessary to raise any more money by mortgages—"

"Certainly, let me see them!" exclaimed Fortier. "One never knows what may turn up among such things."

"They are in my bag. I'll get them."

Aline rose and went below.

Fortier drew at his cigar, sipping occasionally at the lime concoction which Solomon had provided. The three men of the crew furbished away at the brasses, exchanging occasional remarks among themselves in the back-country patois; all three were Cajuns. Fortier, who spoke the tongue as well as he did English, gleaned that they were discussing certain ladies of Latouche, and dismissed them from his mind.

Presently Aline Lavergne returned, putting into his hand a legal envelope stuffed with papers and documents. She sat down with some sewing, and left Fortier to look over the papers undisturbed.

He ran through them rapidly but carefully. Nearly all proved to be documents relating to Cypremort plantation, and some of these went back two hundred years. As he shuffled them, a thin slip of paper fluttered into his lap. Glancing at it, Fortier, to his surprise, perceived that it was a receipt for board and lodging, written in curious English and dated at Port Said in 1905.

"What's this—something valuable?" he said, smiling. He handed the slip of paper to the girl, who glanced at it in surprise. Her eyes softened.

"Oh! No—I suppose father kept that as a memento of his trip," she said. "He was in Syria and northern Egypt about fifteen years ago, on business. He was there for nearly a year, and made a good deal of money. I believe that he always intended to return some day, but of course the War broke up all his plans, and then he died the year after the War. He must have kept this because of its funny English."

Fortier glanced up, to perceive the pudgy figure of the steward before them. Solomon touched his cap apologetically.

"Beggin' your pardon, sir an' miss," he said. "If so be as you wants tea, I'll 'ave all ready, shipshape, an' Bristol fashion whenever you rings."

"Thank you," rejoined Aline. "It's a bit early yet—We'll wait until Mr. Macarty comes."

The girl kept the bit of paper in her fingers. Presently, as though reluctant to sever this link with her past, she slowly tore it into fragments and let the wind carry them over the rail. Fortier had resumed his survey of the documents.

"Your father died suddenly, I understand?" he asked presently.

"Yes. Very suddenly. It was heart failure."

"Then, I suppose, you never learned the meaning of this writing?"

Fortier passed her a legal form. On the blank reverse side of this folded paper were written some words in pencil—evidently a hurried scrawl. It bore an abbreviated date, at sight of which the grey eyes widened.

"Oh! Why, this must have been written just before father died! I never noticed it—"

"Read it," said Fortier. "I don't understand it myself."

Aline read, in puzzled silence:

Memo. Show Aline stones held in trust. Sea-moon, Queen of Sheba, & Gemini in separate case.

"Why, that is singular!" murmured the girl, frowning a little. "What did he mean by stones held in trust? And Gemini—that means the twins, Castor and Pollux—"

Fortier saw the hulking figure of Gros Michel turn and dart a seemingly careless look at the speaker. He quietly held out his hand and took the paper.

"There's no telling," he said, inwardly cursing his lack of caution. "Something that he meant to tell you about, evidently. Perhaps Philbrick will know."

"Oh, of course he will!" exclaimed Aline, relieved. "Philbrick knows everything—my father always told him everything. And there's uncle, now. Shall we have tea served here, Uncle David?"

Macarty came up, and Fortier put away the papers in his pocket. He attached no importance to this hurried scrawl, yet it might have some meaning. He determined to ask Philbrick about it upon reaching the island.

That evening, Aline retired early, leaving the two men to smoke together. Fortier found his host no less charming than at their first meeting; indeed, Macarty seemed exerting himself to make a favourable impression upon the young attorney.

Fortier smiled, for he could read the other man's mind like a map. Macarty fancied that his guest was a raw youth, easily impressed, who could be twisted around a deft finger without trouble. By his studied flattery, Fortier conveyed the notion that he cherished an immense respect for Macarty's opinions. And Macarty was just shallow enough to know no better.

This little game amused Fortier a good deal, and did no harm.

It was ten o'clock when Fortier retired to his little cubby of a cabin. He paused for a word with Wright, who had the bridge, and learned that, barring trouble, they would reach Latouche in the morning. When he had undressed, he crowded himself into his small but comfortable berth, and was asleep immediately.

He was wakened by the sound of his cabin door slammed violently shut.

Fortier sat up, blinking. A glance at his illuminated wrist-watch told him that it was almost exactly midnight. Had his door been open? He was certain that he had locked it upon retiring. Had he been mistaken in the sound?

As he sat there, hesitant, he heard a sudden pound of bare feet on the outside deck. After this, a sharp cry.

"By George, something's up!" thought Fortier, and sprang out of bed.

Throwing on his coat over his pyjamas, he glanced out into the passage, then left the room and passed to the deck. There he found the electric lights switched on, and several men standing about a dark object. The mate glanced at him.

"That you, Mr. Wright?" asked Fortier. "What's the trouble?"

"Murder," said the chief officer curtly. "I had turned over the bridge to Mr. Thompson, and was going below, when I stumbled on him—"

Fortier looked down at the motionless bulk of the quarter-master, Gros Michel. The man had, apparently, been stabbed in the side and lay there dead. Yet, oddly enough, as the body lay on its face, one hand was twisted about to the back of the neck.

The chief officer stooped, lifted one inanimate arm, and examined the knife that still lay gripped by the dead flesh. A startled exclamation burst from his lips, and he straightened up.

"Ask Mr. Thompson to step down here," he snapped at the nearest man. Then, as he stood erect, the hand of Wright shifted to his coat pocket. Fortier caught the gleam of metal.

"No disturbance now," commanded Wright sharply. "Don't

wake anyone. Mr. Fortier, I'll be glad to have you remain, if you will. I believe you're a lawyer?"

Fortier assented quietly, sensing something strange about this murder.

The second officer appeared.

"What's this, Wright?" he demanded. "Gros Michel murdered? Why—"

"Murdered, Mr. Thompson," said the mate. "I'd like to have you look at the knife that did the work. Do you recognize it?"

Thompson stooped. An oath fell from his lips as he straightened up.

"My knife!" he cried, amazement in his sullen face. "My knife! Why, why what—"

"Perhaps you can explain how it got where it is?" said Wright calmly. The second officer stared at him, then swore luridly.

"Here, none o' that talk, Mr. Wright! How the devil should I know how it got here? It's my knife, all right—got my name on it. But I lost that cursed knife yesterday! Must have mislaid it somewhere."

"I'm glad to hear that," said the mate. "Did you mention the loss to anyone? This may be serious, Mr. Thompson—go slow now!"

"What the devil have I to go slow about?" stormed Thompson, perplexed and furious. "Anybody says I'm a murderer is a cursed liar! Yes, I told the steward I lost the knife—that little fool of a Cockney, Solomon! He promised to keep a lookout for it."

"Good! Call Solomon," ordered Wright.

"Here he is," said somebody. "Here he is, sir!"

Solomon was pushed forward. An ulster was flung over his night attire, and he blinked stupidly from the body on the deck to the keen scrutiny of Wright.

"See here, steward!" said the latter brusquely. "Did Mr. Thompson have any conversation with you yesterday in regard to a knife?"

"No, sir, not as I knows of," returned Solomon wheezily.

"Damn your eyes!" burst out Thompson, enraged. "Don't you dare to—"

"Shut up!" Wright lifted his pistol. "Not a word, Mr. Thompson! Now, steward, you think hard about this. Tell me just what Mr. Thompson said to you about his knife."

Solomon started suddenly. "Oh!" he exclaimed. At this word, at his evident recollection, there was a general movement of interest. Every eye was intent on the steward.

"Out with it," said Wright.

"Oh! Yes, sir, it comes back to me now, just like that!" said Solomon. "Why, Mr. Thompson, 'e comes to me and 'e says as 'ow that knife is a werry fine one, and 'as 'is name on it, and 'ow 'e is mortal proud of it! Yes, sir, I remember now."

There was a general relaxation. Obviously, Thompson was cleared. Wright nodded, and his frown vanished.

"And," prompted Wright, "he told you about having lost it?"

"No, sir," said Solomon, with a blank stare. "Not at all, sir. 'E asks me to clean it up a bit for 'im, which same I done, sir, and give it back to 'im—"

Thunderstruck by these words, the group of men stared at Solomon. But Thompson leaped forward, fist upraised, a storm of oaths on his lips.

Without hesitation, Wright intervened and struck at him— hit him across the skull with the pistol. The second mate staggered and went down, senseless.

"This is a serious matter, steward," exclaimed Wright sternly. "Can you swear to this evidence in court?"

"If so be as I 'ad to, sir." The guileless blue eyes of Solomon looked perturbed and frightened. "I 'opes, sir, as it ain't a-goin' to get Mr. Thompson in trouble?"

Wright did not answer the question. He ordered two of the men to bind Thompson and carry him forward. Then he looked around.

"This is a hell of a mess!" he uttered fervently. "Anybody know any cause for this thing?"

There was no response.

"Anybody seen Gros Michel and Mr. Thompson together, the last four hours?"

It was Solomon who spoke up.

"They was 'aving a bit of an argument outside the galley door, sir."

"When?" snapped Wright.

"About an hour ago, sir. I was a-layin' some oatmeal in the fireless cooker, sir, and I 'eard them two talkin' werry 'ard at each other."

"That's a fact, sir," spoke up one of the men. "But there wasn't no harm in it. They was arguing about what colour shirt was best suited to Michel's complexion, sir—"

"That's enough," snapped Wright. "Carry the body for'ard, and get this deck holystoned before daylight."

Fortier, obeying a sudden impulse, leaned over and touched his fingers to the neck of the corpse.

"Steward, fetch some ice water to my cabin, please."

"Werry good, sir," rejoined Solomon.

Fortier went below, switched on the light in his stateroom, and waited. Presently Solomon appeared, bearing a tray.

"Set it down," ordered Fortier. "Shut the door. Now look here!"

Solomon gazed at him placidly.

"That man," said Fortier, "was not murdered by the knife. He was killed by being hit a terrific blow at the base of the skull, Solomon. What do you know about it?"

"Me, sir? I knows nothing and I says nothing, just like that."

The blue eyes were very wide and guileless; the rotund face was entirely blank.

"Confound you!" exclaimed Fortier. "I don't know what to do. I owe you a good turn, but I'm cursed if I'll compound murder!

And I don't believe you're half the simpleton you look, Solomon. Where's that knife of yours—the one with the lead haft?"

"Why, sir, I lost that 'ere knife to-day. Lost it over the side, sir."

"After it struck Gros Michel, it went overboard, eh?"

Solomon made no response, but stood in placid silence.

"See here!" exclaimed Fortier angrily. "I think your testimony
is a mass of lies. Why on earth would you swear an innocent
man into the noose?"

Solomon chuckled. "Me testimony don't count, sir, until it's
took down in court, just like that! And if so be as I change my
mind, why, Mr. Thompson 'e won't be conwicted—"

"Oh!" Fortier gasped at the audacity of the little man. "Then
you actually confess that you murdered—"

"I ain't doin' of no such thing, sir," spoke up Solomon
suddenly; "That 'ere man was not murdered, sir. 'E was killed
in self defence, sir! What's more, nobody can be conwicted for
a-killin' of 'im, 'cause why, 'e ain't inside the law. 'Is right name,
sir, is 'Ennepin, and 'e's the brother o' that 'ere P'tit Jean—"

Fortier sprang to his feet. Petit Jean—Michel! The brothers
who were outlaws!

"Is this a fact?" he demanded swiftly.

"Yes, sir. That 'ere Thompson is a-goin' to get 'eld in jail until
they find out that this Gros Michel was an outlaw. That's all,
sir. And, if I might make so bold, these 'ere papers was in 'is 'and
when 'e was killed, sir."

Solomon held out an envelope, then departed.

Fortier did not prevent his going. He stood there, staring at
those papers like a man paralysed. For they were the identical
ones he had received that afternoon from Aline Lavergne.

It all flashed upon Fortier suddenly—the slam of his cabin
door as Gros Michel had left with the stolen papers, the heavy
fall on the deck.

"By gad, that man Solomon is a smart one!" murmured Fortier
admiringly. "He caught the fellow in the act—and Michel got

killed. Then Solomon threw the blame on Thompson—arranged
to have Thompson jailed—why? Did he know that Thompson
was one of Macarty's henchmen? Did he know—"

Fortier turned out the lights and lay down again to think it
over. The more he thought, however, the more John Solomon
became to him nothing but a startling, perplexing question
mark. Who and what was this little pudgy man?

John Solomon—

BOOK II—THE SEAMAN

CHAPTER I

THE MAN FROM THE SEA

IN THE great white manor house of Cypremort, John
Philbrick sat at dinner with his guest. Captain Tom Wrexham listened without saying very much at first. His protruding
eyes were always staring at the wonders of the huge rooms—
had stared, thus, ever since his arrival. He seemed never to see
enough.

Uncle Neb, black and wrinkled, served the two men punctil-
iously. Wrexham ate like a gentleman. He seemed to appreciate
the silver and glass and snowy linen, as a man who has been
deprived of such things for a long while.

The dining-room was a great chamber, all panelled in black
old mahogany, lighted by candle sconces and a squat candela-
brum on the table—the mahogany table which, fully extended,
would seat fifty guests. In the dark recesses of the room lurked
black shadows and the dim sheen of silver; smoked portraits
about the walls, a mammoth carved buffer loaded with plate.

"I might ha' had a place like this of my own," said Wrexham
suddenly, "only for the law. No use for the law. That was up in
Canada; place like this, all the same."

John Philbrick nodded his shaggy head with a sage air.

"Thought all along you might be a Canuck," he commented. "Funny how folks here brag about Louisiana being settled by the French! It was really Canadians. Iberville and his Hudson Bay bunch—the same crowd hung together, same names and all. All Canadians born. Well, try this venison, now! I don't guess you've had much venison at sea."

"Mighty little," admitted Wrexham. "I'll not go back to sea for a while. I've no crew, and no particular use for one. I've got money enough to loaf a bit, enjoy life."

The talk languished.

Outside, darkness shut down on everything. Out in the bayou rode the schooner of Captain Wrexham, her riding lights dotted against the obscurity. The plantation house was entirely lighted by candles—not even a lamp anywhere, for old ways clung close. Sconces, mostly of solid silver, were everywhere.

In the dining-room the two men partook of a dinner which would have driven Epicurus mad with desire. Crab bisk, turtle, venison, bayou oysters—a dozen things such as can be had in combination only from Louisiana cooks. And all the while the two men were studying each other, as they had done for days past, ever since Wrexham's arrival here.

John Philbrick was a tremendous man, browed and bearded like the "Moses" of Michelangelo, thewed in proportion. The grey shaggy beard hid weak lines, however; somewhere in his face was an unsteadiness, a weakness. Like his guest, he was attired in white, but untidily so. His open shirt collar betrayed a powerful throat, his coat was flung on a nearby chair, his garments were not at all spotless.

Wrexham, on the contrary, was something of a dandy. His whites were tailored. In his snowy cravat glowed a small black pearl, set below the luxuriant, curly brown beard, which was trimmed square and brusque. His eyes, somewhat protuberant, were pleasantly wrinkled at the corners, after the fashion of men who look much into the open depths of sky and sea.

About this sea captain was something puzzling, baffling.

In the carriage of his head was an aggressive challenge, in his sharp look a brusquerie; yet the man was inwardly troubled. His thoughts seemed ever reaching backward, as though he were living through past scenes and days.

John Philbrick felt this oddity. At times his bright eyes, half hid beneath their shaggy brows, would dart a probing glance at his guest. He asked no questions. He knew that any man who showed up here along the bayous, without a crew but with a marvellous boat, and who was content to sit and dream, had some inward confusion in his soul. It was perfectly evident that this Wrexham was no virginal young man, either.

Wrexham betrayed himself often, perhaps from carelessness. Perhaps it was the refinement, the silver and glass and wine, that worked on him. A shadow in his eyes would linger hauntingly; his face would shift into hard harsh lines of cruel purpose. One fancied that this man's crew had left him with good reason. He bore a callous air, seeming unmoved by anything that chanced, as though if he so desired his experiences might astonish anyone.

Something of this crept into his talk.

"I don't like it," he said, apropos of nothing. "I'm used to action, and up in these seas it's a rum go. A rum go, and no mistake!"

Philbrick pushed over the whisky decanter, and laughed.

"You can get your action," he said. "Go shoot up that devil, young Macarty."

The skipper shook his head very decidedly.

"Not we," he said, with emphasis, and poured a tall drink. "I know when I'm well off."

The two men drank. Philbrick chuckled as he set down his glass.

"You can get action in the bayous. Outlaws there, no end of them—honest men they are, too! The sheriff never bothers the canebrakes. I'd not be surprised to be there myself one of these days. You know that big nigger I shot the other night?"

Wrexham nodded, with a curious glance.

"You don't mean they'd get after you? For shooting a black?"

Philbrick shrugged his wide shoulders. "All things are possible. An odd situation, this one! Did you ever see anything to beat it?"

"Often," said Wrexham calmly. "Often. If you want to see queer things, go pearlin', or after bird skins, or even shell. Why, I remember—"

He broke off, smiled thinly at his glass, fingered his beard. After a moment:

"Dashed rum go, down there! I owed a man a debt, d'ye see? Owed him a good deal—passed my word on it. Well, I had the chance to pay it back. In order to pay it back, I had to play a rotten trick on another crowd. I managed it, but it left a bad taste. Two men and a woman, they were. I went away from there in a hurry, I can tell you! Didn't know 'em; never saw 'em before or since. Left a bad taste just the same."

The jerky speech was followed by silence. Suddenly Wrexham went on, thinking aloud:

"I'll make it up some day," he said thoughtfully. "Only I've never had the chance. And I've been lookin' for one, off and on."

"Come in on this deal," offered Philbrick, watching intently. "You know the odds. You know the situation here. If they get me, who's to watch out for the girl? Nobody. Throw in with me."

Wrexham smiled sardonically.

"Not me! You can run your own blessed show—And I don't want to mix with your friend Macarty; don't like his looks. I've got enough enemies now, without taking on more."

His eyes went insolently to the troubled gaze of old Philbrick. He seemed to bristle against some offer which tempted him, yet which he was resolved to reject. Philbrick sighed, and rose.

"Come along to the library, Uncle Neb! Bring out coffee and cigars."

The old darky followed them with the thick Creole coffee and a box of cigars into the library. Here a smouldering fire in the great fireplace banished the damp chill of evening. The two men settled into deep chairs.

"Confounded pretty face!" said Wrexham. He was staring at an enlarged photograph which stood on the mantel. "Most amazin' face, that!"

Philbrick merely grunted. He seldom betrayed in words the poetic urge that was in him. Sometimes it came forth in deeds, but he shrank from talking of it. Not for worlds would he have it generally known that he wrote verse. It was in him, however, and it came forth in more ways than one—sometimes very surprisingly.

"Aline is a wonder-girl," he said. "Looks exactly like her mother, too."

Had Wrexham rightly understood this remark, it would have altered his entire life. But he failed to heed it. He was staring at the picture on the mantel.

The aroma of the parched coffee and good tobacco mingled pleasingly in the room. It was a large room, panelled like the others, and not confined to books. Jewels, both artistic and intrinsic, hung upon the walls. Through a hundred years and more the men of this family had brought their spoils home to this room, spoils of diplomacy and work and battle.

A case of jewelled orders; presentation swords encrusted with gold and gems; four ancient oils worth their weight in hundred-dollar bills. A woman's picture—Aline's grandmother—set in a frame of ivory, studded with huge rough sapphires; and so on, in an infinitude of detail. Wrexham glanced about the walls, a predatory glitter in his eyes.

"Wonder your niggers don't walk off with some of this truck!" he observed.

Philbrick grunted again. "Nonsense! They're family darkies."

"And no wonder your friends the Macartys want to loot this house!" Wrexham's eyes narrowed. "Anybody'd want to. I'd want to myself! Might come and do it some night."

"You?" Philbrick smiled in his grey beard. "You're not that sort."

Wrexham suddenly flung a snarl at him.

"Don't know me. Bah! You fools who live and rot and die here under the hand of the law! You don't know what goes on in the world! I tell you there's no crime worth the name that I haven't—"

He checked himself with an oath. "Too much liquor!" he went on gruffly. "If I could carry it like you, now! Well, it's a rum go."

"So you've pirated in your time?" said Philbrick softly. "Like they do in books?"

Wrexham leaned back in his chair and vented a burst of hearty laughter.

"You *are* a boy, aren't you?" he said amusedly. "I believe on my soul you just wait and scheme to get me talkin' about pirates an' murders on the high seas, and so forth!"

"Well, I like it," admitted Philbrick sheepishly. A wistful note crept into his voice. "I've always wanted to go to sea, and never had the chance."

"With all the sea at your door?" scoffed Wrexham.

"Aye. And I've liked to talk with sailors, and hear them tell things—"

Wrexham sniffed in wondering scorn.

"Then you've learned a fine lot o' profanity and smut," he said brutally. "If you think there's any damned romance—hell! You're a boy, that's all."

Philbrick was silent under this outburst. He was probably ashamed of his own half-confidence. When he spoke again, the subject was changed.

"I wish, now, that I hadn't killed that big black," he said. "They'd like nothing better than to get me off the place long enough—"

"Ain't you got the right to protect your own home and life?" sniffed Wrexham.

"It's not that." Philbrick frowned. "Macarty owns the parish, sheriff and all. He can frame up anything. There's no ultimate danger, of course, but if he could have this place at his mercy for a little while, he'd play merry hell with things. Who's that? Oh, come in, Uncle Neb!"

A knock had sounded at the door.

At the knock, Wrexham jumped. His eyes dwelt upon the advancing figure of the negro with a strange uneasiness, as though he divined something of stiff import to himself.

"Mistuh Philbrick, suh!" exclaimed Uncle Neb, his voice tremulous. "One o' dem slue-footed town niggers jest drapped down to de landin' and left dishyer note fo' yo'—"

He broke off to extend a folded dirty scrap of paper.

Philbrick took it, opened it, and held it to the light. Then he crumpled the paper and flung it into the fire. He leaned back, put his cigar again between his lips, and gave Uncle Neb a calm order.

"Get that little brown handbag out of my room and bring it downstairs. Put in it that bottle of whisky Captain Wrexham brought. And fetch a rifle, Uncle Neb; don't forget a box of cartridges. That'll do."

The old darky retired, and the door closed. Philbrick looked calmly at his guest.

"Some kind soul sent me a warning," he said coolly. "The sheriff will be here in half an hour or so to take me away for that shooting. It's a pretext, but good enough. You can't murder negroes, even in this country. All they want, of course, is to have the place left at their mercy for a while."

Wrexham stiffened in his chair. "What the devil! Are you serious, man?"

Philbrick nodded. "I'm off. Can't take the chance of lying in jail a month or two before I get loose. There's too much at stake. I'll take one of the launches or a canoe, and go into the canebrakes like many a better man! I'll find plenty of friends, never fear."

He spoke calmly of this. Calmly—as though it meant nothing to flee from the law, to live in canebrakes and bayous like a wild beast, in the company of rogues and murderers and devils incarnate. Wonder sat in the eyes of the staring seaman.

"You're devilish cool about it!" said Wrexham doubtingly. Philbrick smiled.

"Why not? There's no rush. Five minutes' start is quite enough—they can't trace me at night, you know. Will you send a wire for me, to-morrow or next day? One of the boys will be glad to take you up to town."

"Of course. Do anything I can."

Philbrick rose and went to a desk in one corner. Here he moved a candle closer, and sat down to write out a telegram. Just to his right was the case of jewelled orders and decorations. After a minute he looked up and jerked his head.

"Come over here, cap'n."

The seaman obeyed. When he walked, it was with the peculiar side sway of one who sets his weight against the swinging heave of a deck, feeling the ground as he treads it.

Philbrick handed him the telegram.

"You'd better read it. But first, look here—"

As he spoke, Philbrick loosened a hook on one side of the case of orders. He swung the case out from the wall, like a door. Behind it was revealed a safe set in the wall.

"Everything's in there," he said calmly. "Money and family jewels and papers."

"Eh? What d'ye mean?" Wrexham's voice was startled.

The door opened. Uncle Neb appeared, carrying a rifle and a small grip. Philbrick came to his feet and held out his hand to Wrexham. He was laughing silently.

"Good-bye, Wrexham! Read the telegram. I'll leave now. I'll perhaps be able to send a message to you in a few days—luck to you!"

Wrexham, astonished, shook hands. Philbrick turned to the old darky.

"You'll hear from me later, uncle. Now give me the cartridges, please, sir! Thanks. I'm off to the brakes. While I'm gone, Cap'n Wrexham will be in charge. Understand? He'll look after things until Miss Aline gets back.

"Wrexham! Young Macarty may show up with the sheriff. If he does, look out! There's a brief note inside the desk, placing you in authority here—you may need it. Good night."

Philbrick turned to the door, and his great figure vanished. Uncle Neb followed him, and the door slammed.

Wrexham was left alone in the room, a picture of blank astonishment, staring after them. Presently he recollected the telegram in his hand, and glanced at it. He seemed to waken from his daze with a start.

"The devil!" he cried out protestingly. Then he realized there was none to hear his protest.

"Why, the old scoundrel! He's a slick 'un and no mistake. Worked me, he did—worked me like a blasted fool!" A note of admiration crept into his voice. "I'll be damned! If the old rascal didn't go away and leave me in charge—*me*, mind you!"

He stood gazing around the dim room as though unable to comprehend it. Thrusting the telegram into his pocket, he went to the centre table. There he took a cigar from the open box, bit off the end, and returned to the desk. He dropped into the chair before it, and held the candle to his cigar. Then he leaned back and surveyed the room again. A struggle was in his face.

"This is a rum go, a rum go!" he exclaimed roughly. "Fancy this, now! What 'ud old Hvarson say to this, eh? What 'ud anyone say, who knew me?"

Presently he rose again and went back to the fireplace. He stood there, his feet planted wide apart, and stared hard at the enlarged photograph of the girl on the mantel. It gazed down at him from wide grey eyes, crystal-clear. The struggle deepened in his face. His brows drew down as he looked at the picture.

"I wonder if that old rascal realized a few things?" he cogitated aloud. "Damn him, I believe he did! Told him too much about myself, that's what I did. Well, young lady, your property is in the hands of a cursed bad rascal, and that's the truth! Nothing to say about it, have you? But it's a damned mess—confound it, don't look at me that way! I didn't mean to swear in front of you!

"Now, ma'am, do you suppose that if I was to stick on this here job, that little matter back in the coral sea would be forgiven me? Do you, ma'am?"

He stood motionless, his head slightly cocked, staring up at the picture. Suddenly, as though some inner answer had come to him, his lips parted in a wide smile. Through his beard flashed strong even teeth like white ivory.

"Well, Miss Aline, it's a bargain!" he cried out exultantly. "Damme if ever I thought I'd look into eyes on earth like yours! Eyes of an angel, that's what. I'm a rotten fool and no mistake— but I'll do it. I expect it'll come to no good end, neither. If this isn't a bad crowd we're up against, I don't know one! But it'll be a novelty to be fightin' for something decent, won't it?"

He laughed again, and bowed to the photograph.

"I'll do it, ma'am, and thank you for the chance!"

CHAPTER II

HIGH TERMS, HIGH RISKS

CAPTAIN WREXHAM, having made his decision, displayed no further hesitation. He turned from the fireplace, walked over to the case of decorations, and planted himself before it.

"Ah!" he observed, blowing a cloud of smoke. "It's only fair to have a look at what I'm in charge of, eh?"

He swung back the case from the wall, held a candle closer, and inspected the wall safe. A chuckle broke from him. White teeth flashed through his beard.

"The old rascal left her in charge o' me, but thoughtfully forgot to tell me the combination! Well, if that safe ain't thirty years old, I'm a Kanaka."

Still chuckling, he leaned forward and touched the knob. For a little while he stood thus, only his fingers moving deftly. Then he straightened up, nodding as though well pleased with himself. The safe door swung open to his hand.

Decidedly, this was not Captain Wrexham's first encounter with a safe!

The scene which followed flung a singular light upon the ethical impulse of this waif cast up by the sea. Another man would have been in thought of the coming officers, and in nervous waiting; but not Wrexham!

The skipper attended to the business in hand with a cool and unhurried enjoyment, an air of relish, of keen satisfaction. Indeed, since he had looked into the pictured eyes of Aline Lavergne and made his decision, there had come a new flash into his eye, a new resolution into his manner. Strange, that a photograph should so sway the mind of such a man, even to altering his very life course!

The safe open, he laid bare the drawers within. One by one he removed them for his inspection. If he had expected treasure, he found it—not in money, but in the jewels of dead women; glittering things, heirlooms of vanity and love. Into the man's face came a fiercely predatory air.

"Lord!" he exclaimed throatily. "I've seen the time when I'd have—"

He did not finish. He had drawn forth a packet of papers, heart-sacred documents of the family's past. These he opened and read, coolly and deliberately, quite ignoring the obvious fact that he was violating the first principles of a gentleman. In five minutes he had absorbed from these papers a tremendous amount of information about the family.

There was little else in the safe to repay his exploration. Last of all, he drew out a thick package, wrapped, sealed heavily, and addressed to Aline Lavergne. After turning it over in his hands, Captain Wrexham calmly broke the seals and inspected the contents. He found it to be a book—rather an astonishing book, too.

Sitting down comfortably in the desk chair, Captain Wrexham puffed his cigar alight, and gave his attention to the volume in hand. Evidently, John Philbrick had had this book made. It was a thick book with blank leaves, bound in leather; upon the cover, stamped in gold, were the words: "The Book of Aline. Her Beauty—For Her Eyes Only—by John Philbrick, Gent."

"John Philbrick, Gent!" commented the skipper sardonically. "A rum go, I call it!"

He opened the volume, and gained his first intimation that John Philbrick was a poet.

Upon the blank pages, Philbrick had laboriously and beautifully inscribed his own verses, most of them tributes personal and delicate to the girl whom he loved. Wrexham glanced through the pages, reading a line here and there.

Then he tossed the book carelessly back into its place and sat in moody silence, his fingers curling about his square brown beard.

"I've lived too long, that's what's the trouble," he said at last, with a sigh. For a little he was silent again, then he broke forth petulantly.

"What've I got out of it all, now that I'm here? Not much. Lechery o' women in the high latitudes, and strength o' men in the low; well, I've held up my end with 'em all, bad and worse! Now I'm here, with some money in my fist—and the picture of a girl tellin' me to be good. That's hell for you! No hell worse than that; to see what you can't ever have again, but might ha' had once!

"Don't know what's got into me, for a fact. Runnin' true to form, I ought to load up this junk in the *Nautilus* an' go about my business somewhere down the Caribbean. Anyhow, I want to sight that girl in the flesh, just to satisfy myself that pictures lie—just to have the pleasure o' saying, 'I told you so!' They aren't made like her, I tell you! Not possible. And who'd think that old grey-beard rascal was a poet, eh? Only last night he was wild drunk. If *I* could get drunk, now, maybe it'd help some."

He sat with his head sunk, his beard brushing over his white shirt, in an attitude of pessimistic gloom, of utter dejection.

What pictures he beheld in his mind's eye, what visions of past years, lost chances, sneered-down virtues, were for himself alone. The wonder was that a girl's picture had compelled this sea-wastrel into such a mood. Yet, perhaps, that picture had only come at the right moment to cast its weight into a long-wavering balance. Who can tell about these things?

Suddenly there was a sound. On the instant Wrexham became a different man.

A trampling of booted feet on the veranda—or "gallery," as is the Southern term—and the man was out of his chair in a flash. So swift were his movements that they were almost incredible. Within five seconds he had closed the safe, swung and locked the case of decorations before it, and was on the other side of the room. He flung his dead cigar into the fire and took a fresh weed from the box.

The hall door opened. Uncle Neb appeared and said something in the patois. Wrexham did not understand. The old Negro spoke in English.

"Sheriff Swords is heah, suh, an' he—"

"Ask the gentlemen in," said Wrexham, cold as ice. He stood passive, waiting, alert.

The two men who entered the room came to a dead halt at sight of Wrexham. Obviously the sight of him astonished them. The foremost, a burly person who wore a holstered revolver prominently displayed, was undoubtedly the sheriff.

"Well?" said Wrexham coolly. "Who are these gentlemen, Uncle Neb?"

The old darky rolled his eyes. "Sheriff Swords, suh, an'—an' Mistuh Macarty."

"Ah!" said Wrexham. "Glad to meet you, gentlemen. My name's Tom Wrexham, master and owner of the *Nautilus,* anchored out yonder. How may I serve you?

"Where's Philbrick?" demanded the sheriff, scowling a bit.

"You refer to Mr. Philbrick?" drawled Wrexham.

"Reckon I do."

"Well, Mr. Philbrick had sad news to-day." Wrexham sadly wagged his beard. "It seems that the owner of this place—a girl, ain't she?—is away in New Orleans or somewhere, and he got word only to-day that she wasn't expected to live after the accident—"

"What's this?" Macarty came forward with a cry. "What's this?"

The skipper regarded him coolly.

"I'm talkin'," he rejoined. "You see, the girl was run over by an auto, and she wanted to see Mr. Philbrick most particular. So he went off to see her, that's all."

The ruse succeeded. Both visitors were flung off-balance for the moment.

"Aline—an accident!" exclaimed Felix Macarty. "See here—we happen to know that Philbrick was on the place this very afternoon!"

Wrexham grinned. "Well, sir, if it makes you happy to know it, I'm not the man to object. Sit down, gentlemen! Have a drink."

Macarty watched him with an angry flush rising in his face. There was no denying that Felix was a handsome young devil, like his father; there was no caution in his face, however. Instead, the face ran to a keen sharp sophistication. It was touched with cruelty.

No weakness in it—none! A quick brain flamed behind the smouldering eyes. From thin lips to level brows, it was the face of one who had fought hard and cruelly. Wrexham knew the type for a bad one, knew well that this type would not break or yield.

"Has there been any accident?" said Macarty slowly.

"For all I know, there might ha' been," and Wrexham chuckled. The sheriff growled and drew forth a paper.

"Here's a warrant for Philbrick's arrest, charge of murder," he proclaimed. "I want him, and I mean to get him even if—"

"Get him, by all means!" said the skipper. "I suppose you'll go to New Orleans?"

"None o' that!" snapped the badgered officer. "He's on this here place, and if you're tryin' to hide him—"

Wrexham broke into a hearty laugh.

"Here's a rum go!" he uttered. "Take him with you, by all means! I don't know where he is this minute, and that's a fact."

"I reckon I'll just take you along, too." The sheriff's hand moved toward the weapon at his belt. "You prob'ly know a good deal—"

Wrexham stiffened a trifle.

"You just try it on!" he said calmly, holding the cigar out in front of him. "You just try it on, that's all! I'll shoot two fingers off your hand before you can pull that gun, my man! If you want Philbrick, you go get him. If you want me—why, you just try it on!"

Felix Macarty touched the arm of the sheriff.

"Be careful," he said quietly. "This gentleman knows nothing. You'd better look for our man, though I'm afraid he's slipped us."

"That's sensible," put in Wrexham. "Oh, Uncle Neb! The sheriff wants to arrest Mr. Philbrick. Show him to where Mr. Philbrick is, and let him do his arresting. Look over the place, sheriff—she's all yours."

Smothering an oath, the sheriff turned and left the room.

Felix Macarty had not moved his gaze from the face of Wrexham. Now he came forward to the table, took a cigar from the box, lighted it. He was as cool as Wrexham himself.

"Pretty schooner of yours, cap'n," he said.

"True enough." Wrexham appeared mollified by this opening. "Sit down?"

Macarty nodded and dropped into a chair. Wrexham followed suit, and lighted his own cigar.

"Fast, isn't she?" asked Macarty. "She has lines, that craft."

"Fast? You ought to see her with a good following wind, not too stiff!" said the skipper with enthusiasm. "Let her out wing-and-wing, and I'll guarantee she'll walk over anything in the trades! Why, I remember once down in the Paumotus, there was a French gunboat poking around after us, one of those old tin pots that can do ten knots aa pinch!

"Well, sir, she pops out around the point of an island, not two miles away. We turned tail, I can tell you! She put two shots over us and two more in the water. By that time the old girl was walkin' away from her with the sails wet down and a bone in her teeth—and we went on walkin, that's all! She'll do her fifteen if all's right."

Macarty nodded at this confidence. He fell to staring into the fire embers.

"Remarkable craft," he said, after a bit. "By the way, I don't suppose you'd consider a charter, at high terms?"

"Might," said Wrexham. "High terms, high risks—eh? It all depends."

Macarty glanced at the door; it was closed.

He shifted a little in his chair, so that he could better study the face of Wrexham.

"I know a man who could use such a craft," he said. "A Chinaman, named Ah Lee."

Wrexham nodded knowingly, and fingered his beard.

"Heard of him from Philbrick—he's makin' arrack and loadin' the black folk into hell, ain't he? Well, I don't mind sayin' that I've carried liquor before this. So he'd give me a good charter? A partner of yours?"

"Of mine?" Felix Macarty smiled thinly. "My dear cap'n, I have no partners. Neither has Ah Lee. I have, however, turned over occasional deals to him, and he's a man of his word. I don't doubt that he'd make the charter to your advantage. What he deals in, I can't say. It might be rice liquor, and it might be other things."

"I see!" said Wrexham sagely. "A touch of hop, eh? All the better."

There was a little silence. Macarty was studying this man, so ready to break the law. Presently he spoke again.

"So old Philbrick got a hint and skipped out, eh? Let him go—he can't do much hurt from the brakes. Perhaps you know that my cousin owns this place?"

"Heard something about it," said Wrexham calmly.

"Very good. Since Philbrick is gone, I'll move in here until she returns from New Orleans. The place should be taken care of."

Wrexham chuckled in his beard.

"What about me?" he said dryly.

"You?" Surprise lightened in the eyes of Macarty. "Why, you—"

"Philbrick put the place in my care," explained Wrexham pleasantly. "Legal enough, I guess. Anyhow, I'm here."

Macarty was silent for a long moment; these words, pleasantly spoken, yet held very strong significance. Captain Wrexham smoked and stared at the fire, ignoring the dark gaze that was fastened upon him.

"See here!" said Macarty suddenly, a stir of anger in his tone. "What's your game?"

Wrexham looked at him reflectively.

"Well, to tell the truth, I don't know! Wish I did. I might load the schooner with some of the pickings around here, and go away. I've been thinking of it, for a fact."

"What's your price?" queried Macarty bluntly.

Wrexham glanced up, met the smouldering eyes, held them with a level look.

"Did you ever see a man playin' straight because he was tired o' makin' crooked money?"

This oblique answer held Felix Macarty thoughtful for a

moment. It was hard for him to understand the skipper. Gradually he had sensed antagonism here—a stone wall, hidden, yet powerful, through which he could find no opening.

Macarty rose and shook his cigar ashes into the fire. As he did so, he asked a question—asked it with elaborate carelessness.

"Ever hear of the Gemini? Or the Sea-moon?"

"Eh?" Wrexham frowned. "You mean a lunar rainbow? I've seen 'em often, off New Caledonia."

Another silence. Wrexham studied that question in his mind—he could not fathom it. Felix Macarty smiled thinly, and rose to his feet.

"I suppose, if you're in charge here, that you know the situation? Philbrick told you about the dam and all?"

Wrexham rose also, and assented. "Philbrick explained all that. Why?"

Macarty took a folded paper from his pocket and laid it on the table.

"There's legal warning that you must install pumps or otherwise contrive to irrigate this plantation at once. Otherwise, the rice crop will be lost."

"Oh!" said Wrexham. "D'you mean—the dam's finished?"

"Yes. The water goes down to-morrow. The rice will need water for another month at least—and it's up to you. You understand?"

Wrexham nodded carelessly. "Yes. All right. I'll attend to it."

McCarty chuckled at this. It was clear that the seaman knew little of a plantation.

"You'd better think the matter over—my offer, I mean. If we can't work together you and I, we'll have trouble."

"Squarely put." Wrexham met his gaze. "We'll see about it."

"Very well. I hear the sheriff returning—good night."

"Glad to've met you," said Wrexham.

He stayed where he was, while Uncle Neb escorted the visitors back to the landing and wharf. Then the skipper sank into a chair and laughed softly. He glanced at the girl's picture on the wide mantel.

"That young devil is a tough 'un!" he confided. "No mistake, neither! Got a head on him; cool as you please all the while. Figured me for what I am, just about. Only he didn't figure on a girl's picture makin' a fool of me."

He was silent again, ruminative, now and then indulging in a soft chuckle, as though he perceived some inward fact to amuse him.

"Trouble with old greybeard," he said presently, thinking now of Philbrick, "was that he was too legal-minded. All his life afraid to run off to sea; reg'lar poet, he was! Civilized! Too damned civilized to take a chance! And the law got him in the end.

"That ain't my way, I tell you! Irrigate? I'll irrigate this place inside o' three days! If I'm goin' to turn plantation manager, then I'll make things happen and no mistake, neither! But what did that chap mean with his question about the Gemini? There's a rum go! He meant somethin' by it, but blessed if I know what!"

The door opened, and Uncle Neb appeared. Wrexham turned to him.

"Gone, have they?"

"Yes, suh, praise be! Done gone a plenty."

"All right." Wrexham's tone was curt, incisive. "You have a dozen boys waiting for me at two bells to-morrow morning—nine o'clock, savvy? I want to lay that ship of mine close in to the wharf here, and moor her steady. Understand?"

"Yes, suh. Yo' all fixin' to stop a while, suh?"

"Well—I might."

And Wrexham glanced whimsically at the portrait on the mantel.

CHAPTER III

THE PAST MAY BE FORGOTTEN, BUT DOES NOT FORGET

UNCLE NEB and Aunt Sapphira, who between them had kept the household arrangements of the plantation running like clockwork for unnumbered years, stood on the front gallery and listened rapturously. They were watching the work at the landing, whence the voice of Captain Wrexham came to them with startling clarity.

Aunt Sapphira rolled her eyes. "Sho' is scandalous talk, Uncle Neb! Dat man is got de mos' masterful use o' langwidge what I heerd sence ol' Jedge Lavergne—"

"Hush, woman!" Uncle Neb put a hand to his ear, and grinned. When he spoke again, it was in the creole patois.

"Laplie tombe, onaouaron chante! The frogs sing when the rain is coming, eh? The waters is going down fast in the bayou; the sheriff went away last night like a monkey in a calabash! And now this man—"

"You and yo' gombo!" snorted Aunt Sapphira. "Is you gotten too stuck up to talk plain speech, niggah? I ain't studyin' 'bouten dat talk you is passin' off fo' creole! If you is gwine talk creole, den talk it; but if you is gwine talk field-hand talk—"

"Huh?" Uncle Neb glared indignantly at her. "Sence dat gal of yours went to de city to study school, you's been talk a heap 'bout Creole an' gombo, ol' woman! Dat gal, she figgers to talk French like quality folks—stuck-up yaller wench! If'n I was you—"

"Hey, Uncle Neb!" broke in a hurried voice. "Cap'n say fetch him a rifle an' shake yo' foot!"

A black boy had run up the walk from the wharf and was panting below the gallery. Uncle Neb caught the message and hastened into the house.

Captain Wrexham was having his troubles. With a dozen half-naked laughing black men at work, he had brought the

Nautilus into the little cove and anchored her bow and stern. He had barely completed this operation when he discovered that she was aground. The water had gone down, swiftly and without warning—Macarty's dam was closed.

The skipper swore and sweated, but in five minutes the schooner was nicely heeled over in the mud; only a tug or a raise of water could float her. It was at this juncture that Wrexham had sent for a rifle.

He stood on the landing, while the black men hastened to get the boats and launches out to where the water would still float them. The wharf was already high and dry. Out midstream in the bayou appeared a launch, floating with the slow current. Captain Wrexham chewed on his cigar and eyed this boat in malignant fury.

The boat carried two men. In the bow stood Felix Macarty, watching the work ashore. At the sudden subsidence of the water, at the grounding of the schooner and Wrexham's storm of curses, Macarty had broken into a wave of hearty laughter. Across the water swept that vitriolic mirth, more deadly than Wrexham's foulest oaths, stinging the seaman like a whip.

"Laugh at me, will you?" Wrexham shook his fist in air. "Laugh at my craft, will you?"

And he sent the boy for a rifle.

Perhaps Felix Macarty made a mistake when he laughed thus mockingly. If there were one thing on earth for which Wrexham held a deep and true affection, it was this schooner that now lay heeled in the mud.

Your true seaman hates the ocean and fears it, most terribly; and with corresponding fierceness he loves the ship which stands between him and the ocean. Yet Wrexham, more than most men, loved this ship of his. She was to him a sensate creature, delicate in the highest degree. He knew every timber of her. Under his hand she would perform miracles. Often he had owed his life and liberty to this knowledge, to this skill, to this hand-in-glove intuition which made the ship a part of himself and him a part of the ship.

This craft was no ordinary trading schooner, lousy with rotten copra, stinking with melted oil in the bilge, her deck uncaulked by tropic suns. Not at all! She was a schooner, but a schooner in perfect miniature, incredibly small and perfect to the final detail.

A trader, indeed, yet with rather the look of a yacht. Her brasses were polished, glittering in the sunlight; her paint was scrubbed and gleaming white. Even her furled canvas showed immaculate. Her varnished spars shone against the blue sky like streamers of cobweb.

It was true that she drew little water, and that her cargo capacity was obviously quite limited. What of that? She had come from far seas, distant horizons of romance.

There are some craft which do not need to carry great cargoes; there are some cargoes which do not need much room for stowing. There are ships that slide across the bar of palm-strewn pearling atolls, and carry a freight of wealth in the compass of their cabin safe. There are ships that swing across the muddy waters of Sumatran rivers, do their trading for gold and diamonds, and slink away before the Dutchman can arrive. There are ships that nestle among the greenery of Dyak creeks, taking aboard their gum camphor, while the British patrol puffs by outside in sheer blissful ignorance.

And now this miniature schooner hung in the mud of a Louisiana bayou, while the man who had trapped her was laughing in shrill mirth to see her crippled!

The black boy, panting, fetched the rifle. Those at work with the boats paused and stared, their eyes rolling. Wrexham took the gun and clicked a cartridge home.

"Laugh, will you?" he roared out, so that his voice lifted and rolled amazingly across the bayou. "Laugh and be damned! You're not dealin' with Philbrick now!"

He lifted the rifle and fired.

With a cry of shrill and startled rage, Felix Macarty leaped upright—the bullet had splintered the wood under his arm. Wrexham threw out the empty shell, clicked another into place, and fired again. Another splinter of wood flew up. Macarty cursed his negro, and his launch swung out and headed away as the power drove her propeller.

Wrexham threw the bolt, lifted the rifle again. His protruding eyes were hard and chill. He sighted on the back of Macarty, and his finger drew on the trigger; then he lowered the rifle and shook his head regretfully.

"No—that's enough. I'll learn you things, damn you!" He handed the rifle to the waiting boy, then looked down at the men below. "Any of you boys know how to handle that mahogany launch and find the way to Latouche?"

"Yas, suh!" shouted several at once.

Wrexham picked out one of them, indicating the handsome mahogany launch which Aline had recently bought.

"Fill her with gas and get her ready. I'm going to town in ten minutes."

"Sho' will, suh! Yas, suh, cap'n!"

Whoops of eager laughter and loud talking, such as black men use to disguise the strain of tense moments, echoed in the ears of Wrexham as he strode up to the great house.

He had brought ashore some of his things. Now he dressed carefully in fresh whites, shaved, clipped his square brown beard, changed into newly-whited shoes. He made sure that he had money and Philbrick's telegram, which was addressed to Fortier. Philbrick had told him about Fortier.

"Some cursed ninny of a lawyer!" thought Wrexham scornfully. "That girl should ha' laid off draggin' a lawyer into this mess."

Informing Uncle Neb that he was going to town for the day, he went to the wharf. The water had ceased to subside. The schooner lay well heeled over, hard and fast aground. Wrexham surveyed her with his lips tightened in a thin line. He beckoned two darkies.

"Carry me over that mud. If you drop me, I'll cut the hearts out of you!"

They grinned at this, picked him up, and waded across the glistening new mud to where the launch awaited him. A moment afterward the craft was chugging up stream.

"Up the bayou," directed Wrexham. "I want a look at the dam o' that power company. Then to town."

"Yas, suh."

Wrexham studied the shores, his brows drawn down in concentration; he was working out an inner problem of his own.

The lay of the land was not hard to grasp. Half a mile behind the plantation house was one outlet arm of the bayou that meandered across the delta, much of which was made land. This arm had now become a tiny trickle, and would soon be dry. Some distance farther up-stream—for a bayou is no more than another name for river—was a large tributary, the commonly used thoroughfare to the town of Latouche.

The rapidly-drying outlet arm had served to water the broad rice acres of the plantation. On the opposite shore of the bayou, a thin strip of land which was really part of the island, stood the Macarty house, hidden amid a clump of trees. These two plantations stood isolated, alone, stately but decaying monarchs of the Gulf Coast. The town of Latouche was miles away through the bayous.

At sight of the dam, Wrexham ordered the engine checked, while he studied the place. It was not imposing. The dam was neither wide nor high—but it was sufficient to serve its purpose. Wrexham discerned only a couple of men idling nearby.

"H'm!" thought the seaman. "Philbrick told the truth. These Macartys are only making a bluff—sheer bluff! Well, they have the wrong pig by the ear this trip, I tell you! Lay my schooner in the mud, will they? Just wait a bit!" And, aloud: "All right, boy. To town."

They glided along through the bayous—long sunlit alleys of water, overhung with clustering, trailing masses of greyish-green moss. They followed trackless ways where slimy green things slid away and vanished, or thin snakes seared through the water and were gone.

Wrexham sat motionless, absorbed in the thoughts that gripped him, unseeing this tropic environment. They could not have been altogether pleasant, those thoughts; his eyes were savage.

Perhaps he was taken back to that other day and place, where he had paid a debt to a man by mortgage of his soul to the devil. Perhaps he was thinking of the two men and a woman whom he had once upon a time betrayed, and whose memory haunted him ceaselessly. Or he might have been thinking of other occasions. He did not lack things to recur to his mind, this man. He had much to remember—and, probably, he had much to forget.

There was, for example, that Chinaman of Macassar, whose junk had been looted and burned under Palembang Island. Wrexham had really forgotten this incident, although one or two long-distance threats had followed him from Chuen Ying. It was only an incident, and lay far back in his life. Wrexham had never learned that it is the incidents which lie far back of which one should be afraid. He had never learned even to be afraid.

The launch popped suddenly into a large and open stream. Bayou Latouche. Here were other boats, horses, men; from somewhere the whistle of a locomotive, bringing first wonder to the eyes of Wrexham, then a laugh. A bend in the stream, and Latouche appeared, rapidly growing in size. Ten minutes, and Wrexham tossed his boy a dollar, then strode up-town to lunch and attend to business.

It was not a large place, this parish seat, but it was strange and interesting. Of late years the Cajun population had been augmented by odd strata of yellow and brown and white, most of whom lived by or from the sea. Filipinos, Japanese, Arab, Chinese—one encountered many such. Except for a few fine houses, and the parish buildings, the town looked hot and listless. David Macarty had a residence here.

After luncheon, Wrexham went to the railroad station and dispatched Philbrick's telegram to Fortier. This accomplished, he sought the post office and went to the general delivery window.

"I ordered mail forwarded and held here, from San Francisco," he said. "Cap'n Tom Wrexham, schooner *Nautilus*."

After a slight delay, he was handed a letter, much marked about and forwarded, and a curious glance followed him as he turned away.

When he was out in the street, Wrexham examined the letter curiously. It was from a man in Zamboanga in the Philippines, a former partner of Wrexham in many deals, a man whom Wrexham trusted.

The skipper tore at the envelope. Into his fingers came a letter, and with it a newspaper clipping. His eyes widened on this clipping. His sturdy fingers clutched it fiercely, his figure stiffened as he read the words. Astonishment flooded into his face, followed by a flush that might have come from some inward relief or deep pleasure.

"If this ain't a rum go!" he ejaculated, with an oath. He lowered the paper and stared blankly before him. "A rum go and no mistake! The only time in my life I was guilty of havin' a conscience—and now to find it's all been wasted!"

He read the clipping again, incredulous. No, there was no error! The two men and a woman, the three whom he had betrayed, had come to no ill-end, after all. His remorse had been needless. There was nothing for which to blame himself; his action had resulted in no harm at all. The clipping told him all this.

The wonder of it oppressed Wrexham. The ironic humour of it struck him and evoked a laugh. On the heels of this feeling, a thought: Why had he learned this fact only today? Because, obviously, he had accepted the duty imposed upon him by John Philbrick and the girl's photograph. Because he had sincerely wished to make amends for his former actions.

In a moment, this conviction became deeply and ineradicably

imprinted upon Wrexham's mind. It was a vague notion, but it fitted well with his vaguely formulated ideas of an over-ruling providence and an offended Jehovah. Wrexham was in no sense religious, but he did have beliefs. His canons were Masonic rather than theologic. It was, to him, indubitable that this information had come to him as a reward for what he had undertaken here.

"A rum go and no mistake!" he repeated, a trifle awed.

He remembered the letter, and glanced over the writing. It made no reference to the newspaper clipping. It was concerned only with business. There was, however, a postscript:

> P.S. I hear that the Chink of Macassar, Chuen Ying, pulled up stakes two or three years ago and vanished.
> They say he went to the States, and I hear he was no Chink at all, but a blooded Manchu. If you meet him over there, give him my regards—and look out!

Chuen Ying! For a moment Wrexham puzzled before he remembered that burned and looted junk under Palembang Island. Then he laughed.

It was a sweeping honest laugh, caused by the newspaper clipping and the great relief this had brought. Wrexham tore the letter across, and watched the fragments flutter away. Once more he had forgotten Chuen Ying. The newspaper clipping, however, he preserved very carefully.

"If this ain't my lucky day!" he reflected. "I'm comin' out all right, I tell you. Now, I'd better buy some stuff and get back home. No time to waste floatin' the schooner and irrigatin' that cursed rice crop. Warn me to irrigate, will you? I'll do it, blast your eyes!"

A furious exultation was upon him for the rest of that day. He could scarcely sit quiet while the launch chugged back home through the bayous.

Immediately he reached the plantation, Wrexham went aboard the schooner, clawed up the steeply inclined deck, and vanished below. He was busied there, alone, until sunset. Then he emerged into sight, yawned and stretched himself, and hailed the bank. A negro in a canoe fetched him ashore.

"Leave this canoe with a paddle in it," said Wrexham. "I want to use it to-night, but I'll do my own paddling."

"Yas, suh, cap'n," came the answer.

Wrexham dined alone that evening. He enjoyed being master of this place, and it was very certain that everyone in the place enjoyed having him for master.

Darkness had fallen when Wrexham called Uncle Neb to the library, and stated that he was going out. He demanded a dark coat, which Uncle Neb produced. With this, he left the house and started for the bayou.

Two hours later he returned. He was met by Uncle Neb, who was excited and nervous.

"Cap'n, boss, dere's been a gen'l'man here two times axin' fo' you-all," said the old darky. "Ol' Mistuh Philbrick, suh, done said he wa'n't to come around heah no mo', but I reckon—"

"Eh?" said Wrexham, coming into the hall, from the gallery. "Someone here, you say?"

"Dat yaller man, suh—Mistuh Ah Lee! He's settin' in by de fiah right now. Oh, my lawd, cap'n, boss! Why, suh, dem elegant white pants is all wet and—"

Wrexham, in fact, was soaking wet to the waist, and stained with mud. He glanced down at himself, and laughed.

"Ah Lee—that's the man, eh?"

"Dat's him, suh. I done tol' him to set an' wait—"

"Quite right, Uncle Neb. I'll change my clothes and be right down."

Wrexham went upstairs to the room which he occupied. He got out fresh clothes, and laughed softly to himself as he changed. Once he glanced at his watch, as though expecting something. Then he shook his head.

"Not yet—a good fifteen minutes yet!" he murmured. "I wonder if Macarty sent this Chink to see me? Wants me to run some liquor, or maybe some hop, for him. That'd be a cute trap to catch Tom Wrexham in, wouldn't it? H'm! After the news I got to-day, the whole bunch can roast in hell!"

He broke into a cheery, albeit tuneless, whistle—a most singular thing for Wrexham. Yet, why not? This day he had received great news. He was a happy man. The load that had weighted his mind was gone. He went down to the library feeling that twenty years had slipped from him. He felt quite prepared for any game.

In this mood, he stepped into the library. He came face to face with the man who rose to meet him. Wrexham stopped dead still.

In the candle-light, his face went absolutely livid. His hand slipped to his pocket, and found that he had left his pistol upstairs. He drew a deep breath and stood waiting, expectant, as though he were facing death.

"Good evening," said the yellow man quietly. "You did not expect to see me, captain?"

"I—I expected Ah Lee," murmured Wrexham. His voice was hollow and dead.

"I am Ah Lee," said the other. The wrinkled yellow face smiled. "Also, I am—or was—Chuen Ying of Macassar. I have hoped to see you for several years. Shall we sit down?"

CHAPTER IV

A NOVEL METHOD OF IRRIGATION

CAPTAIN WREXHAM sat down. Except for the passing pallor of his face, he appeared quite calm.

He was calm enough, goodness knows! Calm, with the deadly certainty that he was trapped. He had not a weapon within reach. He expected not the least mercy. He was too well aware how such men as Ah Lee cherish ancient enmities and relish long-deferred vengeances.

The Manchu was smiling—another bad sign. Despite his years, his frame was tall and burly; his black jacket and trousers were of fine silk, his hands hidden in the sleeves. His bare feet showed through the straps of sandals.

And this man was Chuen Ying! The schooner had been lying here for a week or more, so this yellow man must have known all about her long since. Captain Wrexham felt a trace of cold perspiration. How often in those days had he been stepping close to death? For once all his sang-froid was stricken, his garrulous tongue quenched.

He reached for a cigar, lighted it, and fastened his protruding eyes upon the Manchu.

"Well?" he asked quietly.

"You know, of course, that I have reasons for wanting to see you," said Ah Lee in a conversational tone. "I have had these reasons for a long time."

Wrexham nodded. "I always pay debts myself," he said.

"Of course." The other smiled gently. "I have tried several times to reach you, but failed. Why did you burn my junk, back there at Palembang?"

Wrexham crossed his legs, puffed reflectively, and stared at the fire.

"Well," he answered, "that goes back to trouble I had with her skipper, when we were laying side by side at Timor Laut; and the whole thing started that way. Just how it was, I don't remember. One thing led to another. Finally he drowned one of my Kanakas at Palembang, and after that I left the harbour and laid for him."

"I see," responded the Manchu. "All this was very unfortunate. It cost me a ship and a rich cargo—a very rich cargo."

This was true enough. Some of the loot was still aboard the *Nautilus*, in chests.

Captain Tom Wrexham had been in some tight places in

the course of his life, but in none which pinched so tightly as this one. Being conversant with the world, he knew that he was standing cheek by jowl with death; the only question was just what form that death would take.

For two reasons, Wrexham did not offer to reimburse Ah Lee for that injury of other days. First, Ah Lee would merely have laughed at such an offer. Second and more important, Wrexham was not the kind of man who buys himself a road to immunity.

"I had a long talk with Mr. Philbrick to-day," said the Manchu's level voice.

Wrexham's head jerked. Something in the tone of those words sharpened his glance.

"Ah! Then you know what's going on here?"

Ah Lee smiled. It was a smile of genuine amusement; a smile that ended in a richly musical laugh.

"Yes. Poor Philbrick! He learned something this day. When I left him, he was like a man dumbfounded."

"Oh, ho!" said Wrexham. "You mean, you told him things about me, eh?"

Ah Lee gave him a glance of astonishment.

"Of course not. About myself! You see, he has always considered me something as you or I would regard a lazy, worthless coolie. He knew, or guessed, that I was engaged in the traffic of liquor, and he had threatened to shoot me. What he never knew until to-day was that Miss Lavergne is a very dear friend of mine."

It was Wrexham's turn to be startled. He stiffened in his chair. But Ah Lee continued meditatively.

"We are friends, yes, but not openly. I am not, you understand, a very good person to be considered as the friend of a young girl—in this country. Often we have met and talked. Small favours have passed. During a year and more, we have progressed in our own form of friendship. You should really know her, captain. Asia is supposed to produce wonderful women, yet I have never encountered any with the peculiar charm of Miss Lavergne."

The protruding eyes of Wrexham were filled with a questioning and perplexed light.

This Oriental was speaking in a hushed and reverent voice, as one speaks of some high and sacred thing. Wrexham gradually comprehended that he was being furnished with certain vital information—that the Manchu had a deliberate purpose in what he was saying.

Ah Lee looked up and smiled, but now the smile was thin and dry, very sardonic.

"I will concede," he said, his words smoothly acrid, "that you are a very evil man. You undoubtedly will concede that I am also a very evil person, a menace to the community. Yet, from my talk with Philbrick, I learned something about you.

"For example, that you were impelled to take this plantation in charge because of a singular influence exerted upon you by Miss Lavergne's photograph. In other words, some residuum of basic good in your soul was awakened into life."

Involuntarily, Wrexham glanced at the picture on the mantel, with a frown; Ah Lee glanced at it likewise, but with that same sardonic smile. The Manchu appeared to find some singular and deadly humour concealed in the situation. Wrexham could not understand the smile.

"You may not believe it," pursued Ah Lee, "but a kindred reaction was produced in me by my friendship with Miss Lavergne herself. I am an old man, captain, full of uneasy devils, and in a few more days I shall be dead. I have known for a long while that death's hand was clutching at my bowels, and the things of the body have interested me but little. It is the things of the spirit and mind that have appealed to me. So, perhaps, I could understand your action in taking charge of this place. I had at first thought that you would loot the house and take to sea, but now I understand."

"H'm!" grunted Wrexham, with a wry grimace. He was uneasy and disturbed.

At this instant there penetrated to them a muffled disturbance of the atmosphere—a dull thudding vibration that was felt, rather than heard. Almost at once, it was followed by a second reverberating shock.

Ah Lee started, lifting eyes that were a sudden blaze of light. His hands moved slightly in his wide sleeves. But Wrexham waved his cigar and chuckled calmly.

"Don't worry," he said. "That was my irrigation machinery at work. Perhaps you don't know all the ins and outs of this place—"

"I know," said the Manchu. "But this—"

"Well," put in the seaman, "young Macarty was here last night and served notice on me, vice John Philbrick, to irrigate the rice fields. The water went down this morning. To-night I am irrigating—that's all!"

Admiration gleamed in the oblique Oriental eyes.

"So that was why you were out in a canoe this evening, when I arrived!"

"Oh! You knew that, did you?"

"Of course. You have been watched. And you were—"

"Using up some old dynamite I had aboard the schooner. A time fuse and a float. Now let's get back to first causes. You say that you and Miss Lavergne are friends? But young Macarty intimated that you and he were friends likewise?"

"We have had dealings," returned the Manchu imperturbably. "He does not know that Miss Lavergne is my friend, however. Now, I should like to ask you a few questions."

Captain Wrexham was well aware that a Manchu does not waste words. Further, that this particular Manchu had a deep meaning in what he was doing. His own apprehension began to be distinctly relieved; he began to be reassured as to his own safety.

"Come on, now!" he blurted. "You're drivin' at something, so out with it! There's queer things in these seas, but the queerest of all is you not killin' me when the chance comes! So out with it, now."

Ah Lee regarded him. For a moment the black eyes were chill and terrible.

"Until this morning, I fully intended to kill you, captain. Especially since I have not long to live, and the disease grows on me. But now I have laid aside such thoughts."

"Reason bein' what?" inquired the seaman cheerfully, yet suspiciously.

"That friendship, in the scale of ethics, comes above revenge. Miss Lavergne is in deep trouble; she must have friends to aid her. The gods have sent you to that end."

Wrexham was instantly astonished.

"Eh? Come, now—what about yourself?"

"I am a yellow man." Ah Lee smiled his thin dry smile. "It makes things difficult in this country. You must fight the Macartys openly. Fighting is your business."

Wrexham felt confused and alarmed, as though he were being played with.

"Look here," he said, "you're away wrong! I don't want any more enemies. Lord knows I didn't want to take on any scrap here! I'd give my eye-teeth to be out of it all and fifty miles to sea, and that's the truth!"

For the second time that evening Ah Lee laughed with unaffected mirth. Then, seeing the glance of Wrexham sweep to the photograph on the mantel, he nodded to himself, chuckling.

How was it that this man of yellow skin and alien race, this old man who was regarded as an evil menace to the community, could so piercingly grasp the impulses of Tom Wrexham—who scarcely understood his own mental reflexes? To this query, Ah Lee gave the answer.

"Miss Lavergne is my friend, captain," he said. "You love her as I do, I perceive—with the love that is permitted any man toward an object of rare beauty, whether it be a woman, a delicate porcelain, or a picture on the wall."

In his tone was a fine irony, which Wrexham could not at all understand. For a moment the skipper was tempted to think that there was something odd and queer about this picture of Aline Lavergne—then he forgot the notion instantly.

"What about them questions?" he demanded.

Ah Lee nodded. "Do you know anyone by the name of John Solomon?"

Wrexham frowned over his cigar, stared hard into the fire embers.

"No, can't say that I do—yet the name—hold on! I got it. There was a ship chandler o' that name in Port Said, years an' years ago. I mind the place, now. Lord, I ain't even thought o' Port Said in years!"

"You don't know the man, then?"

"Not personal, no."

Ah Lee removed his hands from his sleeves, produced his cigarette-case, and lighted a tube.

"Did you ever hear mention of the Queen of Sheba? Or the Gemini? Or the Sea-moon?"

Wrexham turned and stared.

"Lord love me! This here is a rum go. And the farther you goes the rammer it gets! Here Macarty comes along and asks some such question, and now you. No, I never heard of 'em—whether it's a lunar rainbow or stars that ain't been charted! What's it mean?"

Across the wrinkled yellow face slipped a mask of impassivity.

"Before he died, Mr. Lavergne—Miss Aline's father—mentioned those words. There was no explanation. Philbrick knows something of it, but has not told me. Never mind!" Ah Lee rose to his feet. "You are not a fool, Captain Wrexham. The rest lies with you. Now I must go, for I have overstayed my time and I must go and drink some Ng Ka Py. Good night, and good luck!"

So saying, Ah Lee extended his hand; Wrexham took it. For an instant the eyes of the two men met and gripped, even as their fingers gripped. In that instant each came to understand many unguessed things about the other. Then Ah Lee bowed slightly and left the room.

Wrexham remained where he was.

For a space the skipper stood motionless, watching the door that had closed. His face was a study in emotions. At length a sigh came from him.

"Lord, but this is a rum go!" he breathed. "A rum go, and no mistake! First I get that letter about the other party, then I run head-on into this chap."

His eyes wandered to the photograph on the mantel, and dwelt upon it in curious wonder. He addressed himself to the picture.

"And what happens? Why, miss, you turn up to save my rotten life, that's what! If I hadn't taken on this job, the yellow lad would ha' done for me. If it hadn't been for your picture, I'd not ha' taken it on. If it hadn't been—oh, Lord! I'm done up wi' thinking about it, and that's the truth."

He sighed again, and lowered himself into his chair. As he himself might have expressed it, Wrexham could have been knocked down with a feather at the unexpected issues of his meeting with Ah Lee. It had not been a long conversation, but it had been frightfully tense for Wrexham, who had, during a good half of it, expected to be killed at each instant. Now he found himself weak and shaken.

"He meant it, about dyin' and so forth," he ruminated, and looked up again at the picture. "Yes, ma'am, he loves you, and no mistake! That turmeric-dyed limb of the devil is in love with you! Just the same as I am, and no harm intended by sayin' so. It's your eyes, lookin' right down into a man! I'm beginning to believe that you do exist, just like your picture. If you do, Lord help me when we meet! I'll turn missionary or something.

"And you saved my life. Instead of killin' me, the yellow beggar wishes me good luck! The rummest thing I ever heard in my life.

And why did he do it? Because you were his friend. Well, the whole thing's beyond me, that's all."

This was a mere figure of speech. The whole thing was not beyond Tom Wrexham, not in the least. As Ah Lee had said, he was no fool.

And he expected trouble when Macarty discovered that the dam was blown up.

CHAPTER V

TIT FOR TAT

CAPTAIN TOM Wrexham made no mistake in judging his actions. He knew that his overt acts had committed him, and that all parley with the Macartys was off. He expected to get some red-hot declaration of war, and was prepared to give as good as he got.

However, to his vague uneasiness, nothing happened. He saw nothing more of Felix Macarty. The *Nautilus,* unhurt by her dip in the mud, floated once more with the full current of water. A sunlit peace and calm brooded over everything.

Wrexham busied himself about the plantation, waiting for something to happen, and meantime keeping hard at work. The task of overseer delighted him; it thrilled him to dig into plantation details and watch the wheels go around under his hand. It fed his vanity and stimulated his itching dignity to dine like a king in the great dining-room.

The days fled swiftly and joyously, the more so that Wrexham found himself now facing the world with clean hands—nothing left to trouble his conscience, no fear of old enemies cropping up. That shock had come and gone again. He was eager, now, for Macarty to open battle. With his fine contempt for the law, Wrexham was quite ready for anything. A visit to the dam showed him that it was finely destroyed, but the site remained deserted. What did it mean? Had the one blow knocked out the Macartys? Hardly probable.

Since there was no lack of labour, Wrexham careened the schooner, scraped and painted her bottom, put every last inch of her into an absurdly perfect condition. Sometimes he slept aboard her. He was hard to reconcile to land hours, and kept much to the sea system of four hours of sleep and another four of wakefulness and work. Thus he was a-prowl at all times. Nothing happened, however, and the enemy appeared quite routed.

This worried him. He saw nothing of Ah Lee, heard nothing from Philbrick. Often he puzzled over those mysterious words about the Gemini and Sea-moon, but in vain. And he approved the aloof retirement of the place. The English strain in Wrexham liked this dignified and stately solitude, although it was distinctly out of place in Louisiana, setting this place apart, branding Cypremort with the brand of the vaguely sinister.

Several times, Wrexham got out that book which John Philbrick had made, and he read it from cover to cover. By degrees, he came to have an appreciation of Philbrick, came to a better understanding and liking of the greybeard who had all his life dreamed of going to sea—and had never gone. Also, that book gave him an idea. He visited the room which belonged to Aline Lavergne—a quaint old room, furnished entirely in buhl.

Wrexham had a red teak chest brought ashore from the schooner, summoned Aunt Sapphira, and set to work upon the room. Upon the dressing-table he laid out a set of exquisite little bottles wrought from moss agate, crystal, and amethyst. Behind and above the armoire he draped a wide brocade of softly glimmering blue and gold, a brocade that had been old and priceless before the days of the great Chings.

Across the bed, so rich in its deep tortoise-shell and brasses, he flung a stole of ermine lined with sun-hued silk, upon which was broidered the name of Shin Tung, the last emperor to stand before the altar of the Palace of Heaven. Upon the wall he hung a sheet of jade, highly carved and framed in silver—inlaid teak—not the cheap Yunnan jade which floods the tourist market, but that rich, reddish-brown jade which has been extinct in China for two thousand years, and which is valued above all products of earth.

When this was done, Wrexham locked the room and gave the key to Aunt Sapphira, telling her to allow no one else inside until Aline returned.

"It's a rum go, miss!" he reflected, looking into the eyes of the pictured girl. "If you knew the history of that stuff, and how I'd got it, maybe you wouldn't take much interest in it. But you don't know—and you'll love it like I do, Lord bless you! You have to get that sort o' stuff as a gift—or else by killin'. Well, well—you'll have somethin' to remember Tom Wrexham, by somethin' better than a puling book o' poems, eh?"

He was feeling well pleased with himself that night as he smoked his after-dinner cheroot and glanced through a magazine. Uncle Neb interrupted him by handing him a note which had been left at the landing by a passing shrimper.

"Ah! The declaration of war!" thought Wrexham, and tore it open.

To his disgust and astonishment, it was nothing of the kind. It contained only a vague and rather maudlin warning from John Philbrick. The pencilled and shaky scrawl read:

Good work with the dam! But I'm sorry for you. No ordinary fight. I don't know; all a puzzle to me—lucky I got out of it no worse, so far. You'll catch it heavy. Ah Lee is down sick, I hear. The Macartys won't strike at the body, but at the heart and soul. That's the thing to watch against. No chance to strike back. No recourse—a blow at the heart. Something's up. I don't know what. J.P.

Wrexham angrily crumpled up the note and threw it into the fire.

"Balderdash!" he cried, twisting his fingers in his square brown beard. "That old fool—and drunk as a lord when he wrote it! Him and his stuff about strikin' at hearts! Why couldn't he up an' say what's what? Wish he'd leave me alone instead of sendin' me nonsense like that. Drunk as could be. Drunk—"

He paused suddenly, as a thought drove home and left him cold. Where had Philbrick any liquor supply, out in the brakes?

Wrexham stared at the fire, his angry eyes wide-set and thoughtful. Whisky was the old man's bane, right enough. Who was supplying him? Felix Macarty? It was a dim conjecture, but there were threads on which to hang it. Felix Macarty was in touch with the outlaws, was said to have a hand in the illicit liquor game. Perhaps Macarty preferred to have the old man drinking himself to death, rather than sitting behind bars!

"Dash it!" exclaimed Wrexham, much perturbed. "Sounds like one o' these here novels! I don't like the looks of it. Sorry for me, is he? I don't need his dashed sympathy! He'd better be sorry for himself, the old greybeard rascal!"

Wrexham wished very much that Aline Lavergne were here; he had a burning desire to know the original of that photograph. When he thought of Fortier, it was with disdain. Philbrick had discussed Fortier with him, and Wrexham regretted the employment of the lawyer. He wished Aline were here, to discuss matters with him. He felt he could be frank with her.

The skipper cherished a frank suspicion and contempt for members of the legal profession. He was convinced that Aline would get no good from this man Fortier. He pictured Fortier as a strutting and crafty shark, and cursed vividly at the thought of him.

Wrexham felt restless that night; he could not account for the sensation. He tried to read and could not centre his mind on a book. For an hour he paced up and down the dock, after setting out the riding lights of the schooner as usual. Then, coming into the house again, he encountered Uncle Neb in the hall.

"See here, do you know when Miss Lavergne will be home?"

Uncle Neb shook his grey head. "I done heard some niggahs specify 'at dem Macartys was a-fixin' to come back right quick, suh, cap'n! Two o' dem Macarty niggahs was over heah las' night, suh. Dey 'lowed de silver was bein' varnished up an' de house cleaned, like de boss was comin' sudden. Miss Aline, she'll mos' likely come, too, suh. Yo' ain't had no letter, suh?"

Wrexham started. He had completely neglected mail, and no one else had gone for any. Mail meant so little in his life, as a rule, that he had forgotten it here.

"No, I haven't," he said. "But I'll go to town to-morrow and see if there is any word. Good thing you spoke of it. You run off to bed, now; I'll stay up a bit."

Wrexham shut himself in the library. Cigar clenched between his teeth, he strode up and down the room, his brow creased in a frown. He was puzzled by the Macarty enmity, by their plans, by the unknown thing for which they were scheming.

"It's a rum go!" he meditated. "What do they want here? What do they want this place for? They ain't poor. Why was old Philbrick so cursed worried about leavin' the place unprotected? Dashed if I can fathom it. Why was Felix Macarty so willin' to step in and take care o' the place, once he'd got rid o' Philbrick? And what's that talk about Gemini and Sea-moon, eh? It's a rum go."

Already his brain was driving off at new tangents. He was nervous; a new, unpleasant, and unrecognized sensation. He wondered what could be the matter with him to-night.

The waiting had told on him. Used always to a direct game, he had encountered only silence since that night he had blown up the dam and met Ah Lee. Now the obscure note from Philbrick, and the intimation that the Macartys might be home soon. All this spelled trouble, but Wrexham could find no opening for trouble to enter by. He was uneasy, confused.

He came to a halt before a window, drew the heavy curtain, glanced out. He could see the riding lights of the schooner, and this quieted him. It was like seeing an old friend, a friend who would never fail him. His eyes softened.

"Good old girl!" he said. "No deviltry about you, eh? You and

I—let the rest of the world go hang! Expect I need a whiff of sea air. We'll get some o' these black boys to-morrow and take a spin, old girl. Good night!"

He dropped the curtain and turned away, a sigh on his lips.

There was a gin bottle in the dining-room, opened but scarce tasted. Wrexham took a candle and went in search of the white fire. He seldom delighted in the liquor, but now he poured himself a tremendous drink and gulped it down. He blew out the candles and went upstairs to his room, a grimace on his lips.

Usually Wrexham woke at four, and in half an hour was out at the schooner removing the riding lights. On this morning, however, eight bells found him snoring—the drink, perhaps, or the mental strain of the preceding evening. It was six o'clock when his eyes unclosed.

Up to a certain point, he could afterward recall clearly what he did that morning. He bathed and shaved, trimmed his beard carefully, dressed with his usual precise nicety. Then he passed downstairs and started for the wharf to attend to the riding lights. He could even remember crossing the gallery and taking up a bit of paper that he saw fastened to the right-hand post. On this paper was a scrawl:

Tit for tat, captain! F.M.

Then, frowning, he had swung down the steps for the wharf. At this point he must have used his eyes. At this instant the full realization of how Macarty had struck at his heart and soul must have rushed over him like a paralysing wave.

Shortly afterward, Uncle Neb came rushing into the kitchen, startling Aunt Sapphira and the two coloured maids with his tremulous excitement.

"Run down to de quarters an' chase up some o' dem field-hands!" he shouted wildly. "Hustle on, ol' woman! All de boats gone—big boat gone—cap'n standin' out dere like de debbil got him! Tell dat slue-foot Charles swim over an' borry a canoe from Macartys—hustle on, woman!"

Spluttering English and creole, old Uncle Neb rushed back outside.

The other negroes soon arrived. They clustered about the figure of Captain Wrexham and stared at him in awe and terror. He stood motionless on the wharf, as a man paralysed. Uncle Neb approached and spoke, but Wrexham only mumbled in his beard. The unfortunate man was stricken terribly.

Every one of the small craft was gone. Gone, too, was the *Nautilus*—gone as though she had never been! The blacks stared and chattered their wonder. Nobody had heard any sound during the night. The paper in Wrexham's clenched fingers conveyed nothing to them. His attitude of stark immobility frightened them more than the loss of the boats.

Presently a canoe appeared, paddled by a dripping boy who had swung to the Macarty place and borrowed it—there were no launches across the bayou. At sight of the canoe, Captain Wrexham started. He seemed to waken into life. A torrent of profanity came to his bearded lips.

"Gone!" he uttered between curses. "Gone!"

He saw the black men staring at him, and a spasm of pain contracted his face. Without a word he turned and strode up to the house. He walked heavily, blindly, stumbling at the gallery steps. Years had fallen upon his shoulders. He went into the library, dropped into a chair, and sat motionless; his mind was awake now, awake and writhing under the blow.

Uncle Neb, who knew in part what the schooner meant to this man, hustled two of the negroes into the canoe and sent them forth to seek the missing craft.

Wrexham sat alone in the library and suffered. Even had there been a launch to use, he knew how futile was any search. Within five miles there were a score of places where the little schooner might be berthed amid the trees, laid up, and hidden. Long ere this, no doubt, she had been perfectly concealed. A dozen boats might search in vain.

"Heart and soul!" groaned Wrexham. "Heart and soul!"

It was the first time in his life that real loss had come to him. He was hardened to most things; but through all the years he had grown in the consciousness that his strength and ability leaned upon an external creation—the schooner he loved.

As he sat here, he recalled scores of little things that pierced deeply. The feel of her puttied seams beneath his feet, the quick swing of her to the helm, the stanch lean and thrust as the wind drove at her canvas. And more intimate things; the times unnumbered he had depended upon her, never in vain! All his life, all his petty world, had been horizoned by her bulwarks. Every scratch in her paint was registered upon his mind. Every rivet in her coppered bottom, every plank in her hull, was an old friend.

He cursed himself for having slept ashore, for having abandoned her. He would have awakened at the first step of an alien foot on her deck, at the first quiver of her parted cable. For her sake he had broken more than one law, had committed more than one crime. She was twined deeper in his heart-strings than any creature of flesh and blood could have been.

For the moment, all fight was gone out of him. For the moment, the spirit in the man was broken. The thought of enemies on her deck, of stranger hands at rigging and wheel, burned into him intolerably. He looked up and saw the picture of Aline Lavergne gazing down at him. From his lips fell a curse. He staggered to his feet and shook his fist, all the worst of him at the surface.

"If it hadn't been for you!" he cried, inarticulately. "If it hadn't been for you—"

He groaned, swept suddenly by helplessness. At whom to strike? There was none. He had come into a web of unseen enemies. Unless he were to go forth and run amuck like a crazed Lascar, he could do nothing. The breathing came from his nostrils harshly, chokingly. Suddenly he flung out his hands and glared at the picture from bloodshot eyes.

"I'm done!" he cried. "I'm done, I tell you! Played the damn fool all the while. Sat in at another man's game and got rooked. Served me right! I'm done!"

He heard Uncle Neb appear and agitatedly invite him to breakfast. Wrexham blasted out a curse, strode to the door, slammed it until the house shook. He wanted only to be alone. He went back to the fireplace. For a space he gazed at the photograph there, looking into the eyes that met his so quietly, so serenely.

"I *am* a ruddy fool," he said at last. "My place ain't here, ma'am. D'you know that you've ruined me, brought me to the gallows? Well, you have! I'll go out now and shoot that cursed Macarty— and the schooner's gone—and they'll get me. Or, I'd better wait here! Macarty will be along soon enough with an offer. If it hadn't been for you, I'd not be here now. And what'll I do? What'll you do about it? Tell me that!"

He gazed at the photograph, as though expecting some answer. Then he shook his head, and plucked at his beard with trembling fingers. His eyes widened strangely, self reproach coming into their depths.

"No, I shouldn't blame you for it," he said at last, struggle in his voice. "No—no! I'm just a fool, ma'am. God or the devil has been waitin' around the corner all this while to hit me when I wasn't lookin', that's all. And I'm hit, no mistake about that! Well, I'm done in. Lost my grip on things. This affair has—well, it's jolted me clear to the keelson. But I can't blame you, girl. I don't know about it. I'm just a fool."

He rested his arms on the mantel and looked into the eyes of the photograph for a time. Presently his brow went down on his arms and he stood there motionless. He was lost to all extraneous things, completely enwrapped in his own wretched thoughts.

Standing thus, at grips with the devils and the angels, he

heard nothing. To him came no sound from outside, no chatter of tongues, no slurred thrum of footsteps on the cypress boards. The man was looking inward, catching up with himself; he was trying desperately to force himself into some coherence of thought and action. A drop of blood from his bitten lip hung pendulous on his square brown beard.

At length, compelled by some agency outside himself, he lifted his head and stood erect. He slowly turned, and perceived that the door was open again. A man, a stranger, was standing there, silently regarding him.

Wrexham returned the look in astonishment. The man was strong, hearty, frank, and keen of eye. One could see that he stood four-square. Wrexham acknowledged inwardly that he liked this man on sight.

"Hullo!" he exclaimed. "And who the devil are you?"

The stranger came in, ignoring the pose in which he had surprised Wrexham. He held out his hand.

"You're Captain Wrexham, of course? My name's Fortier—I just reached here. Glad to meet you, captain!"

Wrexham put out his hand, confusedly. Fortier turned and beckoned another man.

"And this is my friend John Solomon—he wants to lay low for a while, Wrexham, and reach a friend of his up the bayou, a Chinaman by the name of Ah Lee. Do you suppose one of the boys could take him in a canoe? He'll have to be guided, of course—"

Wrexham shook himself alert at this. That is, he shook himself into a semblance of action—only a semblance. He seemed fascinated by the round blank features of Solomon.

"What's this?" he said brusquely. "Ah Lee? You know that beggar, do you?"

"Yes, sir," returned Solomon. "If I can find 'im, sir, e'll take care o' me all right."

Wrexham waved his hand. "Canoe down there," he said

abruptly. "Go get into it. I'll have one of the boys take you—those black devils know Ah Lee, right enough."

"Thank you werry much, sir," returned Solomon, and disappeared.

CHAPTER VI

"DREAMS LEFT WANDERING IN THE DAY"

"AND WHERE'S Miss Lavergne?" demanded Wrexham, with his first show of interest.

The two men sat at luncheon. Hours had passed since the arrival of Fortier. During these hours, Wrexham had gradually recovered himself.

Only in part, however. He was not the same man he had been. Now he was moody, silent, a surly growl in his voice. He had forced himself to talk with Fortier that morning, and to effect an explanation of things. Yet he could think coherently of only one subject—the missing *Nautilus.* He was overwhelmed by his own sense of loss.

It was not until noon that he had asked the question about Aline.

"She's at Latouche," returned Fortier. "She stopped there to spend the day. There are some business matters she must attend to in person. David Macarty had to stop there, too; we had trouble on the way and got held up for a time. Only reached there last night. I got a launch early this morning and came on with Solomon."

The talk languished again. The two men ate in silence.

Jack Fortier could comprehend why Wrexham was so crushed over the loss of his schooner. The seaman had spoken without reserve to him, had laid bare the situation, in a hopeless and listless fashion. He had displayed little interest in Fortier's doings.

"It's an odd thing about Solomon!" said Fortier. He went on

to tell of the murder of Gros Michel. For this murder, David Macarty had turned over his mate Thompson to the sheriff at Latouche.

"That's really why Solomon wants to hide out for a time," he went on. Wrexham heard him in an absent-minded fashion. "That queer chap has brains, Wrexham! He had a talk with Macarty—a frank talk. Expressed himself as ready to help Thompson out of the scrape by disappearing. Without his evidence, Thompson could not be convicted, and Macarty was very glad of his attitude.

"Macarty, you see, does not know that Gros Michel was an outlaw—or, if he knows it, he is keeping quiet. He'd have to, since he had employed the man as quartermaster. You see how clever Solomon was about it? For some reason of his own, Solomon wanted to reach Ah Lee—I don't know why. The fellow is secretive as the devil. Yet he's friendly to us, I'm convinced! Thus, he has contrived to get Thompson out of the way—a dangerous man, that, Gros Michel, another dangerous man, is dead. And David Macarty is convinced that Solomon is doing all in his power to help his employer. It's a queer affair! I can't get any information out of Solomon. I have a notion that he wants to see this Chinaman at once. I don't pretend to understand it. I need information about Solomon as badly as you need it about the schooner."

Wrexham shook his head.

"Don't ask me," he rejoined absently. "All tangled up in my mind, it is. Don't want to think about it. Don't give a tinker's dam about it! And that's the truth."

"You can't mean that," protested Fortier, astonished. "After what you've done here—"

"Devil take what I've done!" cried out Wrexham angrily. "I ain't done a thing! It's what that devil Felix Macarty's done! Where's my craft? That's what I want to know. That's all I care about. Makes my head hurt to worry over you and him and them—needn't come to me about it. Getting old, that's what I am."

"But we need your help—Miss Lavergne and I!" said Fortier. He realized that Wrexham was in an abnormal state of mind, potentially dangerous. The seaman glared at him from angry bloodshot eyes.

"I'm done," he declared bluntly. "I'm done! Shan't worry my head about you and him and them, I tell you. My brain's all fogged up—need to get out to sea. All I want is the schooner. Gone my limit, I have, and that's the truth! This here is a rum go. I'm goin' to take that launch of yours and go look for my schooner. Have a drink first, though."

Luncheon over, Uncle Neb produced a whisky decanter and the two men adjourned to the gallery. By degrees Wrexham lost his sullen air, and talked. At any other time he would have been entirely too reserved to say anything to Fortier about the picture on the mantel. Now, however, with the *Nautilus* gone, the man's mental barriers were down. He spoke frankly enough, in a detached way, as though he were telling some other man's tale. He told of the influence exerted upon him by that photograph, and of the resultant consequences. He apprised Fortier that the Manchu who called himself Ah Lee was a friend and a man to be trusted, and went into reasons for this.

Fortier wondered.

"The eyes of Aline Lavergne," he mused aloud, when the seaman had fallen silent, "seem to have a strange power to reach men, Wrexham! A singular thing—"

"Not a bit of it," said the skipper coolly. "Not a bit of it! Not singular at all. It's like Ah Lee said—that girl has the sweet purity of a flower. Well, then! When a bad 'un like me or Ah Lee looks into eyes like hers, somethin' is stirred inside 'em. A man who has lived hard, who has seen life, knows what a cursed wonderful thing it is to be good. And that's all."

Fortier smiled.

Presently Wrexham departed, by himself, in the launch that

had brought Fortier from town. He was gone for the remainder of the afternoon, searching nooks and corners of the bayous for those missing boats. When he returned, the stoop to his shoulders told its own tale of failure.

During this afternoon, Fortier was not idle. From Uncle Neb, he added to Wrexham's story and gained supplemental details. Also, he learned a most extraordinary fact about that picture over the mantel in the library—a fact which he did not dare breathe to Captain Wrexham, however!

With dinner, Wrexham drank heavily and had fallen into a black and ugly mood. The meal helped to fetch him out of it, but Fortier saw plainly that the man was ripe for any sort of action that offered itself. The mention of Aline, too, made Wrexham uneasy.

"I've been too long ashore," he told Fortier gloomily. "If the schooner was here, I believe I'd put out to-night and get a breath o' wind—and maybe not come back. Anyhow, I've done my work here. I've had my reward and my punishment. If that schooner don't show up by to-morrow, I'll go an' burn the Macarty place, so help me!"

Suddenly his eyes struck up at Fortier with keen incisive force.

"See here! D'you ever hear of the Gemini, or the Sea-moon— ah! So you have, eh?"

Fortier had not been able to repress an involuntary start at those names.

"There's some mystery about it," he responded. "Mr. Lavergne died suddenly. He left those names scribbled on a bit of paper— that's all we know. I'd been hoping Philbrick might have more information. Did he tell you about them?"

"No such luck." Wrexham's face fell. "I don't like mysteries, I can tell you! What's the game these Macartys are playin'? Tell me that!"

"I wish I knew it," said Fortier uneasily. "David Macarty is trying now to induce Aline to take a little cruise aboard his

yacht. There's something here they want to grab. She'll probably be here to-morrow, and we can go over matters in detail."

Wrexham fell into a frowning silence.

Dinner over, they sought the library and smoked. Fortier
showed the skipper that scrawl made by Lavergne on the back
of the document, but it threw no light on the situation. He put
his papers with the others in the safe, and was content to await
the return of Aline before probing deeper.

It was still early when Fortier said good night, and followed
Uncle Neb to the room prepared for him.

Not so Captain Wrexham. After pacing up and down the
library for a long while, the seaman stuffed some cigars into his
jacket and escaped to the open air. He passed down to the wharf
and resumed his ceaseless striding up and down the length of
the planks. Under the glow of starlight, his cigar tip burned
steadily, a red dot of light.

Wrexham was in no mood to meet Aline Lavergne on the
morrow. As he gazed across the bayou at the darkness which
enveloped the Macarty house, he promised himself a raid with
torch and bullet in the dawn, unless something first turned up.
That something would turn up, he firmly believed. Macarty
would come to him with some offer, some bribe; he could have
the *Nautilus* back, upon some sort of condition. Thus, it was
really for the coming of Macarty that Wrexham waited here
upon the wharf.

Time fled, however, and Felix Macarty came not. Wrexham
watched the waters with savagely burning eyes. He had almost
decided to go to bed and get some sleep before his meditated
raid of solitary vengeance, when he discerned a gliding shape
down the bayou—a long sliver of darkness against the starlit
water.

He lighted a fresh cigar, patted the pistol in his pocket, and
waited grimly.

Slowly that dark shape drew near, heading for the wharf, and

Wrexham saw that a single paddler, a man, was urging the canoe forward in silence.

"Come to make a deal, have you?" said the seaman.

A maudlin laugh answered him. "News for you!" said the voice of Philbrick.

Wrexham stifled a curse and went down to the landing. Philbrick, by a miracle, got ashore and stood reeling. He was drunk. Also, he was tattered, mud-stained, disreputable. His beard was a wild tangled mass.

"Just been aboard your boat," he said, with a hiccup. "She's about four mile down the bayou, moored. Nobody there. Got some whisky. Have a drink?"

Wrexham disregarded the proffered bottle. He stood stiffly, staring at this apparition. His schooner—safe! His again, for the taking! It was incredible.

Then a laugh broke from Wrexham, a laugh of mingled astonishment and relief and wonder. He felt a sudden overwhelming warmth in his heart for John Philbrick—a burst of passionate gratitude, of deep and sincere friendship. And despite what was so soon to take place between them, this feeling never quite left Tom Wrexham, for Philbrick had given back his very heart and soul to him.

He shoved a cigar into Philbrick's hand, seized the bottle and drank lustily, clapped the greybeard on the back.

"Good for you!" he exclaimed. "Good for you! Let's sit down and talk it over. There's no hurry. We got all night."

He sat down, and Philbrick managed to follow suit. Naturally, Wrexham's first impulse was to leap into the canoe and go find his schooner. He mastered it, deliberately, and even coldly. He wanted to be sure of himself—wanted to think about what would come next. In the back of his brain, somewhere, was another impulse; to take the schooner and go to sea, and never come back. He was afraid to meet Aline Lavergne. Afraid lest the girl's reality should not come up to his ideals of her. So he sat down and sparred for time.

"You've been drinking a lot, out in the canebrakes?" he asked.

"Aye," hiccuped Philbrick, with a ghastly grin. "Aye. Nothing to do but drink an' dream. You know what Æschylus said about old men? 'Dreams left wandering in the day.' That's me. I'm far gone."

"You look it," said Wrexham brutally. "Why don't you lay off whisky?"

"Can't." Philbrick lifted the bottle and drank again. "It'd kill me."

Wrexham laughed. "Cure you, you mean! I'd cure you quick enough, if I had you aboard the *Nautilus*. By the Lord Harry, but I'd cure you! I've notion to do it, too. I've a notion to shanghai you, make a man o' you, Philbrick! Can do. You'd fight like hell at first, but a few weeks 'ud see you a new man, I tell you!"

"You leave me 'lone," said Philbrick.

"By the way, Miss Lavergne comes home here to-morrow," observed Wrexham.

The effect of this remark upon Philbrick was extraordinary.

For a moment the man sat absolutely motionless, arm outstretched, maudlin grin frozen on his lips. Then over his tattered and filthy body ran a tremulous shudder.

"Oh, my Heaven!" he groaned. The words seemed fairly wrung out of his heart.

"What's the matter o' you?" demanded Wrexham in astonished wonder. "Ain't you glad? Thought you'd be glad to see her. And that man Fortier's here. He's a real 'un and no mistake, I can tell you! A real man. Worth a dozen o' you and me. Here, what's the matter?"

Wrexham rose in alarm. For Philbrick had come to his feet and was swaying unsteadily.

"Can't you see, you fool?" groaned the overseer. "Look at me! I—I'm drunk. I'm all gone to pieces. Can't live an hour without whisky. All gone. Look at me! Think I can let her see me like this—ever?"

It was true. Under the starlight Wrexham could see that the

man's face was working terribly with the fear that was on him. His great body was almost a wreck. Those days of steady drinking must have been frightful in their effect.

"Well, go slow, now," said Wrexham coolly. "I owe you somethin' big, my man! You got to show me where that schooner is laid up, savvy? But wait a minute—I want to ask you something. Ever hear of the Gemini? Or the Sea-moon? Or the Queen of Sheba? Fortier wants to know about 'em. So does Macarty. So do I. What the deuce are they, anyhow? Stars?"

Philbrick put one hand to his head and groaned.

"No, no! They're in the desk in the library—two boxes of 'em. Stones. I don't know what. Lavergne brought 'em home from Asia with him—he's keeping them for somebody. They don't belong to him. Jewels, maybe. Oh, my Lord! To think of her coming home to-morrow—and me like this! A dream left wanderin' in the day—"

"Shut up that talk," snapped Wrexham. "Jewels? Balderdash! More of your nonsense! See here, where's that schooner o' mine? Can you find her?"

"Four mile down the bayou, moored inside that little island," said Philbrick in a dazed voice. He groped for the bottle, found it, lifted it to his lips for a long swallow.

"Ah!" he exclaimed. "I must get out of here before she comes home, cap'n! Mus' get out of here, unnerstand? I'm all gone to pieces. Not as bad as Ah Lee, though! He'll be dead in a few days. Says so himself. Devils eatin' him up inside—arrh! But I made him laugh, all right, when I told him that joke on you. Made him laugh!"

"Huh?" growled Wrexham. "What joke's that?"

Philbrick uttered a wild laugh and flung out his arm.

"Joke, all right! You and that picture. Fell in love with that picture—ho, ho!"

Wrexham's hand fell on his shoulder, twisted the man around suddenly. The fingers gripped and bit like iron. The seaman's voice was cold as ice.

"Spill it! What's that joke, old fool? What about it?"

"Picture of a dead woman!" mouthed Philbrick wildly. "Dead woman—Aline's mother! And you thought—you thought it was her all the while—you—"

There was a quick low sound as the fist of Wrexham went home. Philbrick staggered, flung out his arms, whirled half-around, then fell heavily. He lay on his face, motionless.

For a moment Wrexham stood over him, looking down. One would have thought that he was about to lash into the senseless old man with his boot—perhaps, indeed, he was. But he stood motionless, silent, for a long moment. Whatever emotion lay in his bearded face could not be seen under the starlight.

Suddenly he stooped. His hands caught at Philbrick's rags, ripped them savagely. In a moment he had bound the old man hand and foot, bound him hard and fast. Then he lifted the bound senseless body, and laid it in the canoe.

Without a word, Wrexham turned and strode up to the house. As a matter of fact, his brain was in a whirl, yet he knew exactly what he was going to do. It all came to him in a flash—came to him as he had stood there looking down.

Despite his confusion of mind, despite the jumble of thought, he knew exactly what he must do.

He quietly walked into the house, went to the library, and sat down at the desk. There he penned a short curt note to Fortier, telling him what he had learned from Philbrick. His lips curved in a sardonic twist at the mention of jewels. He concluded:

> The old fool's drunk as can be. He'll be dead in a week if I don't take a hand. So I'm taking it. I'm going to make a man of him yet. We're off to sea.
> The plantation's in your hands. I've resigned. Yours truly,
> Tom Wrexham.

Wrexham folded the note, placed it in an envelope, sealed it, and left it lying on the desk in plain sight. Then, a candle in his hand, he rose and walked to the mantel.

For a space he stood there, looking into the pictured eyes of the girl.

"So you're not Aline Lavergne—but her mother!" he said at last. He was quite calm now. "It's a rum go, this—a rum go, I tell you! If it hadn't been for you, young Macarty 'ud be here now, and no mistake. Were you watchin' over her, I wonder?"

This thought must have wakened strange things in him. He stood there, fascinated by those eyes which gazed down so sweetly and frankly into his. At last a sigh came surging from his lips.

"Oh, I knew it wasn't possible!" he said at length. "I knew no such bein' as you was living on this earth; and it's so. Maybe your girl's like you—I don't know. I ain't going to wait and see, neither."

He half turned away. Then, as though loath to go, he turned again and looked at the picture. Those protruding eyes of his, which at times could blaze with so fierce and predatory a light, were now strangely softened. There was even a diffidence in his air.

"Maybe," he said, hesitant, "maybe, now, you—you wouldn't mind going along to sea with me and old Philbrick? The old rascal has dreamed o' goin' to sea all his life, and never dared. Now I'm taking him—goin' to make a man of him. Do you think it 'ud be wrong o' me to take you along, miss? Would you mind goin'?"

He blinked at the picture. Then, suddenly, a smile touched his bearded lips. He reached up for the enlarged photograph, took it down from its place.

An instant later he blew out the candles.

He had gone.

CHAPTER VII

THE VOICE AND THE EYE

A H L E E lay gasping, until the pellet of opium eased his pain.

He who had worn the imperial yellow, now lay half-naked. He, who as prince-delegate had guided the plough before the altar of Earth, now lay, a dying yellow man, on the threshold of death. The glorious tiled roof of the Manchu palace no longer covered him, but the thatched roof of a hovel in the cypress swamp. Instead of sandalwood incense, there drifted across the night the sour odour of rice mash, from the vats where the coolies worked at the bayou's edge. He who had been served by princes and lords now had but one companion to witness his departure to the long home.

This companion was John Solomon.

Since these two men had last met, in the dirty restaurant in New Orleans, the Manchu had changed. Fate had overtaken him. His face had become a contorted mask of suffering; his body, a gauntly helpless machine that had suddenly run down.

Of his former condition, but two things remained unaltered. One was his voice, neither enfeebled nor obscured, since the voice of the spirit. The other was his black and glittering eye, since the eye is the window of the soul.

"Did you ever read," said Ah Lee suddenly, "the books of a Frenchman called Hugo?"

"Not to speak of," answered Solomon wheezily. "I've tried werry 'ard, but I don't like to be mistook in me details, as the old gent said when 'e was took up for bigamy. That there man was chock full o' details, 'e was, and a mortal lot of 'em wrong. 'E never bothered to look up 'is facts—'e just went it blind."

"Yet he was wise," said Ah Lee. "In one of his books he asks a question. It is this: 'Is there a providence of demons, as well as a divine providence?' He was right. The Macartys are served by a providence of demons. We are beaten and helpless."

"Look 'ere, you're all wrong!" said Solomon earnestly. "That's natural, 'cause why, you're a Manchu, and you take stock in such things! Not me! Prowidence is Prowidence, I says, and I don't 'old with demons and such."

Ah Lee made a weary futile gesture.

"What can we do? Nothing. I am helpless. In an hour I shall be dead. You are alone. Felix Macarty controls the outlaws, his father controls the law. Something new is being planned—what it is, I don't know. Their legal contrivances have failed. Now they will go about their work illegally. They are desperate, and they will win."

"I 'ave me 'opes, just like that," said. Solomon. "That 'ere Fortier, 'e ain't nobody's fool. They can't twist 'im around their finger."

"But what do they want?" said the dying man. "Why do they persecute her? What is the meaning of those words—the Gemini—Sea-moon—Queen of Sheba?"

"Didn't Philbrick know?" parried Solomon.

"He did not know. He guessed—he knew nothing. Perhaps he lied to me about not knowing."

"I know."

The eyes of Ah Lee turned to the face of Solomon. Upon that expressionless visage they rested in a species of horror. Nearby, a candle lantern fumed and smoked. It made the black eyes glow like *han yu* jade.

"You know?" said the Manchu.

"I know."

Ah Lee caught his breath. A spasm of pain shook his face.

"And I know—of you," he said, a catch of pain in his inflexible voice. "I have known of you for many years, before ever we met. They say that devils serve you."

"No," said Solomon. "It's me as serves Prowidence."

"No matter. Promise me one thing! That you will protect her."

Solomon looked at the dying man, and nodded. His eyes widened. For an instant they held a singular glow of feeling, of emotion, of expression.

"Yes. 'Er father was me friend; that's why I'm 'ere. Years and years ago I knowed 'im werry well indeed—in Port Said, it was. We done some business together. But you 'aven't no notion o' what them Macartys are plannin' to do?"

"None. Felix Macarty was here yesterday, but I could learn nothing. Hennepin is his chief man—Petit Jean. What is the reason? What do they seek from her?"

"A fortune," said Solomon reflectively.

"But the girl is poor! That is to say, she has little money—"

"Yes, but 'er father 'ad a fortune. 'E was keepin' of it for me in trust, thinkin' as 'ow I might need it some day and call for it. Them 'ere names you mentioned—"

Ah Lee lifted a warning finger. "I hear steps."

John Solomon sat in silence. Presently he produced pipe and tobacco, and began to smoke. He had been on the point of explaining what was meant by those three names—the Queen of Sheba. Gemini, Sea-moon.

Ah Lee, who had checked that explanation, was destined never to hear it.

As Solomon drew a match across his sole and held it to his clay pipe, a figure glided into the hut and sat down at one side. It was a man dressed in corduroys—a large and powerful man, whose face was bearded thinly, lined with seams of evil. In his hand the man held a long, slightly curved knife. As he sat there, legs crossed, he began automatically to whet the knife back and forth on his boot.

This man was Petit Jean Hennepin.

"Not dead yet, eh?" he said, looking at the Manchu.

"Not a-goin' to die, neither, I 'opes," said Solomon cheerfully. At these words, a ghastly grimace was for an instant visible on the contorted face of Ah Lee. The Manchu's lips opened, and he spoke.

His voice was now no longer the same. It was clear, but faint.

"Money in the trunk, yonder. You will pay my men? Six coolies. Two Arabs, good men who know arrack. You will attend to this?"

"I will," said Solomon. There was a slight silence. Then Solomon glanced at Petit Jean. "You was a-lookin' for me, sir?"

"Yes." Petit Jean Hennepin replied in oddly accented English which defies reproduction. "Yes. I've just had word from David Macarty. It shows your story was true. You're one of us. It's all right."

"That's werry kind of you, sir," said Solomon.

"The message also said," and the outlaw fastened upon Solomon a steady regard, "that your evidence 'ud hang Thompson for killin' my brother, Gros Michel. That so?"

Solomon nodded. "That's why I'm 'ere, sir. Mr. Macarty, 'e didn't want that 'ere Thompson to 'ang."

"Neither do I," said Petit Jean, and fell silent. In those three words, in the slow whetting of that knife, lay a dreadful significance. Suddenly the outlaw glanced up.

"When they discover who Michel was, Thompson will be set free. Then he'll come after you, Solomon! But don't you worry. I'll take care o' you."

"Werry kind of you, I calls it," said Solomon, with a nod. "Werry kind of you, sir, I says!"

Again silence. The candle guttered in its glass, and flamed higher. Solomon's pipe sucked empty; he knocked it out and leaned forward, looking at Ah Lee. Then he rose and took the lantern, and held it close to the face of the Manchu.

Something in the pose of Solomon, something in the way he stood there and gazed, caused Petit Jean to rise and join him. They both stared at the sick man. But Ah Lee was no longer sick. The voice was fled. The jade-like eyes were filmed over.

A wheezy sigh escaped the lips of Solomon. He blew out the lantern and went out of the hut.

Walking stiffly, he followed a curving path from the hut,

and this path brought him to an opening at the edge of the bayou. Here he stood, gazing at the scene before him—flaring, smoky torches of pine knots lighting the vats, the working, flitting figures of naked men vanishing and appearing again, the sketched suggestion of the swamp and forest behind. Behind Solomon came the figure of Petit Jean, standing there with him.

After a moment, Solomon filled his pipe again, and lighted it. As though the flare of the match had been a signal, a dark figure glided to him—one of the two Arab overseers. He addressed Solomon respectfully, in Arabic.

"Has my father Suleiman any orders?"

"No," returned Solomon in the same tongue. "He is dead. There is nothing to be done now. I shall pay off the coolies to-morrow, and they may depart. Tell them so."

"It shall be done as ordered," was the response. "And let Suleiman be satisfied that I and yonder Hassan, who is also the son of my father, are awaiting his commands."

The man departed. Petit Jean touched the arm of Solomon.

"What'd he say?"

"That the stuff 'ud be drawn off to-morrow," said Solomon. "And that the coolies wouldn't work no more, now that Ah Lee was dead. They're a-goin' to quit."

Why did John Solomon lie to this man?

BOOK III—THE DEVIL

CHAPTER I

FATHER AND SON

DAVID MACARTY and his son were sitting in the library of the Macarty house on Cypremort Island, while the yacht swung to her moorings in the bayou.

The library was a dark sombre place, and David Macarty did not like it—or the house either, for that matter. He lived mainly at Latouche. Felix, however, did like the house; Felix liked anything that served his own purposes. Perhaps David disliked it because of the memories it held for him; memories of dead days and dead women. Whenever he was here, David Macarty felt ill at ease. Whenever Felix was here with him, he felt at odds with his son; the place seemed to have a sneering and ironic influence upon Felix.

Father and son did not get on any too well. Felix felt that his father was too cautious, too "picayune", as he expressed it. David felt that his son was too impetuous, too headstrong.

As the two sat together in the dark old library, the afternoon heat hung heavy on the air outside, but its warmth did not penetrate the house. David Macarty held a paper in his hand, upon which was an abruptly broken paragraph of writing. He had read this writing a thousand times since the death of his relative, Aline Lavergne's father.

"Here," exclaimed Felix, holding out his hand. "Let's have another look."

His father gave him the paper. Felix spread it out, frowned over it. The writing, which had been written by Lavergne an hour before his death, read:

My Dear Aline: In confiding to you a great, an immense, treasure, I do so with the injunction that it be held as a sacred trust. It does not belong to me, but to a friend, whose name you will find inside the larger box. In the smaller box are the Gemini, the Queen, and the Sea-moon. Three of these are pearls, probably the finest ever taken from the Gulf of Aden; when I brought them home, their customs valuation was ten thousand dollars each, and this was many years ago. The Queen of Sheba is a diamond, of still greater value. In the larger box are—

Felix Macarty looked up, uttered a curse, and crumpled the paper in his hand.

"Here!" exclaimed his father, startled. "You young fool, be careful—"

Felix turned on him with a snarl, his dark eyes smouldering.

"What good is it to us? Not a hint in it of where the stuff is placed! It's bound to be in the library, somewhere! We know from the way you pumped Aline that she knows nothing of it—therefore, her father hid it. Well, quit being cautious! I tell you, we've got to get down to business, and do it quick! Building that cursed dam has cost too much money. That's what we get, with your slow and cautious ways. Failure!"

The graver features of David Macarty looked disturbed. "I know we've failed, my boy," he said weakly. "But why? From unforeseen accidents, that's all. That confounded Wrexham ruined all our plans. Now we're back where we started from—"

"Oh, are we?" snapped the younger man. "What about that man Fortier, eh? He's wise."

"Nonsense! Aline herself suspects nothing—"

Felix Macarty broke into a torrent of profanity. "Open your eyes!" he cried out savagely. "Can't I read behind all the story you've maundered along with? The girl is wise to us. So is Fortier—her lawyer. You've fiddled away the time, playing your own sort of game and I've backed it up. Now that's done with, understand? You've failed. Your game has failed. Can you deny it?"

David Macarty fingered his lips. His complacency was shattered, riven.

"No," he responded at length. "No, I can't. So far, it has failed. Nevertheless—"

"I backed you," intervened his son coldly. "Now I'm done with your way of playing. I'm going to play my own game, understand? In my own way. Either you back me or you don't. Which is it to be?"

David Macarty gazed at his son with pleading eyes, but met only an inflexible purpose, an iron determination. He met no affection whatever.

"Do you forget that I am your father?" he said, donning his usual dignity.

"No," flashed the other. "That's why I'm giving you a chance, one and only chance, to sit in my game! I'm out of yours. You'll get nowhere. Get behind me, and you'll share a fortune—a whopping fortune! You know the kind of man Lavergne was. He'd never play any picayune game. He had two boxes of jewels, and you can bet they meant something! Yes or no?"

"Yes," said David Macarty in a low voice.

Felix dropped into a chair, lighted a cigarette, and surveyed his father with a cool appraisal. Somehow, those smouldering eyes made the elder man wince.

"I shan't bother you with details—you'd only whine about 'em," said Felix brutally. "What you'll see will be results, that's all! I can use you. You'll come in handy when it's a question of covering tracks and stepping soft. That's where you shine. But for the present, only two men will know what cards I hold. I'm one of them. The other is Petit Jean."

At the mention of this name, David Macarty lifted his head. Now he responded, and in his voice was an unwonted earnestness.

"Felix, let me tell you for the last time—I'm afraid of that creature! He is no man. He is a devil! That's what he is. A devil. There's no crime he'd hesitate to commit; he has no more conscience or ethical sense than a wild beast.

"You talk of using me," went on the father, with gathering force. "That's your whole attitude toward everyone—even me, your father. Using me! Have you no love for me, Felix?"

"Certainly I have," said Felix Macarty, with a quiet assurance.

"Sometimes I doubt it." David was on the offensive now, and remained there. "When I found that this Fortier was employed by the girl, I set Petit Jean on him. And with what result? None—"

"You probably did it half-way," said the son scornfully. "Told

Jean to lay the lawyer out. You should have told him to kill Fortier then and there. But that's not your way."

"No, it's not my way!" exclaimed David Macarty, a singular expression on his face. "I can't trust that Petit Jean, I tell you! Ever since the first time I encountered the devil, I've had an uneasiness about him; I've read danger in his eye—danger to you and me! You think you can use him, but I tell you to beware! You're not so worldly-wise as you think, Felix. Go to extremes if you will, but don't go leaning on the arm of Petit Jean!"

Felix Macarty smiled thinly, his hot eyes showing no sense of having been reached by his father's appeal.

"You made a fine botch of things," he observed. "I needed Gros Michel, and you got him murdered by that fool Thompson. What's the result? Thompson is being held in jail, and Petit Jean will knife him like a shot when he gets out!"

David Macarty nodded unhappily, as he gazed into space. His son continued at once.

"Wrexham is out of our way. He took his schooner and went—took that old fool John Philbrick with him, too! The Chinaman, Ah Lee, is dying; he's probably dead now. That will end my income, for there's no one I can trust to fill Ah Lee's place. The job is too slow for Petit Jean. Therefore, we'll have to grab those jewels, and do it at once! In spite of your kindly advice, the man to do the job—or help with it   is this same Petit Jean. As you say, he's not a man, but a devil. So much the better! If I could drag Satan in person into this game, on my side, I'd do it!"

David Macarty put out his hands with a gesture of futility.

"I don't understand it!" he said helplessly. "All we have to do is to get inside that house, search the library. It's such a little job—yet we can't do it—"

"And you know why?" snarled the son. "Because you've blundered it into a big job, that's why! Tried to grab off the whole plantation, in order to keep Aline in ignorance of our object! You tried to be so cursed careful that you stepped on your own feet all the time. Now she suspects what we're after—of course, you fool yourself that she doesn't! But she does. You bet she does!"

"What will you do about it?" queried his father.

Felix smiled thinly and leaned back in his chair.

"I'll do what you failed to do," he said. "Petit Jean will be here to-night, sure. He was to come when Ah Lee was dead, and I had word that Ah Lee wouldn't last out the day. I'll have all the liquor business cleared up out of the way in an hour or so. That'll be off my mind. Then we'll go to work at once."

David Macarty flung him a startled look.

"Not to-night, surely? You can't mean—"

"Wait and see." Felix laughed, swung to his feet, yawned. "Maybe not to-night; don't know yet, but we'll try for it. If anything goes wrong, we'll need the yacht—and you. See you later."

He swung off out of the room.

David Macarty sat in perturbed thought. It was the tragedy of this man's life that he had no hold upon his son—that he must stand by, helpless, and see Felix go his own way. Nor could he very well preach. Felix knew too much about him, too many little things! And there, too, lay tragedy—they were all little things. David Macarty had no great crimes behind him; he was a man of small deeds and petty tricks. Nothing to steel his soul.

A great crime will at least argue a strong man. Pettiness holds a man to small dimensions—small thoughts, small acts, small soul!

As he sat thus, Macarty could well enough guess what Felix meant to do that night. Plain burglary and robbery, nothing less. Why was the notion so uneasy in his mind? He could scheme and plan and trick, in order to take what vaguely belonged to somebody else; yet he found it repugnant to face the simple act of robbing Aline Lavergne.

It was not goodness in David Macarty that made him balk at robbing Aline—no, no! It was caution, furtiveness—what you like. He shrank terribly from letting her know what he was about. He was willing to rob her, if he could keep her in ignorance of the fact. He was, simply, a moral coward through and through.

Now that Aline knew or suspected about those pearls, he was uneasy. He had surprised that paper under the hand of the dying Adrien Lavergne, had hidden it, had kept its contents a secret, as he thought. He dreaded any open rupture with her, shrank from meeting her clear eyes bent upon him in scorn and reproach.

The talk of marriage between Felix and Aline had fallen through, nor did David Macarty care that it had. Marriage would not have secured the jewels to him and Felix. On the contrary, the Louisiana law would confirm Aline in their ownership, or trust.

"No, that's a dead issue," reflected David Macarty. Then he brightened. "Unless there were some way of obtaining title to them after marriage! Then they would be community property—and the law tucks that away in the absolute control of the husband—ah, perhaps I haven't failed yet, my fine Felix! But I shall have to think—"

So David Macarty fell to his thinking, although it was destined to bear no fruit. For while he thought, tragedy was sweeping close under the reckless hand of Felix.

At dinner that evening, David Macarty informed his son that he was going aboard the yacht and meant to stay aboard her.

"Good enough," assented Felix. "Don't tell Wright we may put to sea to-night—let him sleep and know nothing until the time comes. By the way, I told Petit Jean to bring your man, Solomon, whenever he showed up. There's no sense having that fool steward hiding out somewhere in the brakes."

"It seemed safest—"

"There you go again with your cursed caution!" exclaimed Felix heatedly. "His evidence will never be needed, and you know it! Thompson will be released soon enough, when it's discovered that the dead man was Michel Hennepin. I only hope Thompson won't be released too soon—liable to happen at any minute! You discharged him, of course?"

David Macarty looked troubled.

"Certainly not! He's been useful to me—"

"More picayune business!" said his son angrily.

Just after the coffee was served, the negro houseman entered with word that a boat had come in to the landing, and two men were coming up to the house. Felix uttered an exclamation and rose to his feet.

"That'll be Petit Jean and Solomon. I'll send the steward aboard the yacht, eh? And take Jean into the library."

He hurried outside. At the gallery steps he encountered the two men, whose identity he had rightly guessed. The three figures made an indistinct group under the starlight.

"Ah Lee?" queried Felix Macarty.

"He's dead." Petit Jean made answer in Creole and jerked his thumb at the pudgy figure of Solomon. "He told this one to handle the accounts and pay off the men. It was well done, too. No fuss about it. This creature could talk with the two Arabs, and all's done."

Felix looked at Solomon. "So you talk Arabic, do you? How come?"

"I've knocked about quite a bit, sir," returned Solomon. "Some o' them 'ere 'eathen tongues comes in 'andy at times, sir, and I've picked 'em up."

"Be careful that you haven't picked up too much information about my business," said Felix Macarty coldly. "You settled Ah Lee's accounts, did you?"

"No, sir—paid off 'is men, that was all. I wouldn't make so bold as to open 'is account books, sir. They're all together in the canoe."

"Very well. Take 'em out to the yacht and settle back to your position. Tell Mr. Wright to send a boat ashore for my father whenever a lantern is waved from the landing. And have things in shape aboard—we may put out for a cruise, to-night."

"Werry good, sir." Solomon touched his cap and stamped away toward the landing.

Sitting alone in the dining-room, over his coffee, David Macarty heard the stamping of feet as his son and Petit Jean Hennepin came into the house. He heard the door of the library slam upon them. A slight shiver ran up his back—a cold *frisson* that made him jump.

"Rabbits running over my grave!" he muttered, and tried to smile. But it was a sad smile that sat on his lips.

Could he have seen a few hours into the future he would have understood.

CHAPTER II

WHEN A MAN SEES LOOT

THAT SAME evening, Jack Fortier sat up late in the library of the Lavergne house, with Aline.

Work held them; there was much to be done. Aline Lavergne was coming to a full and definite grasp of her own affairs, and under Fortier's guidance she was reaching it. Papers were gone over. John Philbrick's accounts were found exquisitely taken care of, the wall safe was given a thorough overhauling. When they had finished, Fortier felt cheerful.

"Things are in fair shape, Miss Aline," he reflected. "You're not pressed for money. Thanks to Captain Wrexham, there'll be no need to irrigate, at least this year—that dam can't be rebuilt in time. And I notice it is not being rebuilt."

"It was queer about Captain Wrexham!" said the girl. "And he took my mother's picture with him, too—well, he's welcome! Those beautiful things he left in my room—"

"Wrexham thought that picture was of you," said Fortier dryly. "I honestly believe he fell in love with it. Probably he discovered his mistake, and decamped—a queer chap!"

"I'm glad," said Aline very simply. "Glad, I mean, about the picture and all. There must be fine things in that man; I hope that he'll come back some day, and bring Philbrick."

She said nothing of the book which John Philbrick had made for her; that was reposing in her own room.

Fortier took up the letter which Captain Tom Wrexham had left behind him, and tapped it reflectively. He laid it down again on the table.

"This letter," he began, "and the information in it—"

"Oh, about the treasure!" The girl's face lighted up swiftly. "Do you suppose it could really be jewels?"

Fortier laughed. "My dear girl, how should I know? Didn't your father ever mention it?"

"No. And we've been all through the desk, and there's nothing in it. Unless—"

"Unless what?"

She was looking at the desk—a large massive piece of rosewood, much scrolled in the old style.

"Unless there's some secret compartment in the desk. It's quite possible."

Fortier shook his head. "We'd have to tear the thing apart in order to find it. Do you care to do that?"

"If nothing else shows up—yes. But not to-night; I'm tired."

"You're not going back to the yacht to-night?"

"No." The clear eyes of the girl were slightly troubled. "I'm afraid—I want to stay here, Mr. Fortier. Something about that yacht makes me afraid. Madame Dubois will arrive to-morrow from Latouche—she's a dear old lady; I've known her all my life, and she's coming to stay with me."

"Then I'll return to the yacht to-night and—"

"No, please!" Her hand went out to his arm, her eyes sought his with a suddenly startled look. "No! I don't want to be alone in the house—the servants all have their own quarters. I think I'll go upstairs now, if you'll excuse me. Uncle Neb will bring you the keys when he locks up. Good night!"

"Good night, Miss Aline," returned Fortier.

Left alone, he sat smoking and thinking for a space. Again he read over that letter which Wrexham had left, frowning at it in puzzled thought. Certainly there was no trace of any treasure or other mysterious objects in or around the desk, as Philbrick had intimated to Wrexham was the case. Fortier laid the letter down again on the table. Afterward, he remembered having left it there.

"There might be a secret compartment," he reflected, eyeing the desk, "as she thinks. If so, it'd be a hard thing to find. The only way would be to rip off the back of the desk. Well, time enough to-morrow!"

Uncle Neb appeared with the keys, bringing word that everything was locked up for the night, and Fortier went to the east guest-room, which opened on the upper gallery.

When he had undressed and turned out the lights, he stood for a little at one of the French windows, gazing out across the bayou. There were the riding lights of the *Watersprite,* out in the deeper water of mid-channel. Farther along, amid the trees, a light gleamed from the Macarty house. Frowning, Fortier turned away at length, and sought his bed.

He lay for a while, wondering if the Macartys would try anything further, or if they had had enough of the fight. On the morrow he might be able to tell. He had left his suitcase aboard the yacht—Aline, too, had left her things aboard. On the morrow they would get those belongings, refuse the cruise David Macarty was planning. This would mean a rupture with the Macartys, a plain talk, a defiance. And so much the better! The truth must out.

At length Fortier fell asleep.

A strange dream came to him. He dreamed that Captain Wrexham was sitting on the edge of his bed, discoursing about precious stones. He could distinctly see the skipper, fingering his curly brown beard and speaking in his jerky, abrupt fashion.

The presence was so vivid that the words were deeply printed on the mind of Fortier:

"Jewels? All balderdash, I tell you! Never come true. But when they do come true, they play tricks on people—never hit two persons alike. It's a rum go, that! You watch out for it, now. You can't bank on what'll happen when a man sees loot before him—jewels! Like as not, he'll go out of his head. Watch out for it!"

Fortier woke up. He blinked and peered around for the seaman—the room was quite empty. None the less those words still rang in his ears—"Watch out for it!" Fortier was actually brought wide awake by the reality of this dream.

As he lay there, he heard a faint slight sound—like the sound of cracking wood, of rending, splintered dry wood. It was only a faint sound, almost obliterated in the splashing of the bayou waves. Yet Fortier sat up and listened. He imagined that he caught other faint sounds, proceeding from downstairs.

"Confound it, that dream has put my nerves on edge!" he muttered.

He glanced at his watch—it was one o'clock.

Rising, he slipped a dressing-gown over his pyjamas, and quietly left the room. He walked to the stairway, and paused there. To his astonishment, he was now certain that he heard noises coming from below. Was Aline down there, searching for those jewels?

No thought of danger was in his mind as he descended the stairs; he did not try to quiet his steps. The heels of his loose slippers flapped dully on the carpeting. The sounds from below ceased abruptly.

Coming to the foot of the stairs, he saw a gleam of light below the library door. He went to the door, opened it, and paused in astonishment at the scene which met his eyes.

Where the desk had been was now a wreck of smashed and splintered rosewood, and over the wreck, staring at Fortier, stood Felix Macarty. Even at this first sight of the man, Fortier realized instantly that it was no other than Felix Macarty—the resemblance to David was strong enough to show forth.

The two men stood gazing at each other for a moment. Fortier was astonished to find the room in a full blaze of light, young Macarty caught in the very act of wrecking the desk—and yet quite calm about it. Felix showed no consternation. He must have heard Fortier coming, then. And, of course, he had found that letter which Fortier had left lying so carelessly about, and had at once gone to the desk.

"Hope you have found what you were looking for?" said Fortier.

Felix Macarty nodded.

"All right," he said. "All right. Get him, Jean."

Fortier spun around, not quickly enough to escape. A blow from behind caught him over the head. Before he could recover, a scarf was about his throat and he was being neatly garrotted. Felix Macarty looked on with interest.

Strangled though he was, however, Fortier did not go down altogether tamely. He had a glimpse of a frightful face bending above him—the seamed, evil face of Petit Jean Hennepin as he had seen it that night in New Orleans. That thinly bearded face glowed with an infernal delight in the task underway, gleaming teeth, glittering eyes, savagely dilated nostrils, all expressed a diabolical fury.

Fortier, before he fell, struck at that face and felt his fist drive solidly home. In response, he got another blow across the skull that dazed him again—and the garrotte drew tighter. He went to the floor, fell heavily, with the powerful figure of Petit Jean on top of him. The crash of the falling figures seemed to shake the house.

"Tie him up, quick!" snapped the voice of Felix Macarty. "Get a couple of the men from the boat—carry him out."

"Here!" said Petit Jean, snarling over the word. "Here—finish it now!"

"Do as I say, curse you!" snapped young Macarty. "Think I don't know what I'm doing? Carry him aboard, and do it quick!"

For a little Petit Jean bent over the figure of Fortier, then came erect and slipped away like a shadow. Felix Macarty closed the library door, darted to the desk, and began wrenching away the fragments of its back.

A moment afterward he produced two boxes of plain wood. One was quite small, the other was larger—barely large enough to be slipped into a coat pocket. Both boxes were fastened only with brass catches. They had lain in a secret compartment at the back of the desk.

Felix Macarty bent over and searched again in the ruins of woodwork. There was nothing more—not even a scrap of paper. The two little boxes, and nothing else, had been concealed there.

Satisfied of this fact, Macarty went over to the table. For a moment he hesitated, looking down at the two boxes. Then he thrust the larger box into his pocket, and with a deft movement unfastened the cover of the smaller one. The lid flew back.

The man caught his breath as he stared down.

Lying bedded in a deep pad of black velvet, were four precious objects. Two of these were pinkish pearls, an evenly matched pair of great globules, staring up at the man with a soft lustre as of concealed fire in their depths.

"The Gemini!" murmured Macarty in awed tones.

The third pearl was a most peculiar and extraordinary creation. It was not pure white, nor was it round. Instead, it was shaped like the moon just before the full—an elliptical form whose perfection was none the less remarkable. So, too, was its hue, which was a clear and most delicate *clair-de-lune,* transfused by that sheeny lustre which comes only to the nacre of a pearl.

"The Sea-moon!" murmured Macarty.

He looked at the fourth gem—this one a stone, the Queen of Sheba, a pure white diamond as large as the nail of his little finger. From the black velvet this thing blinked up at him with a thousand little tongues of flaming fire that licked at his brain.

Lost to all around him, the man stood transfixed, staring down at what lay in his hand. Like most other people in the world, he had rarely seen a perfect jewel; the sight of these four at once was a revelation to him. As he gazed, a transformation came into his face—a subtle change.

In the dream-words of Cap'n Wrexham. "You can't bank on what'll happen when a man sees loot spread out before him". When that loot consists of four jewels, among the most perfect and beautiful in the world—jewels which, even in the Orient, had been deemed worthy of personal names—then all probability is lost. No two persons will be affected in the same way. What renders one man sane, will evoke the devil from another. The inmost hidden depth of a man's nature surges up and takes command of him.

Thus, a slow change took place in Felix Macarty as he gazed at those four precious objects. The cold cruelty of his face became smoothed out, so that he looked more like his father. He had the things in his hand—they were his. The game was won. As he stared at them, the smouldering eyes of him deepened into a steady blaze of thought. One would have said that these four jewels set the brain of this man to work.

Such was actually the case.

When he caught the slight creak of the opening door, Macarty coolly shut the little box and dropped it into his pocket. Then he turned, perfectly calm and self-possessed. He saw Aline Lavergne standing on the threshold and watching him. Her eyes were comprehending and perhaps a little sad.

"Felix! So you dared this much?" she said quietly.

Macarty merely nodded. His gaze darted past her, and he perceived that the body of Fortier had vanished. A sudden blaze of exultation leaped into his eyes, as he saw how everything was cleared away for him—now the game was won! Never in his life had his evil brain worked so fast, so coherently, so perfectly, as at this moment.

"Of course, Aline, of course," he said, and approached the

door. "Listen, now! You are coming aboard the yacht—now, this moment! My father is there. We must have a straight talk, settle everything up—"

"So far as I am concerned," returned the girl quietly, "everything is settled and—"

"Listen to me!" Macarty lifted a hand. So strange was the authority in his face and voice, so vibrant had his personality suddenly become, that Aline paused, yielded. "If you make a noise, that fool lawyer of yours will be down here to investigate—and I'll shoot him. This is a family matter. You come aboard with me; the boat's waiting."

Perhaps the thought of Fortier struck Aline very hard. If Fortier came down he would doubtless attack the intruder—and the pistol which had leaped into the hand of Felix Macarty was menacing. Besides, what had she to fear?

Her calm deep eyes dwelt upon the man speculatively, a bit puzzled by the singular change that had come over him.

"Very well," she said unexpectedly. "Perhaps it is best that I go with you. A frank understanding will clear up things once and for all. Wait until I get a wrap."

A silken thing was flung around her. She turned and went to the stairs. So well did Felix know the deep serenity of her, that he actually stood in silence and let her go. When she had vanished, a deep breath came from him.

"Won!" he said to himself. "Everything's clear now—everything! The game's in my hands, and it's won. Safe—perfectly safe!"

He stepped to the light switch and plunged the room in darkness, then passed out into the hall. There he turned on a dim light, and waited.

Presently Aline reappeared, descending the stairs. About her figure was wrapped that long stole of ermine lined with sun-hued silk on which was broidered the name of an emperor—the stole of ermine which Wrexham had left in her room. Felix, gazing up at her, caught his breath again, so greatly did the ermine enhance the delicate beauty of the girl.

He held out his hand to her, but she quietly ignored it, and went past him. He followed. In silence they went through the open door to the gallery, and so down toward the landing. Across the starlit waters a boat was heading in and Felix laughed softly to himself. He realized that Fortier had been taken aboard the yacht. Aline knew nothing of this.

Two of the crew were at the oars of the boat; Petit Jean Hennepin was in the bow. No words were exchanged. Aline stepped into the stern of the boat, and Felix Macarty followed; he made a gesture, and the boat shoved off.

As they approached the gangway of the yacht, a canoe was seen swinging there. It was the same canoe which had fetched Petit Jean and Solomon out of the bayous.

"Come below, please," said Felix to the girl, when they had gained the deck of the yacht. David Macarty was not in sight.

Aline followed him down the companionway. At the foot of this, Felix paused and threw open the door of the cabin which Aline had previously occupied.

"In there," he said. "Wait until I send for you."

She looked at him a moment, her eyes disquieted. Perhaps she meant to refuse? Before she could speak, Felix quietly took her arm and pushed her inside. He shut the door, turned the key in the lock, and pocketed it.

"Caught!" he said to himself, and laughed. "Won—the game's won!"

A slight sound at his elbow. He turned, to find Petit Jean standing there.

"Well?" demanded the outlaw hoarsely. "Well? What luck? Find them?"

Felix reached out, clapped the man on the shoulder, broke into a low vibrant laugh.

"All the luck in the world, *mon ami!*" he cried. "Come along now. I'm running this game, understand? The orders come from me."

"Certainly," murmured the other. He looked at Felix admiringly.

Felix led the way along the passage to the little saloon cabin—a tiny room. Here, beneath a cluster of electric lights, a card table had been set up. David Macarty sat smoking nervously, a bottle of brandy and glasses at his elbow. At sight of the two men, he sprang to his feet.

"Felix! What—what luck?"

Felix looked at his father, and smiled in a singular fashion.

"Where you failed," he said slowly, "I have won."

"Won! You have them?"

Felix nodded, and dropped into a chair. He took a cigarette from his pocket, lighted it. Petit Jean dropped into a chair, likewise.

"Let's see them!" said the outlaw.

"Yes, yes!" exclaimed David Macarty, seating himself again. "Where are they?"

Felix blew a thin cloud of smoke, gazed at them for a moment from narrowed eyes, and then spoke.

"Kindly remember, both of you, that while you may be sharing the proceeds equally with me—it is I who am giving the orders. You understand?"

They assented with a nod, a gesture, in eager silence.

"The stones are in my pocket," went on Felix, "but we are not going to inspect them just yet. First, there is going to be some talk—by me. We are in a situation that demands quick and sure action. A false move will ruin us. I have the whole thing in my brain, and I am going to tell you exactly what is to be done. You understand?"

Again a silent assent. David Macarty reached for his glass and gulped down its contents. The brandy had heartened him, fired his constitutional caution into life and action.

"You're a wonder, Felix!" he spluttered, and wiped his lips. "A wonder! What've you gone and done?"

"Enough," said Felix. "Now, kindly listen—and pay attention to me!"

CHAPTER III

WHAT MAKES SANITY IN ONE, MAKES THE DEVIL IN ANOTHER

LEANING OVER the table, Felix swiftly described to his father what had taken place ashore. His eager assured manner held both listeners intent on his words. He was fully in command of the situation.

"Aline's locked up in her cabin," he concluded, "and Fortier's bound and gagged on deck—both safe temporarily. Wright is sound asleep, and must be made safe. Now, Petit Jean and I will take one of the Lavergne launches and go to Latouche at once—before dawn. We'll take Wright with us and leave him there on some pretext; the less he knows, the better."

"But why," and David Macarty wet his lips, staring at his son, "why do you go?"

Felix laughed shortly.

"To get a marriage license, of course. Aren't you a captain, with regular papers? Well, we'll go to Latouche by the back way, through the bayous. You go around with the yacht by sea, and meet us to-morrow afternoon. On the way, you are to drop Fortier overboard."

David Macarty jerked slightly.

"Hold on!" he said. "Leave Petit Jean here with me. Petit Jean can attend to that—"

"He goes with me," said Felix. "He can find his way through the bayous at night, and I can't. You'll not need to worry about Fortier. We'll instruct a couple of the men what to do—and it'll be done as quick as you get to sea. We can't risk having his body found in the bayou, later on."

His father was about to venture some further objection, when Felix snarled at him with a savage word.

"Be quiet, you! I'm giving orders here—do as I say, and shut up! You're to keep Aline locked in her cabin. After you pick me up off Latouche, you'll marry us. I'm going to have her as well as the stones, understand?"

"Maybe she won't have you," interjected Petit Jean, with a low laugh.

"Then I'll break her," and the eyes of Felix leaped into a blaze. "Even if I fail there, she'll at least be my wife by law, and what we've done to-night will never come out to public sight. If we gain nothing else, she'll be so glad to get rid of me that she'll keep her mouth shut. I don't think she knows very much, anyhow. Fortier is the one who's dangerous—the one to be put away. If we were planning to disappear, it wouldn't matter; but we're planning to stay here, you and I. Do you understand?"

David Macarty nodded, and poured himself more drink from the brandy bottle. His face had become a bit blotched, his fingers were unsteady as he drank. Once his eyes went to the visage of Petit Jean, and a slight shiver passed over his body; he reached quickly for the brandy again.

"I suppose so," he assented. "It looks good enough. But marriage with Aline won't give you her property; under the State law it's hers. Community property is only what's acquired after marriage. It won't give you title to the jewels—"

"Title be damned!" said Felix, with some irritation. "Marriage will close her mouth, won't it? She's too cursed proud to go dragging a scandal around for the sake of jewels—"

"Oh I see!" David Macarty nodded and chuckled. "You're too clever! It's a good plan. Her mouth will be shut, yes. So will Fortier's. Petit Jean, here, is the only other one who knows anything about the jewels—"

"And he leaves for South America as soon as we split," concluded Felix.

"But, yes," said Jean at once. *"Certainement, oui!* But, m'sieu'— the jewels? The results of this little *razzia?"*

"Are here."

Felix Macarty took from his pockets the two little boxes of wood, and laid them before him. Petit Jean leaned forward with a good-natured interest in his wild eyes. David Macarty knocked over a glass with his unsteady fingers, and cursed at the crash of it. Retaining the smaller box in front of him, Felix handed over the larger box to his father.

"Open it—I don't know what's in it. Unhook the clasps, there."

David Macarty seized the box between his hands, and fumbled away at the clasps. After an instant the lid flew back. Beneath the lid was a scrap of white paper, which he brushed impatiently aside. The paper fell to the floor, not heeded by any of the three men. And small wonder that it was unheeded!

For there, under their eyes, was revealed a flame of precious stones. The box contained two shelves, padded below and stuffed above with soft cotton. In one of the shelves was a glittering sheen of crimson blood; in the other, a layer of white fire.

Felix Macarty craned forward to peer at them, and then smiled softly.

"Not large stones, but all good ones—rubies and diamonds, eh?" he observed. "Plenty of quick money there for all of us. We can turn over those things in a day's time. However, you might be interested in what's in the smaller box—"

And he opened the smaller box, shoved it out before them into the centre of the table.

From David Macarty came a hoarse cry of astounded wonder at sight of those four precious things. He sat as though in a stupor, hands gripping the table-edge, eyes bulging. His breath came with a whistling noise. He was, temporarily, paralysed; he could only sit there and stare, incredulous, awed, silent.

Like his father, Felix Macarty fell silent and staring. He took the Queen of Sheba and set it on the table between his fingers, playing with it, fascinated by the brilliant fire that flamed forth from its heart.

He might better have been watching Petit Jean.

For the outlaw sat motionless, unstirring, his eyes riveted upon the jewels. They moved, those eyes of his, from the smaller box to the larger, from the kingly pearls to the glimmering rubies. And as they flitted back and forth, those alert cunning eyes took on a gradual change.

In fact, the entire face of the man beneath its thin and straggling beard might have been seen to alter slowly but terribly. Never in all his life had Petit Jean Hennepin seen such jewels as now met his eyes—and the effect upon him was frightful, had it been noted. Yet his companions saw it not.

Once, as though fearful lest Felix see the thing that could not be kept from his face, the eyes of Petit Jean darted up craftily. But Felix Macarty was fascinated by the great diamond between his fingers, was playing with it, smiling as he did so. Again Petit Jean looked down at the other gems.

The lines of his face, seamed with evil and guttered with vile thoughts, intensified his savagely wild expression. The nostrils dilated thinned, dilated again with each breath. Beneath the table, the man's fingers were gripping tightly on each other. But it was in the eyes that this change, this alteration, was most intense and frightful to see—for into the glittering eyes had crept an inhuman and devilish look beyond the power of words to describe.

From the deeps of this man's soul, the devil had been evoked—and had answered the invocation.

It was not long that the three men sat thus, in silence; but it was long enough to change the life-currents of all three, and to change the lives of all connected with them. Captain Wrexham, who knew the world pretty well, would never have made this fatal error of showing forth all those jewels, particularly to the eyes of Petit Jean Hennepin. But Felix Macarty was not the skipper.

Felix was the first to break the silence. He sighed, and put the Queen of Sheba back into the smaller box. Neither of the other two men had touched the stones or pearls.

"Well, time to be stirring, I guess," he said, his voice singularly soft. "Jean and I must get off. We'll have to get Wright up and dressed, to go with us. I want a drink—any whisky here?"

David Macarty bestirred himself and indicated the brandy bottle. Felix sneered.

"Not for me. I want some whisky. Oh, by the way, what about this steward, Solomon? You know him, Jean. Is he safe enough to leave alone?"

Petit Jean looked up. His eyes were glazed slightly, and by an effort he had rid his face of all expression.

"Eh? Oh, that one!" He made a gesture of contempt as he responded. "Yes, I know him. He is a fat little fool—not worth the killing, m'sieu'. He'll give us no trouble. Do with him as with the men—a hundred apiece will shut their mouths. Besides, they know little. I have some whisky in the canoe—good whisky. Shall I get it?"

"Yes," said Felix. "And have one of the men wake Mr. Wright. Tell him to dress."

Petit Jean came to his feet. It seemed hard for him to turn from the table, where those stones glimmered and shone under the lights, but he turned and went to the door. There he paused and glanced back.

David Macarty had put out a shaking finger and was turning over the loose rubies. Felix was staring down again at the diamond, smiling to himself. Across the face of Petit Jean flitted a wild and terrible look—for an instant, the devil in the man looked out of his eyes.

Then he was gone, silent as a shadow.

With stealthy lithe step, the step of a wild beast, Petit Jean gained the deck. He stood there a moment, his eyes darting about. The lights had been doused; the little craft swung obscurely beneath the stars. Dawn would not be long in coming, now.

Glancing along the deck, Petit Jean discerned a knot of men grouped together in the bows—the five men of the crew. Of those five, one was the engineer. They were his men, all of them; his men, not Macarty's! But Macarty did not know that. Petit Jean turned and glided forward, making no sound as he went. In his face was the gleam of an unholy light, the glimmer of an infernal joy.

He came upon the five men so suddenly and silently that they were startled. He laughed at that. The laugh made even those careless brutes shiver and fall still.

"Wright—the mate—is asleep?" he asked softly.

"Yes."

"And the steward also?"

"Yes."

"No need to worry about *him*." Petit Jean chuckled, then stabbed with his finger at two of the men. "You, and you, lift that fool Fortier and set him in the canoe alongside. Then cast off the canoe and let it float away. See that you make no sound doing it."

"But—he knows—" protested one.

"He knows nothing of us!" said Petit Jean quickly. "Let him live or die—what matter to us? But he'll go out to sea on the tide. Now, go!"

Two of the men rose and slipped away. Petit Jean leaned forward and spoke very softly to the other three. They uttered low-breathed oaths of admiration. Petit Jean lighted a cigarette and inhaled it. Presently the first two came back.

"It is done," said one of them. "The canoe went with the current at once."

Again Petit Jean leaned forward and spoke. More low oaths. Then he rose to his feet.

"You understand perfectly?"

A low chorus of assent. He dropped his cigarette and stepped on it.

"Very well. You, Alcee, go and inform M'sieu' Macarty that Fortier wishes to speak with him at once."

The man designated slipped back to the companionway. After him, a veritable shadow, went the figure of Petit Jean.

Perhaps three minutes of silence ensued. Then the scrape of feet from below, and the brandy-shot voice of David Macarty rose puffingly.

"Give that *vaurien* a piece of my mind! I'll show him something—"

Through the companionway rose the head and shoulders of David Macarty. The arm of Petit Jean swung slightly; there was a dull sound, and David Macarty stopped moving. From his lips came a grunt of expelled breath. Then his head sagged, and seemed about to fall backward, except that the body was supported from below.

"Up with him," said Petit Jean calmly, and caught Macarty's collar.

The man below shoved, and Petit Jean pulled. An instant later, the senseless Macarty lay on deck, while Petit Jean was going through his pockets and transferring money and papers and keys. Then Jean rose.

"Not badly hurt," he said, and glanced around. Four other shadows hovered close at hand—the four other men. To one of them Hennepin handed the keys he had just taken.

"Go lock the door of Wright's cabin. Lock the steward in also. The rest of you, get him gagged and tied."

Above the figure of David Macarty worked the silent shadows. They gagged the unfortunate man cruelly, and bound him. Then over his head one threw a ragged coat, another threw a shirt about his body. These were bound about with cord, so that the man resembled a wrapped mummy.

"All right," said Petit Jean, and went down the companionway.

He came back into the little saloon cabin, where Felix

Macarty sat beneath the light cluster at the table, and whistled between his teeth as he came. Felix glanced up at him, not without a trace of suspicion in the smouldering eyes.

"How the devil did that fellow Fortier get free of his gag?"

Petit Jean Hennepin lifted his brows, shrugged carelessly as though to intimate that the question could not be answered, and sat down at the table. He put forth his hand and drew toward him the smaller box, that in which reposed the pearls and the diamond. Felix Macarty watched him like a hawk, saw that he wished only to gaze, and made no objection.

As he looked, once more the eyes of Petit Jean dilated and flamed, then narrowed into crafty slits of evil light. Suddenly he lifted his head, startled. From the deck above there sounded the stamping of feet, an oath, a wild cry—then a splash alongside.

"The devil!" exclaimed Petit Jean. "What's that?"

Felix Macarty darted forward his long arm, seized the smaller box, and closed it. He closed the larger one also. Swift as light, he shoved them into the pocket of his coat, and whipped out an automatic pistol.

Swift as he was, however, he had barely come to his feet when the door was burst open and one of the men appeared there— the man Alcee.

"M'sieu' Macarty!" gasped the man, his horrified eyes on Felix. "The prisoner—that Fortier—had a knife—he stabbed your father—"

With a wild oath, Felix Macarty brushed the man aside and leaped for the ladder.

As he came out on deck, Felix saw the shapes of several men struggling in a confused mass before him. He kicked at them, forced them apart with a storm of oaths and blows. He saw that they had been trussing up a figure, which was hidden beneath rags and bonds.

"My father?" he cried out.

"There," said one of the men, pointing overside. "This one, this Fortier, stabbed him twice in the throat, m'sieu'. He must have been quite dead before he fell across the rail. We fell on this one and stifled him—"

They drew back. For a moment Felix Macarty stood there in silence; under the veil of night his face could be seen only as a contorted mask of fury and passion. Twice he lifted the weapon in his hand as though to shoot the bound and motionless figure at his feet.

That figure moved slightly, with a wrenching motion. It moved as though the man inside those wrappings and bonds were sensible, knew what was going on, and was trying desperately to get free of his confinement. At the slight contortions, Felix Macarty laughed horribly, stepped forward, kicked the bound figure.

"Tie a weight to his feet," he said, "and throw him over. Quick!"

From the men came something not unlike a gasp of horror, of incredulous fear. But behind Felix Macarty uprose the figure of Petit Jean Hennepin, with an imperative gesture. The men saw that gesture, and obeyed.

They produced a weight of some sort, tied it to the recumbent swathed figure. They hesitated then.

"Over with it!" commanded Felix Macarty, his voice harsh.

Three of the men lifted that close-wrapped figure. In their hands it seemed to twist with a frightful effort, to be contorted as though the man were struggling in his bonds. A low throaty noise came from it.

At this, Petit Jean made another imperative gesture. The three men dropped the body on the other side of the rail, then drew back quickly as though in horror of what they had done. There was a muffled splash, and then silence.

"So much for him!" said Felix Macarty. "Where'd he get the knife? How did he get free?"

Felix stepped to the rail and looked over at the indistinct ripples widening under the stars.

As he stood there, gazing down, the shadowy figure of Petit

Jean approached behind him, making no sound. The long keen-whetted knife flashed for an instant in the dull light of the stars.

Felix Macarty uttered no cry, but fell forward half-across the rail. The pistol fell from his hand. Petit Jean coolly caught the body and drew it back on deck.

At this instant there came a furious hammering and pounding from the door of the mate's cabin. Mr. Wright wanted to know what was going on, and said so in no uncertain tones.

The face of Petit Jean leaped into a grin of infernal delight. Snatching up the pistol that Felix had dropped, he slipped across the deck like a shadow. A moment later two reports reverberated across the water. The hammering at the cabin door ceased.

"Get up the anchor," said Petit Jean, his voice hoarse with exultation.

His men obeyed.

CHAPTER IV

HOW A KNIFE MAY PERISH
AND COME TO LIFE

IN THE obscurity that precedes the dawn, the *Watersprite* moved away from her anchorage. Her engines purred into life. Petit Jean, standing in her tiny bridge-house, ordered full speed ahead. She leaped through the dark waters, down the bayou toward the open gulf.

Petit Jean summoned the four men who were on deck. One, who knew the waters, he placed in charge of the wheel. With the others following him, he sought the mate's cabin and unlocked the door. Mr. Wright had been shot twice through the body, and must have died at once. Petit Jean commanded his three followers to get rid of the body over the side, and turned to the little cabin of the steward, adjoining the gallery.

The men obeyed him in fear and trembling, jumping at his

every look. This was not the man whom they had known; this was a new Petit Jean, who held them in a grip of horrified fear. They would no more have questioned his orders than those of the devil in person.

Indeed, they muttered among themselves that it was no other than the devil which now leered out of the eyes of Petit Jean! But they knew nothing about the two boxes of gems which Jean had taken from the pockets of Felix Macarty. Previously, they had seen him as an outlaw, a hunted man; now they beheld him a fiend in human shape. And they were afraid.

They had reason to be afraid. The coldly savage diablerie which shone from the face of this monster was frightful and inhuman.

Unlocking the door of the steward's cubby, Petit Jean flung it open. A light was going, and Solomon sat on the edge of his bunk half dressed. He blinked up at the intruder, who inspected him with an amused scrutiny. Indeed, there was something ludicrous in the aspect of this pudgy little old man, grey hair tumbled about his blank blue eyes, with just now a tinge of alarm in his expressionless face.

"The shots woke you up, did they?" queried Petit Jean.

"Why, sir," returned Solomon wheezily, "I thought as 'ow I 'eard shots, yes, sir!"

The eyes of the other man suddenly blazed forth at him.

"I've taken over this boat," shot forth Petit Jean. "The Macartys are dead. I'm going to lay her up somewhere down the coast, to-day, and then skip out. The other men will loot her for their share. Come in with us on the deal—I'll give you two hundred cash and set you ashore safe. You know nothing, and you can't hurt us. What say?"

Solomon stared up, agape at this information.

"Dead!" he muttered. "The Macartys dead!"

"No talk," said Petit Jean. "Two hundred cash. Speak up quick!"

Solomon recovered himself.

"Why, sir," he said, "that 'ere cash is a werry good argument. But I ain't so young as I was, sir, and I'd be werry sorry to be took up an' jailed, sir—"

"No danger." Petit Jean laughed thinly. There was a diabolical edge to this laugh of his—the sound of it made Solomon shiver slightly. "You're safe enough. No tales to be told, and there'll be no investigation until we're all scattered and safe. What say?"

"Why, sir," and Solomon bobbed his head. "I'll be werry 'appy to accommodate you, as the old gent said when 'e kissed the 'ousemaid. If so be as I could touch a bit o' that 'ere cash, sir, and—"

With a slight sneer, Petit Jean drew a handful of bills from his pocket—money taken from the Macartys. He counted out a hundred dollars and tossed the bills at Solomon.

"Now, get up and get busy," he snapped. "Throw some breakfast together. I'm going to snatch a bit of sleep. We ought to be out of the bayou in a couple of hours—by sunrise. Call me then."

"Yes, sir," returned Solomon humbly, stuffing the money into his pocket.

"Here's the key of Miss Lavergne's cabin." Petit Jean threw a key at him. "Give her something to eat and drink, and mind you keep the door locked. I'll send for her later."

Solomon bobbed his head, and the figure of Petit Jean withdrew.

As for the outlaw, he went to the cabin of David Macarty, dropped on the bunk, and was instantly asleep. He was the only person aboard who knew of the existence of the jewels. He was quite safe, especially as his cabin door was locked. And in his sleep, an infernal smile played about his cruel evil lips.

The crew, left in charge of the yacht, clumped together and talked in low tones. Terror of Petit Jean was upon them. They brought the engines down to slow speed and let the yacht crawl along with the tide and current. At sight of Solomon, going about his duties with his usual apologetic cheerfulness, they fell silent, watching him warily. They would have murdered him at the first hinted suspicion, for they were in panic at thought of the things which had taken place that night.

Dawn was breaking when Solomon finished his job of tidying up the saloon and getting things in shape. In the course of this work, he discovered on the floor a scrap of paper, which he examined and then pocketed.

Soon afterward, he brought food and hot coffee to the group of men about the wheel. The yacht was a little below the place where Wrexham's schooner had been concealed, and was several miles below the plantation. When the steward set down his burden, the helmsman threw a loop over the wheel and turned to snatch a cup of coffee. Solomon made his way back to the galley.

Calling up their comrade from the engine-room, the men ate and drank. The sullen mood fell away from them. Before the coming of the day, their panic vanished slowly.

"Better take the wheel yourself, Alcee," said one of the men, glancing at the shore. "She's making toward that mud flat—current swinging her, probably."

Alcee turned over the wheel, advanced the loop a spoke, and began to fill his pipe. The man who had just spoken leaped suddenly to his feet with an oath.

"Up with her, ye fool! We don't want to fetch up on that mud bank—"

All five men sprang up, in sudden astonishment and alarm. For the yacht was certainly headed direct for the right-hand bank of the bayou! Alcee threw off the loop and twirled the wheel. Into his sullen Cajun features came a look of bewilderment.

"She don't answer!" he complained. "She don't turn—"

"Tiller rope's busted!" cried somebody. "Shut off the engine—"

The engineer went leaping below. From the group of men broke a storm of oaths and curses as they realized that the move was useless. The yacht refused to answer her helm at all, and was now darting directly at the shore. There was a sudden thrum and throb as the engineer gained his post and threw the gears into reverse—but he was too late.

Before reversed propeller could take effect, the yacht gave a long and creepy shudder, as her keel nosed into the mud of the bottom. Her prow still a dozen feet from shore, she drove herself firmly into the mud, and stayed there. With each instant, the tide was running out fast. As the wild vibrations of the screw shook her and it became evident that her own power would not get her off, the men fell to cursing anew. The engine ceased work.

She carried no launch. Her small boat towed alongside from the gangway, and two other boats were chocked and in davits on the upper deck.

It was at this instant that Petit Jean Hennepin appeared on deck again.

"How did this happen?" he said, with an appearance of calmness.

"We don't know—the steering gear is broken—the tiller rope has parted—"

Hennepin's deceptive manner burst into a furious demoniac storm of rage. He whipped out that knife of his and rushed at five of them; foam touched his lips, wild oaths were on his tongue. In his eyes blazed the devil of murder.

Armed though they were, the five men broke before him in mad terror. They ran here and there, evading him, shouting hoarsely, leaping out of his course. In the way this murderous creature sent those five men running and screaming, was something horrible. Then, suddenly as he had let drive at them, Petit Jean halted, wiped his face, put away his knife.

"All right, curse you!" he cried hoarsely. "What's done can't be helped. Come here!"

They suspected some ruse, held off, watching him. Petit Jean cursed them, and began to make a cigarette; he walked to the rail, eyeing the shore and the water, then turned and beckoned.

They perceived that the madness had left him, and sullenly approached, albeit with much precaution. Now it was seen that

a new change had come into the face of Petit Jean, the hereto-
fore glittering eyes had become bloodshot, overspread with a
crimson murk.

"I shan't hurt you, little ones," he said, and laughed. "Come
and do what papa says! You two," and he stabbed at two of them
with his finger, making them start back, "get into the boat, row
up to the Lavergne place, and bring me down a launch. If those
niggers ask any questions, say that everybody has gone for a
cruise; say anything you like! Better bring a canoe for yourselves,
too. I'll be off as soon as you get back. Then you can loot what
you want from the yacht here, and set fire to her. Understand?"

They assented, gradually regaining confidence in him.

"You other three," he went on, "stay aboard. Do what you like,
but see that one of you remains on watch. If any boats pass and
ask questions, say that we ran ashore and that M'sieu' Macarty
has gone to Latouche to get a large boat to pull us off. Let no
one aboard. You understand?"

They assented again. Petit Jean watched them shrink from
his lurid eyes, and smiled.

"I shall sleep for an hour; at the end of that time, waken me.
The boat will heel over a little as the tide goes down. When the
tide comes in again this afternoon, she will float. Do what you
like with her—she is yours. But I advise you to loot and burn
her at once. That is all. Off with you, now!"

He turned, walked back to the companionway, and vanished
there.

The five men looked one at another, exchanged a shrug and
a muttered word, and obeyed his orders in a species of dumb
terror. Two got down into the trailing boat, and began to row
her up-stream. The other three conferred for a moment, then
two of them went to their own quarters, for they had gained
little sleep the preceding night. Alcee, chosen to stay on watch,
seated himself on the deck, took a fishing line from his pocket
and cast it over the rail, and began to smoke his pipe.

The eastern sky broke into a flame as the new day arrived.

The ensuing hour dragged its slow length along without incident. The only busy man aboard the yacht was the steward, to whom the brooding Alcee paid no attention.

John Solomon, indeed, went about his work in an unconcerned and placid manner, as though no sequence of tragedy had invested this yacht with a tragic veil of horror. He carried a tray to Aline Lavergne's cabin, and was in there a long while, talking with her. When he came out, he was puffing at his clay pipe, and appeared quite satisfied with himself.

A little later, he returned for her tray and bore it to the galley. Then he went down the companionway again, but this time he was not smoking; this time he went directly to the cabin that had been occupied by David Macarty. The door was locked, but for a little the steward worked softly at the lock. Presently the door opened under his hand. He saw Petit Jean stretched out in the bunk, snoring lustily, and beside him was the automatic pistol taken from Felix Macarty.

After a time he was on deck again, Alcee, the man on guard, paid him no attention.

When the appointed hour had gone, Alcee went below and wakened Petit Jean by pounding at the door. Hennepin opened the door and came out, sleepily.

"Not back yet with the launch? Tell that fool steward to fetch me some coffee, here in the saloon cabin. Then stay on watch."

The man departed. Petit Jean went into the saloon and dropped into a chair at the table. He did not observe that the place had been tidied up, nor that the scrap of paper had disappeared from the floor. He was thinking of something else.

With the falling of the tide, the yacht had heeled over quite a little, so that her decks were inclined. The skylight above the saloon was pointing toward the eastern sky, and all the glory of the morning sunlight came through the clouded glass, filling the place with a diffused glare of light.

From his pocket. Petit Jean drew out the two little boxes, and set them on the table before him. He left them unopened. A moment later Solomon appeared, with a tray, and set coffee and fresh-made toast before the outlaw.

"Fetch Ma'm'selle Lavergne here in ten minutes," commanded Petit Jean, "and see to it that she does not go on deck instead."

"Yes, sir," returned Solomon, and disappeared.

Petit Jean wolfed the toast, gulped at the coffee, and then shoved the dishes back carelessly. With a quick catch of his breath, as though he had been awaiting this moment, he opened the smaller box and displayed the four great gems. He relapsed into a motionless silence, staring at them with new amazement.

If they had been glorious on the preceding evening under artificial light, now, beneath the flood of new daylight, they were splendid beyond words, indescribable in their beauty. Few men have ever looked with the pride of ownership upon four such jewels as these—the great smoky pearl, lustrous as some lost star plucked from Erebus; the twin pink gems, luminous sisters that reflected the rosy refulgence of the morning; and the diamond that coruscated in its bitter dazzling acerbity.

What did Petit Jean Hennepin see in these four precious things? Not money alone, nor beauty, nor rarity; none of these could have drawn into his face such a devil of inhumanity as was compelled there as he gazed! These things, which react alike on no two men, wakened all the beast in this man.

Did his evil spirit divine the lust and blood which these precious objects had aroused in the past, and would rouse again? Was it this which evoked into his face that frightful devil of malign virulence?

A movement attracted his attention. He looked up, and saw Aline Lavergne standing in the doorway.

Under his look, the face of the girl whitened. Yet her eyes did not lose that clear serenity which so distinguished her; she met his keenly piercing regard, and baffled it by the sheer magic of her virginal spirit. His eyes fell from hers.

"What do you want with me?" she asked quietly.

Petit Jean stirred a little. By an effort, he became composed.

He came to his feet and stood gazing at her ermine-cloaked shape. He looked at her eyes again, and now his gaze was quick and hard, terrible in its evil menace.

Hatred of her serene purity flamed in his face.

"I want you," he said, speaking the guttural patois which came naturally to his lips. "You shall go away with me now. You belong to me."

Perhaps he was astonished to find no fear, no terror, in her face. She was afraid, yes; the pulse at her throat, the quick colour in her cheeks, betrayed inward fear, yet none showed in her eyes. And her voice was steady, cool—it maddened the brute before her.

"You are an evil man, P'tit Jean," she returned calmly. "I know what you have done here; you are not a man, but a degraded beast. Go your way and await your punishment. What have you to do with me?"

Petit Jean started. "You know—nonsense! You know—nothing!" he snarled. "I say you are mine—understand? You belong to me—like this!"

And he came toward her, with the devil dancing in his eyes.

Meantime, outside at the head of the companionway, John Solomon was standing, his blank blue eyes fastened upon the burly figure of Alcee, the guard. Alcee had hooked a fish on his line, and was standing, half-leaning over the rail, peering down.

Solomon shook his head half regretfully, and stuffed his clay pipe into his pocket. His hand came forth, and brought with it a queer knife, with a haft of heavy lead. He poised it in his hand, and looked again at the figure of Alcee.

This knife was the same which had supposedly been lost when Gros Michel was slain.

An instant later, the knife left his hand. The haft of lead struck the man Alcee just at the base of the skull.

This time, the knife actually did go overboard.

CHAPTER V

IT DOES NOT PAY TO FORGET TRIFLES

AS JOHN Solomon descended the companion-ladder, a sound came to his ears. It was a low involuntary cry—the only one that Aline Lavergne uttered.

She stood against one wall of the saloon cabin, shrinking from Petit Jean and yet having no fear in her eyes. In the body, she shrank back; in the spirit, she met him fairly and unafraid. The outlaw, who had seized her wrist, stood leering into her face as though seeking to overwhelm that spirit of hers with his evil power.

"Come!" he was saying. "Come, look at the pearls which shall be yours, the pearls which shall glimmer on your bosom when you are mine—"

"Beggin' your pardon, sir," said the apologetic voice of Solomon, "but I'd like to 'ave a word with you about them 'ere pearls me own self."

Loosing the girl's wrist, Petit Jean turned. He glared at the steward, not comprehending what had been said.

"Get out of here," he ordered.

"Yes, sir," said Solomon, "but I wants to 'ave a word with you first, just like that."

Solomon was stuffing tobacco into his clay pipe in his placid manner. He appeared quite unconcerned, and the gaze of those blank blue eyes fairly staggered Petit Jean for an instant.

"What are you talking about?" snarled the outlaw. "Didn't you hear me say to get out?"

Solomon scratched a match and held it to his pipe.

"You and me," he said wheezily, "are goin' to 'ave a bit o' talk. This 'ere paper was in that box o' stones, sir. If you'll be so good as to read it, you'll see what I'm a-gettin' at. And if I was you, I'd take it calm, as the old gent said when 'e kissed the 'ousekeeper."

Solomon extended a scrap of paper. Astonished and perplexed by this attitude of humility mingled with cool defiance, Petit Jean took it and glanced at the lines of writing. His eyes widened with astounded surprise. Aline Lavergne, at a sign from Solomon, remained motionless where she was.

Dropping the paper, Petit Jean took a step backward, against the table. He was now staring at Solomon; one hand crept behind his back, fumbled with the two little boxes of wood, slipped them into his pocket. Still he stared, an incredulous, uneasy wonder in his eyes.

"You—what sort of joke is this?" he croaked. Hoarse fury crept into his voice. "You fool, have you gone crazy? Lavergne never left this stuff for—for you—"

"Yes 'e did, just like that 'ere paper says," returned Solomon.

He puffed at his pipe a moment; he was absorbed in this, quite ignoring the menace of that half crouching devil-eyed figure against the table. Then he resumed, placidly, as though conducting a perfectly matter-of-fact conversation.

"You see, sir, me and Mr. Lavergne was werry good friends, jest like that! I give 'im these 'ere things to keep for me, 'cause why, he'd never ha' took them as a present. Later on, I wrote 'im sayin' they was 'is—but I'm afraid that 'ere letter never got to 'im."

A hoarse incredulous burst of laughter broke from Petit Jean.

"You!" he cried. "You—fool that you are! What mad dream is this?"

"Why, sir, it's all gospel!" exclaimed Solomon, looking slightly injured. "So when I come to see me old friend, and 'eard as 'ow them 'ere Macartys were a-plannin' some injury to Miss Aline, why, I ups an' makes me own plans, just like that! Them 'ere two Arabs in Ah Lee's gang, they was werry good friends o' mine. So was Ah Lee."

Solomon came to an end, and went on puffing calmly at his pipe.

Petit Jean, who was transfixed by the calm placidity of these disclosures, at length began to believe them. His astounded brain was forced to believe them. Yet, as he stared at Solomon, he could only believe that the pudgy little man was a blundering fool.

"So it's all true, is it?" he exclaimed, and broke into a demoniac cackle of mirth. "You expect me to give you those two boxes, do you?"

His laughter shrilled horribly. He thrust one hand into a pocket, and produced his automatic pistol.

"Wait a minute!" exclaimed Solomon, clapping one hand to his pocket. "If you'll be so good as to look at these 'ere accounts with you, sir, in the matter o' these stones, I expect as 'ow you'll find them all shipshape—"

He drew out a little red notebook, as though quite unconscious of the pistol that was trained on him. He thumbed over the pages of the notebook, nodded with a satisfied air, and stepped forward. He ignored the pistol that jerked at him, and extended the notebook.

Petit Jean was held in leash by curiosity, like any wild beast. He could not figure out what this little old man, so absolutely helpless in appearance, was driving at. There was no menace in the air of Solomon. When Petit Jean took the notebook, Solomon stepped back again and went on smoking. His face was quite expressionless.

Aline Lavergne looked from one to the other, spellbound by the scene.

Holding the notebook in one hand, Petit Jean looked at what was written in it. As he read, his face changed horribly; his eyes dilated, his lips curled back from his teeth, an atrocious contortion seized on the muscles of his face. With an oath, he dashed the notebook to the floor and glared at Solomon.

"So it was you—" he mouthed, and stopped, panting.

"Yes, sir, it was me as cut that 'ere tiller rope this morning," said Solomon calmly. He paused, listening. In the silence, all three persons were suddenly aware of a trampling of feet on the deck above.

"Them 'ere are me men, I expect, and Mr. Fortier with 'em," went on Solomon. "It was me as put this 'ere yacht ashore. I had 'em waitin' for a signal from me, you see. And it was me as killed that 'ere brother o' yours, Gros Michel. A werry bad man 'e was, too, and—"

From Petit Jean burst a horrible cry. He jerked up the pistol and fired point-blank. Aline Lavergne uttered a scream.

Solomon calmly knocked the dottle from his pipe.

"There ain't no bullets in them 'ere cartridges, sir," he said. "If I was you I—"

Petit Jean burst into the inhuman diabolic cry of a tortured wild beast. He dropped the pistol, whipped out that long knife of his, and flung himself forward.

At this instant, the figure of Fortier, followed by the two Arabs, appeared in the doorway. Solomon was jerked aside.

The mad rush of Petit Jean was checked by the fist of Fortier. From the lips of the outlaw shrilled another howl, so instinct with utter ferocity that it chilled the blood. He plunged at the group of men, his knife darting in and out with the swiftness of light.

But, if he was swift, the hand of Fortier was swifter. Gripping that lean wrist, Fortier held it in fingers of iron. His fist crashed again into that snarling demoniac visage. Both men lost balance on the inclined deck and fell. Over them thrust the two Arabs, in whose hands were short lengths of line.

At this moment there was a slight shock, as another craft bumped gunwales with the yacht. It passed unobserved by those in the saloon.

"All right!" Fortier sprang to his feet, laughing excitedly. "He's safe!"

Petit Jean still struggled, but his frantic efforts availed him nothing. One of the Arabs stooped over, took from his pocket the two little boxes of wood, and handed them to Solomon. The latter nodded.

"Rope 'im good, now! 'E's a-goin' to answer in court for them 'ere murders. Mr. Fortier, I 'opes as 'ow you got them two men up above?"

Fortier nodded. "They're tied up."

"They'ad a 'and in the murders. The other three will be along after a bit, too. If we—'ello! Dang it, if she ain't went an' fainted!"

The figure of Aline had slipped to the floor.

Fortier tried to catch her, too late. He raised her head, supporting her in his arms, and was about to speak. The words died on his lips. Solomon, catching his fixed gaze, turned and looked at the door.

In the doorway stood Thompson, pistol in hand, eyes fastened on Solomon.

"You dirty little Cockney!" exclaimed the second mate. "You will swear my life away, will you? Well, you won't do it again, blast you! I'll fix you so that—"

The pistol in his hand vomited flame. With a cry, the two Arabs flung themselves on the man, knives flashed; the figures went reeling away from sight toward the companionway. Thompson's voice sounded in a choked cry, then was silenced abruptly.

"Dang it!" said Solomon. "If I 'adn't clean forgot that 'ere man! This is what comes o' bein' careless, as the old gent said when 'e married 'is third and—"

His voice failed. His knees crumpled suddenly, and he pitched forward across the bound figure of Petit Jean.

CHAPTER VI

HIGH TWELVE IN THREE PLACES

A T A dirty table in a filthy restaurant of the old quarter of New Orleans—a restaurant huddled in one portion of an old house that had been built by the great Marigny—sat a man in whose hand was a newspaper.

This man was reading the newspaper with attention. It was

not a fresh newspaper; it was an old and crumpled copy, which he had found in his chair. He was reading, in that paper, an account of the trial and sentence of Jean Hennepin and his accomplices. The date of execution had been set for noon on the tenth of the month.

Suddenly the man lifted his head.

"Why!" he exclaimed, with a startled air. "Why—sure it is! This is the tenth—to-day! What d'you know about that, now! To-day!"

A slight noise attracted his attention, and he looked up at the wall above his head. Upon the wall hung a clock, dirty and fly-specked, with broken front glass, but still proclaiming the time. From the clock proceeded a faint whirring noise—then the clock struck.

The man stared at it, fascinated, a species of terror in his gaze. At the twelfth stroke, he shuddered slightly, then drew a deep breath, as though something had missed him narrowly.

This man was Thompson.

N O O N   O F the same day was witnessing a very different scene at Cypremort plantation. In a comfortable chair on the front gallery sat John Solomon, puffing at his clay pipe. An old red tarboosh was cocked on one side of his head, and a silk dressing-gown enveloped his pudgy figure.

One of his two Arabs, now clad in snow-white garments, appeared and salaamed.

"Master, the hakim effendi!"

The doctor from Latouche came forward cheerily, followed by the smiling Aline Lavergne. Solomon laid down his pipe and allowed the physician to inspect a cicatrix in his left side. The doctor straightened up, and turned to Aline with a laugh.

"In another week, Miss Aline, your patient won't have even a dimple to show for it! You'll not need me again, I'm glad to say."

"Oh, good!" exclaimed the girl quickly. At sound of a step, she turned to meet Fortier. Her face was beaming. "Doctor Dubois isn't even coming again, Mr. Fortier—it's absolutely all right, just as we thought! You will stay for luncheon, of course, doctor. What's that you have, Mr. Fortier?"

Smiling, Fortier held up a half-blown pink magnolia blossom.

"The big tree down yonder," and he nodded toward the garden, "is just coming into full bloom—it's away ahead of the others! Here is the first blossom for you—"

"Oh, I must see it!" Seizing the waxen bloom, the girl carried it to Solomon, and, with an affectionate pat, laid it in his hand. "For you—I'm going to run and look at the tree quickly—we'll get some more of them for the table!"

She departed, Fortier at her elbow. Smiling to himself, Doctor Dubois sat down and lighted a cigarette.

"I don't suppose as 'ow you brought any mail in your launch?" inquired Solomon. "I was lookin' for a parcel that—"

"Brought a whole bag of it," returned the physician. "Ah—your man has it!"

One of the Arabs appeared, bringing a box. Solomon commanded him to open it. From the box was produced a large flat case, of morocco.

This Solomon took. He pressed the spring, opened the case, and glanced at what lay within. Then he nodded, and chuckled wheezily.

"A werry good job they made of it, too," he said. "It's a bit of a trick, mountin' up some o' the werry finest stones in the world and a-makin' a necklace of 'em! It ain't everyone as knows 'ow to do it right, as the old gent said when 'e kissed the 'ousemaid. Mebbe you'd like to 'ave a look at 'em, sir?"

He handed the case to the physician. The latter opened it, and at sight of what lay within, a gasp escaped him.

"My heavens, Solomon! I never dreamed such things existed—"

Solomon took up his pipe and chuckled wheezily.

"That 'ere, sir, is a-goin' to make a werry nice weddin' present, so to speak! That is, if I ain't mistook. And I ain't often mistook, as the old gent said when 'e 'ired the pretty cook."

Somewhere within the house a deep-toned clock was striking noon.

HIGH NOON in still another place—this time, amid a waste of great hills of green water where a tiny schooner, like a toy ship, was driven up and across the surging crests with endless insistence.

Upon her forward deck three black men, naked Bahamans, sat in the lee of the booming tight-bellied foresail and rolled dice—talking, laughing, shouting with the glee of children. Aft, beside the helm, stood a gaunt, powerful man, in whose face were the marks of suffering; lines of weakness about the mouth were offset by the blazing strength of the hollow eyes, by the determination and latent power of the whole face.

Down in the cabin Captain Tom Wrexham adjusted his cravat carefully, then looked up at a picture which had been framed and set near his bunk. It was the picture of a girl, whose eyes looked out at him with a deep, clear serenity. As he met those eyes, the face of Wrexham softened.

"So you like the schooner, lass?" he soliloquized. "Aye, she's a sweet craft! Well, I'll have to be leaving you a bit, miss—time to change watches and see what that cook's got dished up!"

He stamped up on deck. At sight of him, the black men up forward ceased their shouting abruptly, ceased their dicing and laughing, and scrambled to their feet. Captain Wrexham went aft, glanced at the binnacle, and nodded to his mate.

"Well, Mr. Philbrick! You're looking fine and hearty today. Making a new man of you, I am. It's a rum go, this. Sorry you came to sea, are you?"

The deep eyes of Philbrick rested steadily on the gaze of Wrexham.

"Yes," he answered. "Yes—and no."

"Ran away to sea at last!" Wrexham chuckled. "Hullo—what you lookin' at?"

Philbrick had turned to look at the empty horizon behind them. He started quickly, and shook his head.

"Nothing."

"Nothing, eh?" Wrexham chuckled again. "Thinkin' about that girl back there, are you—that Cypremort place? Want to go back? Homesick?"

"Yes," said Philbrick, with a helpless gesture.

"Oh!" Wrexham fingered his curly, square cut beard for a moment. "Well, if you want to get back there, the course is nor'-west by three-quarters north, Mr. Philbrick."

The gaunt grey man started suddenly. Eagerness filled out his voice.

"What!" he exclaimed. "What! D'you mean we're going to head back? Back home?"

Wrexham gave him a hard cynical look.

"No, I don't. I was just tellin' you for your own information. What's the course?"

"South-east by a half south, sir," and Philbrick's voice was dead.

"Very well—keep it so," said Wrexham coldly.

A long moment passed. The ropes twanged and sang, the long churn of foam under the lee rail trailed whitely out behind. Suddenly Philbrick spoke again.

"Eight bells, sir. Noon."

"Make it so."

Wrexham took the wheel. Philbrick went forward to the polished brass bell, and struck it. With the last two strokes, he released the cord and went to the companionway. There, for a moment, he stood looking out across the horizon—the empty horizon to the north-west.

Then he lowered his head and went below.

"I'll make a man of him yet!" said Wrexham, and chuckled.

THE WISDOM OF SOLOMON

JUST OUTSIDE the white mud walls of Maan, on the line of the pilgrim railroad from Damascus to Medina, was a little encampment; a few men, a few low tents, a few camels. Away off to the right in the empty deserts was the bleak railroad station, with its shed and a new hotel and gleaming red-headed water tanks.

The day was declining fast, the cry of afternoon prayers were over. At the door of his tent sat a man enveloped in a worn brown burnouse, which revealed only his sunburned features, his bushy black brows and hair, his vigorous eyes. Before him on the sand was a bubbling water-pipe.

As he smoked, this man gazed meditatively at the throngs about the city gates to his left. Here were fezzed Turks and soldiers, for those things happened in the days before the war—black slaves, swaggering Arabs of Hall or Nejd, merchants and beggars, camels and donkeys all in readiness for the harvest of the tourist season. The month of Shawal was close at hand, and soon the white-clad pilgrims in their thousands would pour though Maan en route to the holy cities of Mecca and Medina.

Frederick Sargent, who sat thus observing and smoking, was in all appearances a wealthy Egyptian merchant, by name of Nur-ed-Din ibn Saleh. He was an explorer and knew Arabia and other parts of the Moslem world as well as he knew New York city or perhaps better.

Now, as he loosened his heat-resistant burnouse at the throat to enjoy the refreshing sunset breeze, Sargent had good reason to congratulate himself. He had accomplished a difficult business. The camel loads heaped behind his tent were presumably of merchandise; in reality they contained reins and rubbings from an ancient Christian cathedral in the heart of Arabia. Ahead of him he had only the trip down to Egyptian territory and safety.

When Sargent lifted the stem of his *nargile*, a silver ring was visible on his hand. It was such a ring as any tourist may purchase in the Rue Sultan Osman in Port Said, a cheap silver band. Upon the bezel was graven a rectangle with lines from corner to corner. This design, among certain tribes, is known as the Seal of Solomon.

Had any of the passing throng guessed the identity of this Egyptian merchant a wild riot would have resulted. Only last Shawal had Hamdi Bey, who commanded the garrison here, crucified at the gate a Frenchman who had tried to make a pilgrimage in disguise. Yet Sargent had not even grown a beard to aid his imposture, so thorough was his knowledge of the East that he was in no fear of detection.

Now he watched a scruffy beggar come from the roadway toward the little encampment, uttering a pious whine for alms. He went first to the group of camel men, who rebuffed him with many jeers and took his curses with full repayment in kind. Then he wended toward Sargent with his plea.

"Alms, protector of the poor. Alms, in the name of Allah the compassionate, the merciful, the forgiving. Alms O blessed one in the name of Allah."

"Allah grant them to you for he is richer than I," said Sargent indifferently.

"Nay, worshipful protector." The beggar drew closer in persistence. "In the ineffable name grant alms. Droppings of mercy from the table of abundance. Then will the angels draw thee from hell by the scalp-lock saying that here was a man worthy of Paradise." The whining voice fell to a lower key. "Alms in the name of Suleiman!"

At this name, a slight start escaped Sargent. He gave the beggar a swift comprehensive scrutiny, looked at the upthrust palm. Against the dirt of that palm shone a glint of a silver—a ring identical with his own, the bezel of which was turned to his view.

Sargent produced a coin, dropping it into that hand.

"Add unto thy prayers," he said, "a *ratib* for him that gives."

"Allah requites thee, protector!" cried the beggar joyfully, stowing away the coin. "May he pluck thee from hell to the day of misfortune. Tell thy name, that it may be reached to the mosque, attaining sanctity for thee in the eyes of God and men!"

"Nur-ed-Din, the son of Saleh, of the house behind the Abou Dahab mosque in Cairo."

"It is well, Light of the Faith." The beggar thrust his hand into the sand—a swift, nervous gesture. "Thy generosity shall be known here as it is known in Al Kahireb!"

The man withdrew and departed the city gates. Sargent watched him, calmly smoking as he pondered. This circumlocution in the delivery of a message puzzled him, for there appeared to be no need for it. His men were faithful. They knew him only as an Egyptian, but they obeyed implicitly the token of the silver ring, and asked no questions. Why then, was the beggar in such secrecy?

After a little Sargent leaned forward and began to play negligently with the sand, catching it up and running it through his fingers. When he came upon the folded paper which the beggar had thrust there, he palmed it out of sight.

Some time later, he produced the paper openly, unfolded it, and read the message. Few men could have deciphered it. The beautiful script was ancient Arbi, written without vowels; only a scholar of the old tongues could read it. The note addressed to Nur-ed-Din ibn Saleh, ran:

> "I cannot meet you at Port Said as arranged. I write this from Damascus. By the wisdom of Allah, there is greater work for you than smuggling Christian relics out of Africa.
>
> "Go swiftly to the Hilaj wells, 10 miles from Maan, and camp. I will join you or send a messenger within two days. Trust no one unless his camel bears the personal brand of Ibn Rashid. I depend on your help.
>
> "Beware of one from the South who comes to the same place. His name I know not, but shall now be joining you. He has racing camels marked with the brand of the Sawarka tribe of Egypt; you cannot mistake it. He is an emissary of the Senussiyeh. Beware of him.   Suleiman."

This Suleiman was no other than John Solomon, a ship-chandler of Port Said.

The final paragraph of this letter, as he calmly burned it, caused Sargent some hard thought. John Solomon did not waste words, and the warning was repeated. Also, that mention of the Senussiyeh showed that big game was afoot—in all truth, desperate game! Sargent became acutely aware that he was not only entering upon danger, but that John Solomon himself was in deadly peril.

He knew John Solomon well, had known him for years past. He knew that the pudgy little man who sold ships stores in Port Said was in real life a person of vast underground influence, that from the dingy shop of the ship-chandler radiated threads which led into palaces and coffee-shops, throne-rooms and chancelleries, and that the little cockney who sat at the center of the web had the pulsing life of the eastern world under his fingers.

John Solomon held secrets rigidly guarded from most Christians. The sheiks and emirs of Arabia were his friends. More than once had he clashed with all the power of Turkey itself, more than once had he defied the sinister forces of the Senussiyeh—and always he had won. His seeming ability to control destiny had made him a legend.

Yet behind his amazing successes were definite reasons. He controlled a devoted secret-service system which had attained an incredible perfection, and allied with him were persons in every walk of life. John Solomon was not, as some claimed, a renegade; yet he was thoroughly conversant with the customs and language of the Arabs. He could pass for one if necessary, and he respected their belief. About his uncanny mental powers, about his very name, clustered legend and story.

Behind it all, stood the fact that the Arabs hated the Turks, and feared that strong but much over-rated secret society called the Senussiyeh. The stronghold of this order, the followers of Beni Snuouas, had moved from Western Algeria to the Libyan Desert. Its power extended throughout Africa and reached into Asia, for it was a missionary order, and the Arabian empire feared it would stretch into the holy land and seize their power. Even the Christians, in these days before the great war showed the reality, stood awed before the Senussiyeh, dreading revolts in Egypt, Algeria or Libya.

"Hm," reflected Sargent casually. "I understand the Senussiyeh have a price of 50,000 lbs on Solomon's head—they must be trying to collect! That's certainly queer about the chap coming from Egypt, too—on Sawarka camels?"

Livestock in the orient is and has been branded for 3,000 years and more, on exactly the same principles as in the wild and woolly Occident; some of the brands, in fact, can be traced back easily that length of time. Personal brands, in the case of powerful men, are used in connection with the more common tribal brand; as many of them are identical, their position on an animal serves to differentiate them.

Sargent knew his Egypt. He knew that the Sawarka tribe of El Arish used a very peculiar and unique brand, named El Zenad. The word Zenad means the iron used in striking fire, and the shape of the brand like an arrow head, clearly indicated the thing referred to.

"Probably," mused Sargent, "this chap got hold of some fine racers from the Sawarka breeders and is using them over here, taking for granted that the brand will be unknown. Or perhaps he cares nothing about his brand. Wonder who he's going to meet at the Hilaj wells? And why the deuce should I beware of him?"

Another uncertainty was the messenger of whom Solomon wrote, for there were two groups of Ibn Rashid tribes. Sargent feared that the note referred to the emir of Nejd, who ruled independently the interior of Arabia and whose relations with John Solomon were intimate. If this were an affair in which the Nejd emir were personally involved then it must be extraordinary indeed; the emir was as remote from the outside world as were the Manchurian emperors of China, and was supreme over all the tribes ruled by the Chammar family.

Sargent called his five men, and issued orders. They knew where the Hilaj wells were located, a now abandoned spot near the railway line off the main caravan route, owned by the Alawayine family of Maan.

"After the prayer of darkness load up and be off," said Sargent. "We go to that place at once."

They assented without protest, for did not this Egyptian wear the seal of Solomon?

An hour later, then, one of the men held down the head of Sargent's camel. The American stepped up to the neck, desert-fashion, and as the beast raised its head, gained his saddle with one agile movement. The bells of the lead and rear camels tinkled with silver echoes. The six men and the twelve lumbering, swaying camels padded softly into the night and were gone on the quest of adventure.

The Hilaj wells composed the scene of beauty. The water of the wells was brackish and of small quantity. Besides these, there were only a dozen ragged date-palms of inferior species and the desolate remains of a mud wall around what had been a house.

Sargent reached this place about midnight and his men pitched the little tents near the walls. At dawn the camels were turned out to graze on the thorny grassed growths, and Sargent sat down to wait what might befall. Upon his lips was the resigned "Ma aleah!" of his Egyptian character, but his heart was a live and alert curiosity. Those wells were close to Maan, an ideal point of meeting between Egypt and Arabia or Turkey, yet the place was abandoned and presumably secure. Of his own part in Solomon's plans Sargent could guess nothing; he might be kept here waiting for a day or a week.

So, having his rubbings to keep him occupied, he opened one of the packs and began to catalog his treasures.

The morning drew into noontide heat, blazing and intolerable. All around the desert spaces were empty, the horizon drawn in upon a yellow bowl of sand. A hot wind came out of the southeast and all the brazen sky in that direction was tinted with the brown waves of impalpable sand from the nefuda. The camels grunted and gurgled, the men prayed and slept and prayed again, and the consuming bath of blinding sunlight gradually lost intensity and assumed an eerie, sickly tinge as the wind-borne waves of sand drifted across the zenith.

Sargent did not miss the glances of his men. The Arab despises the Egyptian tremendously, but Sargent had overcome this feeling. Now he summoned the chief of his men, Yusuf by name.

"The mercy of Allah is infinite to the faithful," he said ironically, and waved his hand toward the low mud wall and ruins.

"And the wisdom of Suleiman is infinite," responded Yusuf, understanding perfectly the allusion and the order. He departed, rallied the men, and they fell to work getting the loads and camels inside the walls. The tents were pegged out afresh and weighted with sand. All was made ready against the hot breath of destruction which threatened.

Sargent watched. "They probably think," he reflected, "that Solomon ordered us to here so that we might be protected against the sandstorm; or else, that because they serve Solomon, Allah provided this well! Well, no matter; they are faithful men."

When his own tent had followed the others inside the mud wall, Sargent sat at the gateway and smoked, awaiting the event. This was not far distant. By imperceptible degrees the sun had vanished from sight, and two-thirds of the sky were mildly brownish yellow; over the desert hovered a gloom which was pierced by a most unearthly light as the advancing sand clouds filtered the sun's rays. The wind was strong and steady, and out of the sky came a singularly sibilant moaning, not unlike a whistle, so that the Arabs rallied upon Allah to protect them against the devils.

Now the first sparks of sand began to sting and burn the skin; the men were making ready water-soaked cloths. Sargent rose and stiffened. He uncased the prismatics underneath his burnouse, leveled them to the southern horizon. That horizon was fast vanishing in sand, yet he made out certain objects. He called sharply to Yusuf.

"Five camels come from the south. Let all of you beware.

Mention not the name of Suleiman, talk not with those who come."

Yusuf grimly unwrapped his rifle.

"Here is my tongue, oh Nur-ed-Din. Light of the Faith!" he responded. "Allah brings these men to destruction since there is no room in this place for them. Look to it, Egyptian!"

Sargent nodded, for the space inside the wall was filled, crowded to capacity.

"Room for the men, but not for their beasts," he said.

The men grumbled at this, but dared not cross his will. Sargent examined the approaching camels, which were plunging forward at full speed for shelter, the horizon quickly closing rapidly behind them.

"Hello!" he muttered. "*Mehari*-racers every one of them! Five riders, no baggage; and coming from the same south or west. They must be the ones I'm looking for; yet Solomon spoke of only one. One man, of course, and to escort him—"

Those long, gaunt *mehari*, with their spidery legs weaving fast, plunged in upon the walls, knowing perfectly what threatened them. The keen eyes of Sargent noted that they had come fast and far; the saddled riders were mere bundles of camel hair, for already the sand was stinging them deep. The storm-burst was not five minutes away.

At sight of Sargent and his men occupying the walled space, evident consternation fell upon the five. Swift shouts among them; a rifle was flourished. Sargent, at the gateway, quietly shifted his revolver into sight. Then one of the five dove forward ahead of the others, halted, swung to earth, and stood facing Sargent, who would see only a rather short figure completely muffled from sight. Their eyes were visible.

"Room, in the name of Allah!" came the words. "Entrance for us!"

Hoarse and thick was the voice, from a thirst-swollen throat; yet Sargent frowned as he tried to place that veiled wrapping. Something in the tone of the voice—

"As you see," he rejoined, "it has pleased God to bring us here first. There is room for you and your men, and water is plenty. Let your *mehari* wait in the lee of the wall."

The shrouded eyes searched him for a moment, flitted to his men as though weighing the chances of force. The two parties were almost equal. Then, abruptly, the stranger turned and shouted; the other four men left their beasts in the lee of the wall, on the outside, and came running back.

The first gusts of the storm came in this instant.

Everything was blotted from sight. Sargent groped forward, shouted, felt one of his men thrust a wet cloth upon him. This he wrapped about his head and face, while he was seeking the wall. It arose before him, a brief respite from the driving, penetration and burning of the sand; he bumped into another figure, recognized the leader of the five from the mouth, and flung himself down at the foot of the wall, where the little tents had been pitched. After a moment he crawled under the nearest, and again found himself beside the newcomer. Momentary respite again; the murky obscurity allowed little to be seen.

"Here is water," he said, thrusting forward a canteen.

The other accepted. Water gurgled. Then a long sigh, and Sargent felt a groping hand upon his. The darkness was now almost complete. Even under the tent, sand penetrated and burned in a fine-sifted cloud.

"Allah be praised!" said the other, and Sargent thrilled to the voice and touch. "You have come from the north or east?"

It was the voice of a woman, and the hand was the soft hand of a woman.

Before Sargent could answer, before he could recover from his astonishment, the roaring blasts of the wind were pierced by a faint, shrill scream of wild fear. Something struck the tent heavily. A ripping smash and crash resounded. The whole tent was suddenly pinned down by an enormous weight.

The mud wall had yielded in the pressure of the wind and sand.

Somehow, Sargent extricated himself, dragging the sense-less figure of his companion. The body in his arms, he sat in the open, head bowed, a black whirlwind of biting sand all around him. He could do nothing, dared not move. Even through the water-soaked cloth, the air that he was breathing was suffocating and harsh.

Thus passed time uncounted, hours that dragged as days. Thirst tortured him; his canteen was under the tent, and he suffered in silence. After a time the figure in his arms stirred slightly, then remained motionless. Sargent drifted off gradually into a doze, and so into deeper sleep.

He came broad awake with a vigorous start, and stared around in stupefied wonder, at first unable to place himself. Time and storm had passed together, now a glittering flood of moonlight poured down upon the desert, everything was cold and calm and still. Only one sound broke the silence—a low groan, repeated with monotonous reiteration at every catch of breath.

Sargent shook off the sand that half buried him. He leaned forward, looking at the woman in his arms. He stripped off his own head covering, and, loosening the hood of her burnouse, shamelessly lifted the veiling cloth beneath. He drew a sharp breath. Woman, indeed! A woman gloriously beautiful, her features touched by the moonlight into singular and delicate perfection, who lay breathing regularly in the slumber of exhaustion.

Again the groan intruded upon him. Sargent lowered the woman gently to the sand and, by an effort, drew his legs clear of the sandy weight. He rose, looking around, and his eyes widened. Dismay and horrified comprehension gripped him.

The place was not as he had last seen it. Gone was the mud wall on one side, where the tents had been pitched in its lee; gone, too, the tents, and in place of these things was only a great mound of yellow sand, that the night wind was ruffling into wavy curvatures. The camels had vanished likewise. On the other side, the remainder of the wall stood intact.

Once more that groan—Sargent turned swiftly, seeking its source. A huge pile of sand marked his camel-loads, heaped together. He approached this, and knelt over the half-buried figure of Yusuf. Under the man's side the sand was black and caked, and the shaft of a knife protruded from the burnouse.

Among the loads were two skins of water. Sargent uncovered one of these, knelt above Yusuf, saw that the man had been drained of life and could live only moments. Presently the Arab's eyes opened and recognition came into them.

"Who did this?" demanded Sargent. "What has happened? Where is everyone?"

Yusuf drank again and formed faint words.

"It was written; what is to be will be! The wall fell down on us. I was crawling out, when one of those dogs smote me with his knife to crowd past. Allah! Part of the wall fell again and broke his back. I am here."

"The camels?"

"I know not. Perhaps they fled when the wall fell—God, The Compassionate, The Merciful! Deliver me out of the hand of the evildoer—"

He fell into a mutter of words from the Koran. Then suddenly he came to his elbow, his right hand clutching at the sky.

"There is but one God, Allah the eternal, who begetteth not nor is begotten—nor is there any like him—"

So, the credo of his faith upon his lips, passed Yusuf to his fathers.

Sargent lowered the dead face to the sand, rose, strode around the outside of the remaining wall. There he came upon two of the *mehari*, kneeling and complacently regarding him; the other three had vanished, perhaps in pursuit of his own camels. As he stood there, he looked at the left thigh of the nearer animal, and compressed his lips. The brand burned into the skin was the brand of El Zenad.

"So this woman, then, is the emissary of the Senussiyeh!" he murmured.

He came back again to the enclosure, utterly dismayed by what had chanced. His men and animals were gone, he found himself suddenly stripped of all externals and help. Piled amid the sand was the fruit of long months of arduous labor, and if the Turks learned of what lay in those camel-loads, trouble would be swift and sure to ensue. There were Turks in Maan, no lack of them.

"And I'm at the mercy of the first party of thieving Hedawi who pass this way!" thought Sargent. "They'll plunder those loads and take the news to Maan—"

He recalled Yusuf's pious and simple belief that Allah and John Solomon had sent them to this place for a reason—and an ironic smile twisted his lips at sight of Yusuf's body sprawled on the sand. He turned to the woman, and stood as though petrified.

She was standing facing him, her burnouse removed. He perceived that she was no Arab, but Caucasian—a white woman!

To Sargent it was as though they two alone were left in an extinct world.

Under the mounded sand, under their very feet, was desolation and death. The palm trees rasped harshly in the night wind. The light of the moon poured down on a greenish, pearly effulgence whose deceptive clarity heightened the mystery of the desert night, softening all things, revealing all things, hiding all things, in the paradoxical fashion of that master-paradox of creation.

And the woman beautiful, her features young, delicate, surreal with masses of golden hair glinting Medusa-like under the moon's rays—struck upon his senses like a fairy. Then her voice came to him, mellow and rounded, speaking the harsh Arbi with such fluency that he realized she must be English or American.

"What has happened? Where is everyone?"

Sargent's hand swept to where the wall had been. Barely in time, he remembered his assumed character.

"Dead by the dispensation of Allah. The wall fell. The camels are gone. Two of your *mehari* remain."

"Then," she ordered coyly, "take one of them and go. Maan is not far distant. I do not wish you to remain here."

Sargent laughed curtly, Then native-wise he fell into towering rage.

"My goods and my money—O woman, truly as is written that folly lieth in the words of women! Allah upon thee! Shall I desert my goods, leave my children paupers, be myself once more who begs for alms at the door of his mosque? Peace, fool! Nor does it become a woman to give orders to a man. Who are you? Some slattern of the bazaars married to an Arab?"

Thus was true to type. The woman's mien changed instantly. A smile broke on her lips.

"Your pardon, protector of the faithful! I am Fatima, and was journeying under escort to meet Hamdi Bey whose third wife I am to be. For your own sake I bode you because, since if Hamdi came here to meet me and found the two of us alone—"

She flushed with an expansive gesture, but Sargent had learned much. Hamdi Bey! A true buzzard of the Osmanli, in charge of the garrison at Maan; a strong man, who robbed and ravished at will and whose name was a curse in the mouths of Arabs.

Sargent shrugged, gave his name and dismissed the entire matter by saying that he chose to remain here. He had a small Arab pipe and some tobacco in his pouch and sat down to light it. The woman, who was clad in serviceable khaki, reclined in the sand near him, her eyes fastened upon his face. He made a sign to avert the evil eye, and she laughed softly.

"Cursed is the hairy woman and the hairless man!" she quoted. "Where is thy beard, Egyptian? Did the storm scatter the hairs of it?

"Chatter not," responded Sargent dourly. "Lie down in a corner and sleep."

To his infinite relief, she wrapped her burnouse about her

shoulders and obeyed his command. She was, obviously, still in the grip of desperate weariness from her travel.

When she was fast asleep, Sargent removed the burnouse from the dead Yusuf, and gently spread it over the woman. As he did so, he paused. The moonlight struck down upon her figure and disclosed a flat leather case strapped to her belt.

That her story was a lie went without saying. He knew already that she was here on behalf of the dreaded Senussiyeh. What, then, was in that case?

With all precaution, Sargent knelt and loosened the flap of the case. The woman stirred, her hand fell down on her bosom. Sargent stared down at that hand, and slowly his exploring finger drew back. Upon the woman's hand glittered a silver ring bearing the seal of Solomon—and those rings were confided only to John Solomon's most trusted emissaries!

What did this mean? Sargent was perplexed and bewildered. His first instinct was to waken the woman and demand an explanation, but he rejected it. Over the leather case, he hesitated a while and finally drew back. No, morning would be time enough. Perhaps this woman was an agent of Solomon's who had been with the party of Senussiyeh. All things were possible.

It did not even occur to Sargent that this woman might have previously observed his own ring, or that she might not at this minute be more than shamming sleep. Nor did he observe the smile that touched her shadowed lips when he left her and rolled up in his own burnouse. Considering all his perplexities unto the morrow, and knowing full well the value of sleep when it could be obtained, he passed again in slumber.

When Sargent awakened, the morning had arrived.

He lay for a moment in startled surprise, wondering at his singular feeling of constraint. Then, when he tried to move, he found himself helpless; he lay on his back, staring at the cloudless sky, with his wrists tied together across his breast, his ankles likewise bound. After the fashion of Northern Arabs, he had worn about his legs tasseled fillets less for ornament than for

ligatures in case of scorpion-bite, and with the cords he had
been securely fastened.

Who had done this—the woman?

Unable to rise, Sargent slowly turned his head about, and
finally rolled on his right side, directed by a sound of voices.
Nearby a camel stood, waiting to be unsaddled; on the sand sat
a man who the woman Fatima was serving such food and drink
as she had been able to obtain from Sargent's half-buried loads.
Seemingly this man had arrived here very recently. The two were
thirty feet from the American.

Accepting his position coolly enough, Sargent made use of
his eyes. This was a short chap whose face was nearly hidden by
an enormous green turban proclaiming that he was a Hajjt, who
had made the pilgrimage or was a descendant of Mohammed;
and by the muffling throat of his burnouse which was much too
large for him. He sat facing Sargent, who even at that distance
discerned a stubby gray mustache and a pair of blue eyes, nothing unusual in Arabs of pure stock. The woman was assiduously
waiting upon this man.

Sargent transferred his attention to the camel, a fine blooded
racer, and suddenly he stiffened as he lay. On the left thigh of
the beast was branded a large X and lower down above the foot,
a straight vertical line. This latter was the brand El Chahed, the
personal brand of Ibn Rashid Emir of Nejd; the former was the
brand of the Chammar tribe.

This man was the emissary of Solomon whom Frederick
Sargent had come here to meet.

Now the Hajjt refused further food and motioned the woman
to be seated. His curt words came clearly to Sargent.

"Tell me what happened here."

"Nay, holy one," she responded. "You have eaten my salt, tell
me then, whence you come and whither you go and who you
are. My errand may not be lightly told to everyone."

"First I look at this man."

The Hajjt grunted, came to his feet and came to the side of

Sargent leaving Fatima where she was. The holy man stooped, pretended to feel Sargent's bonds and whispered low words which left the American absolutely petrified.

"Dang it, Mr. Sargent, we're in a most uncommon fix, just like that. That 'ere female will bear watching, as the old gent said when 'e blamed the 'ousekeeper. Lie low, sir, and if so be as I gives you a clue, why, you up and grab it. There's a 'orde of Turks as'll be 'ere in less than half an hour, dang it, they're fair got me this time and a werry bad job it is."

With a wheezy sigh John Solomon turned and rejoined the woman.

Sargent stared blankly, astonished by the revelation. That momentary close-up had given him a glimpse of the little cockney's features—pudgy round face masked by a stubble of gray beard, an expressionless, motionless face, lifted into distinction only by the china blue eyes which held the innocent wondering look of a child.

This man playing the part of a holy man of Islam! Why, he would be torn to bits were the imposition discovered! Then Sargent gathered himself together, recollected that he was doing the same thing, and smiled at his own quick dismay. After all, there was little risk. John Solomon had passed for an Arab ere this.

What an Odyssey the cockney had experienced between writing that note in Damascus and appearing in this place, Sargent could well imagine. Little things were significant. He had come alone, absolutely alone, riding a camel that was the personal property of the Nejd emir—and with word that the Turks were close behind! And now, as Solomon rejoined the woman, Sargent heard swiftly enough the exact situation.

"I am Suleiman Ibn Yusuf," said the cockney, "and I am pursued. Take my camel, which is lame, and some money, and give me another on which to flee."

"Nay!" The woman laughed harshly. "Last night two of my *mehari* remained; now they have wandered away."

"It is the will of Allah!" said Solomon, and the words were earnest enough. "Know, then, that I came hither in order to meet another servant of my master, one whom I was bidden to seek at this place."

"His name?" queried the woman.

"I know it not. I was to know him by a sign."

"Was this the sign?" Eagerly Fatima lifted her hand. From Solomon broke words.

"W'allah alim! Truly Allah seeth all things and ordereth the event!" He pretended to examine the ring on her finger. "Aye, it is the sign! Tell me what has passed here!"

"I came here on the business of our master Suleiman," she answered boldly. "Here I found yonder dog," and she motioned toward Sargent, "encamped with his men. There was sandstorm upon us, we took refuge here and during the storm, which was terrible, a wall fell upon our men and the sand smothered them. Our camels ran away. This was last night—"

"Truth," broke in Solomon eagerly. "Men say in Maan that it was greatest storm in twenty years. Allah bear witness."

"And last night," went on the woman, "yonder Egyptian made proposals to me and spoke words of shame in my ear. I pretended compliance, but taking him off his guard I bound his hands and then his feet. That is the tale."

"By the ineffable names," quoth Solomon admiringly. "What is your name, woman? It seems to me that you are a Frank."

She laughed. "Have you never heard of Miriam. English Miriam?"

Sargent choked back an oath of consternation. English Miriam! Why had he not guessed it? He wondered now that the woman had left him alive.

English Miriam! All the East knew the name, knew something of the story. She was not the first English or French woman to be brought to Algeria as governess to the children of some wealthy sheik—and then to vanish in the gulf of the

Sahara. Unlike the others, however, this English Miriam had risen again from the void; and she had risen terribly.

According to the report, she had become the wife of some Turkish sheik, had murdered him, and had taken his wealth in the secret city of the Senussiyeh, by whom she was employed of missions in Egypt and elsewhere—places a white woman might go unquestioned. About her name clustered legends of murder, of assassination, of intrigue. How much of all this was truth, how much rumor, was hard to say. The fact seemed to be that she was used by the Senussiyeh to accomplish strange purposes, and she was endowed by Dame Gossip with marvelous powers and clairvoyant faculties.

So this English Miriam had been sent to kill John Solomon!

"No," rejoined Solomon to her questions. He appeared quite unmoved. From beneath his burnouse he drew forth an old clay pipe, into which he whittled some tobacco from a black plug. He was quite absorbed by this occupation.

The woman was obviously disappointed. She drew back, rose to her feet.

"The hour of prayer is past," she said. "There is water here for thy ablution. I will get a little, that Allah may bless us."

Solomon struck a match, cupped both hands about his pipe; Miriam passed him, then swerved like a flash, threw herself down on his back, knife flaming in the sunlight, and drove in a blow with all the weight of her falling body in back of it. So swift and deadly was that glittering thrust, so unexpected, that Sargent had no chance to cry a warning.

Nor had Solomon the least chance of avoiding it. The knife-point smote him behind and in the left of the shoulder blade. Miriam lost balance, plunged forward in the sand.

Solomon calmly tossed away his match, without moving from his position.

"If I were you, me dear," he said in English, "I wouldn't lose no more time a-tryin' of that 'ere game. 'Cause why, it don't work."

Sargent, himself slow to realize what had happened, found

himself staring at a terrible tableau. John Solomon hitched himself slightly around so that he was facing Miriam. She, coming to her feet, stood there inarticulate, terrified beyond measure, fear and a wild agony of dread stamped in every line of her face.

Now, seen under the pitiless sun, the beauty of that face appeared harsh and seamed, lined with cunning evil, a death-mask of the days that were no more for this woman. And the aureole of her golden hair was faded and unkempt. Her eyes, as she stared at Solomon, were frightful to behold. So great was the terror and fear in them, yet she summoned one final flash of energy.

"I know you," she cried, gasping the words. "You could not fool me." Suddenly she broke off, shrank back again. "Magic! They say that the devils served you—"

Solomon, puffing at his pipe, wagged his head sadly.

"Providence, alas, beggin' your pardon," he rejoined. He leaned forward and picked up the knife. It had snapped asunder. "Providence, and that 'ole coat o' chain-mail me werry good friend ibn Rashid up and give me."

Under the immobility of the man the restraint of Miriam snapped.

"Kill me, then—kill me and end it all!" she uttered in a hollow despair. "O, I am sick of living; sick of it all, sick! Go and kill me."

Solomon removed his pipe.

"Miss, I ain't never yet done no 'arm to a woman. Werry sorry for you I am, just like that. But sorrow don't butter the parsnips, as the old gent said when 'e buried his third. No, miss. I ain't a-goin' to kill you. Take that 'ere gun off your belt an' throw it down."

The hand of English Miriam dropped to the revolver holstered at her hip. For a long instant she seemed to hesitate, yet that motionless little man had cowed her. Even now, though she understood why her knife had snapped asunder, she was cowed for the moment. She took out the revolver, dropped it in the sand.

Solomon leaned forward and quietly raked the sand over the weapon. A slight action this, which passed unnoticed.

"So you're the one as was sent to murder me," he said, and chuckled wheezily. "And what was the price, English Miriam? Out with it, Mary! 'Ow much for me 'ead?"

A shiver took the woman.

"Freedom," she said in a low voice. "Freedom. Money, and liberty—I was to go back home again—"

Her words died away.

"And who's that 'ere man tied up yonder?" demanded Solomon.

She lifted her head, stared incredulously into his calm blue eyes.

"That man! I don't know. But he wears your ring—he is one of your men—"

"'E ain't nothin' of the sort," said Solomon bluntly, and in a sense truly. "If I ain't mistook, 'e belongs to the Senussiyeh—himself, just like that. A werry good job as 'ow you tied him up, I says. Are you tryin' another trick on me? Or was this someone as was set to keep watch on you by the Senussiyeh?"

Sargent drew a deep breath of relief. Whither all this tended he had not the least idea, but he recognized that John Solomon had given him his cue.

Well as he knew that little cockney, he had scarcely credited Solomon with such crafty guile. Miriam looked toward him, in her features a mingling of hope; and why not? Sargent must have seemed to her a spy of the Senussiyeh, indeed, stationed here at this place to watch what she did and report on it to the monastic order. Well she knew that the grand master of this brotherhood trusted few.

So her face was a fantastic medley of emotions as she gazed. Solomon rose to his feet, emitted a wheezy sigh and came to the side of Sargent. He spoke in a low, tense voice that barely reached the ear of the bound man.

"Dang it! I 'oped as 'ow she wouldn't recognize us. Women are very extraordinary critters, as the old gent said when 'e kissed the 'ousemaid. Now, sir, 'ere are them bloody Turks—use your 'ead, sir! Game's up. Spar for time, just like that—"

A curt voice, a sudden thud of hooves in the sand, and around the corner of the remaining segment of wall rode a squad of Turkish cavalry, headed by a glittering officer. Even Miriam broke a sharp cry.

"Bluff it!" came the voice of the little cockney. "None o' them here Turks knows a blessed thing about the Senussiyeh—bluff it 'ard, sir!"

And Solomon knocked out his pipe as he faced about.

The officer dismounted and strode forward, four of his troopers followed while the remaining six waited with the horses. Neither men nor horses were of the ordinary type; the latter were bred animals, the former were obviously picked men. The officer, who had thrown back his handsome white burnouse to reveal a medalled breast, was a tall and striking man, a boy in rank, his face vigorous and brutally powerful.

English Miriam darted forward.

"Hamdi Bey!" she cried out. "I am the messenger come here to meet you—that man is Suleiman—John Solomon! Release the man on the ground, for he is of the Senussiyeh—"

Hamdi Bey! Sargent stared. He wondered how Solomon could stand there, imperturbable, motionless; the burnouse flung back revealed his pudgy features, his calmly poised gaze, his entirely unencumbered expression.

The Turk flung upon Miriam a questing, curious glance, waved his hand carelessly as though bidding her be silent, and riveted his gaze upon Solomon. "In my hands!"

"Yes, sir." Solomon's air was almost apologetic. "Werry sorry I am to say so, but that 'ere is the truth."

"Search that man," exclaimed Hamdi in Osmanli.

Two of his men stepped forward to Solomon, who did not resist. They went through him swiftly, efficiently, producing nothing except his smoking materials and a small red notebook, which Hamdi disdained. Then the Turk glared at the prostrate Sargent.

"Who is this?" he demanded. "Speak, dog!"

Sargent made answer.

"Effendi, I am called Nured Din the Egyptian, but in the grand lodge of the Beni Snouss I have another name which is not for your ears. It is I who am sent here to meet you; trust not that woman, I warn you! Order your men to release me from these bonds. The woman is English Miriam—have care!"

"English Miriam!" The Turk whirled, hand on pistol, a startled expression leaping into his face. Plainly enough, he had heard tales of this woman. As for Miriam, she stood amazed and bewildered before Sargent's words, unable to tell whether his claim were true or false. Sargent seized the opportunity to drive home his blow.

"I am a mokkhadem, a missionary of the Senussiyeh," he went on, his voice biting into the morning silence. "This man and this woman waylaid me here and robbed me. Seize them swiftly, effendi! About the woman's waist you will find the dispatch case stolen from me. Quickly!"

Hamdi Bey snapped an order; his men closed in upon Solomon and the woman. At this, English Miriam recovered from her stupefaction and flew into a storm of furious cursing, reviling Sargent and Solomon and Hamdi Bey in a flow of richest Arbi. Some realization of how she had been duped stole in upon her brain, but instead of keeping cool she lost her head and poured vituperation upon those around her.

Only when the leather case was taken by force from about her body did the woman cease her struggles. Then she relaxed, her gaze fastened steadily upon Sargent, only the heaving bosom and glittering eyes betraying her emotion.

As for Sargent, he had worked desperately with his fingers

until the silver ring slipped into the sand beside him and was covered by a movement of his body.

"Look at her hand, effendi," he exclaimed. "Upon her finger is the seal of this man Solomon whose servant she is! There is proof!"

One of the men held up Miriam's hand, showing the forged ring.

"Bind her," said Hamdi Bey. "Guard this fat fool."

Stooping, the Turk produced a knife and cut Sargent's bonds.

"Peace be with you," he said, helping the American to rise.

"And upon you, peace. Give me eat and drink, for I have tasted nothing this morning. My men and camels were scattered in the sand storm yesterday and I barely reached this place alive."

"Aye, Allah blessed us with a sweet taste of hell yesterday." Hamdi Bey sent one of his men to the horses for a canteen and food, and then turned to Solomon. Upon his face was insolent triumph and scorn of the man before him. He fingered his glossy mustache, and smiled.

"So you are the famous Solomon! I have heard of you. But I thought to find a man, not an insignificant dog of a Nazarene."

Solomon lifted his blank blue eyes.

"Yes, sir," he responded. "And I've 'eard tell of you likewise. It was you as crucified two Armenian women at Damascus last muharram. It was you as murdered an American missionary six months ago and stole 'is wife. It was you as 'ad ten Greeks impaled—"

"Two on the same stake—a very original idea," struck in the Turk, with a burst of hearty laughter. "So you have heard of me, eh? Good. Your head shall hang at the gate of Maan tomorrow morning—and between now and then you shall learn more of me." He glanced at his men and spoke with a deadly intense-ness. "Guard this man. If he escapes from your hands, you shall be crucified. Look to it, you twain."

Hamdi turned and regarded the woman with unconcerned interest.

"So this is English Miriam!" he said musingly. "Well, I perceive that rumor has lied again. The famous Solomon is a petty rascal trading on the name of a great king. The famous English Miriam scarce justifies her reputation for beauty. My men are not particular, woman, but you would not even interest them. Hah! My brother Yacoub Pasha wants an Englishwoman for his harem; I shall send you to him—a pretty jest, is it not? I can imagine Yacoub's emotion when he beholds you and hears your name. He will probably have you strangled lest you poison him; poor Yacoub always imagines that there is intrigue in his harem. Well, keep her guarded for a little, you two."

The woman responded no answer, but the flashing glance of her eyes caused a frown to crease Hamdi's brow. He turned from his prisoners, produced a cigarette case, seated himself on the sand, and lighted a cigarette.

"Now, Egyptian!" His dark, full eyes rested on Sargent. "Sit down and let us come to business. As an officer of the Senussi-yeh, you are of course learned in languages?"

Sargent assented. "I speak English, French, German and the Arbi dialects, effendi."

"Then let us speak English," said Hamdi, "for it is not desirable that my men should know which we say. As for the other two—" He broke off, shrugged, and smiled slightly.

Sargent seated himself, for he had been eating and drinking as he stood. Now he drew the leather case before him and opened it. It was imperative that he should glance at any letters before turning them over to the Turk, for he had not the faintest idea on what errand English Miriam had come.

Hamdi fortunately gave him a clew.

"When your Damascus agent came to me last month with the preliminary proposals," said the Turk, "it was agreed that I should be furnished all the data in your hands regarding this Solomon. That is now, of course, unnecessary. I learned that he was in Damascus, wrote my brother Yacoub, who is Governor there, and he was very nearly caught, but slipped away. Fortunately, he came directly into my hands."

"Allah is bounteous to the faithful," said Sargent, with a nod of assent.

He had drawn forth a number of papers written in Osmanli. A glance showed him the name of Suleiman, and he replaced them in the case.

"These are the notes in question, effendi," he said. "But here is the main document—"

He unfolded a sheet of vellum on which was very fine and elegant writing. Affixed to this was the signature of the Emir Idris Kaimakaan or Grand Master of the Senussiyeh order, followed by those of his waikils. The face of Sargent was stony as he glanced swiftly through the writing; only by tremendous effort did he repress the eagerness that threatened to fill his eyes.

"Here is the letter, over the signature of Emir Idris, whom may Allah bless!" he said, and extended the roll. Hamdi accepted it and began to read.

Small wonder that the powerful, vulpine features of the Turk began to glow as he scanned the lines. For by this agreement the Senussiyeh were to plant a branch of their monastic order in Maan, another in Damascus—thus controlling the pilgrim railroad. Hamdi Bey was to obtain a *firman* from the Sultan to this end, which could be purchased, and was also to obtain clear title to certain enumerated lands and buildings in the two cities. He was guaranteed all expenses and the sum of 10,000 Turkish pounds.

A neat and simple scheme it was, by which the Senussiyeh would be firmly entrenched in Arabia—and once in, they would not easily be ousted. One curt sentence, however, had been etched into Sargent's memory:

"Once the death of the Englishman Suleiman is assured."

It was John Solomon who stood like a rock between the Beni Snouss and their ambitions. Behind Solomon were the Arab tribes, politically almost helpless in the hands of their Turkish masters.

Hamdi Bey finished his perusal and tucked the roll inside his tunic. He lighted another cigarette and regarded Sargent with a crafty smile.

"Excellent!" he said. "You see how the will of Allah is demonstrated? We meet, we make agreement; at the same moment Solomon is delivered into our hands! It is written."

"What about the *firman?*" questioned Sargent. "You will have no difficulty in obtaining it from the Porte?"

Hamdi waved his hand and laughed.

"Certain expenses, of course—no matter! Between the Wahabi tribes at the other end of Arabia, and the Senussiyeh planted at this end, these pestilent Arabs will be held its subjection; an excellent argument, I assure you! Now, there are certain minor arrangements to be settled between us, Egyptian. For example, the price which your order has placed on the head of this Solomon."

"He is not yet dead," returned Sargent.

"Oh!" Hamdi chuckled. "You will see his head at the gate of Maan in the morning, unless he dies too soon. My men are not bunglers, however. They shall see to it. You return to the city with me?"

Sargent reflected swiftly. John Solomon had ordered him to fight for time—why?

"Yes," he assented. "I must obtain camels and a few men to escort me as far as Jerusalem or Beirut. Perhaps I had better return by ship to Egypt. I can bear witness to the death of Solomon, and the reward will be sent you immediately."

"Agreed," said Hamdi. "But there was a little matter—a draft was to accompany this letter from your emir—you understand?"

Sargent cursed himself. A bribe for this Turk, of course! Yet there had been nothing else in the leather case.

"Everything was taken from me by those accursed infidels,"

he answered, but in upon his words broke a shrill of laughter from English Miriam.

The woman stood passively between her two guards, and from her lips came that shrill, almost hysterical laughter.

"Ask him the sum, effendi!" she cried out. "Prove him, prove him! Fool that you are, to let him betray us all! He fooled me too—nay, he is no believer in the holy Snouss. I was wrong. His words showed me the truth. Prove him quickly, Turk—ask him about the draft, and then ask me, and prove which one of us lies."

Sargent, as he listened, felt a cold chill steal upon him. He was caught.

The Turk listened to that shrill cry, listened with a flicker of suspicion in his dark eyes. The flicker became a slow gathering flame at the next words from the woman.

"I was the true messenger, fool! It was this devil Solomon whose tongue tricked me, made me believe the Egyptian was also of the Senussiyeh. He is not! Prove the truth!"

A wheezy sigh, almost inaudible, came from the lips of John Solomon in that sigh. Sargent read his doom. Yet he forced a satirical smile to his lips.

"A woman babbles and the sun stands still!" he quoted, with the true Moslem sneer.

Hamdi Bey sat smoking, his eyes flitting from one to the other of the three. Those dark and cruel eyes told the thoughts passing in his brain. The words of Miriam had shaken him badly, had struck of incredulity. He knew not whom to believe, yet he feared the little cockney who stood quietly and eyed him from blank features. And moreover, it appeared that the bribe which had been sent him was lost and Turkish cupidity was swift to be aroused.

"I doubt you not, Egyptian," said Hamdi slowly, watching Sargent's stony face. "Yet the woman speaks well. What was the amount of the draft, and its nature?"

Sargent smiled slightly.

"As Allah knoweth, who am I to be told such matters?" he

responded disdainfully. "I am a servant. An envelope was among these papers; now it is gone. Doubtless the money was in this envelope. Who am I, to break the seal of Idris himself, on whom be blessed? Either this woman or this man has the money taken from me. Search them!"

"Search Solomon," ordered Hamdi. His two men obeyed. Beyond revealing the chain-mail next to the cockney's skin, nothing was found. The little red notebook which Solomon held was shaken out vainly. Then from Miriam came a scornful laugh.

"Aye, search!" she taunted. "Search for that which does not exist—an envelope bearing the seal of Idris! Is the emir a fool, then? Here is the envelope from the banking house sealed by the banks! Now judge who has lied, effendi."

From her bosom she snatched an envelope. One of the soldiers took it, brought it to Hamdi, who had risen to his feet.

Sargent, whose revolver had been taken from him when he was bound, perceived that he was lost. He sat motionless until Hamdi whirled upon him in a blaze of anger.

"Explain thy lie, Egyptian!" he cried furiously in Arbi. "By the prophet, the woman has caught thee in a cleft stick!"

Before Sargent could reply the woman's voice broke again.

"Ask him what lies under the sand yonder, effendi!" She pointed to the mound that marked Sargent's loads. "I found him here when I arrived yesterday—there are his camel loads, beneath the sand! Open the packs and examine into this thing fully!"

Now all was lost. Once Hamdi took this advice, as he would, everything would be discovered, and Sargent's identity revealed.

"What sum is this draft, woman?" demanded the Turk, tearing at the envelope.

"One thousand pounds on the bank of Egypt."

In silence Hamdi drew forth the slip of paper, examined it, pocketed it, his gaze struck upon Sargent in a glitter of fear and hatred.

"Liar!" he said coldly. "You shall ride to Maan with us, and my torturers will get the truth of this matter from you, for the words of the woman have damned you! And your head shall swing beside that of Solomon.

He turned with a gesture to his waiting man.

"Hither! Bind this Egyptian. Bind Suleiman yonder. Mount them both on one horse—two of you double up—and tie them in place. Clear away the sand from these loads."

The waiting man dismounted and came forward. At this moment, however, Solomon leaned over, picked up the red notebook, which had fallen to the sand, and spoke to Hamdi Bey.

"One minute, sir! I'd like werry much to 'ave a word in private, if so be as you'd oblige me."

His face was quite blank, his calm blue eyes were quite devoid of expression, as he proffered this request in his apologetic fashion.

Hamdi regarded the little cockney searchingly. Solomon's huge green turban had been plucked away in the search of his person, and there remained a battered tarboah cocked on one side, from the edge of which protruded wisps of grayish hair. In one hand Solomon held his pipe, which he had just refilled, in the other, his notebook. Taken all in all, he was anything but an object of menace.

"What do you want?" demanded the Turk.

"Why, sir, a little matter o' business, if you'll be so good. I 'ave me accounts to settle, all shipshape an' proper. Business is all werry well in its place, I says, and this 'ere is the place, just like that!"

The Turk fingered his mustache with an air of reflection. Beyond question, he scented a bribe, for Solomon was reputed to be very wealthy. A glitter shot through his eyes; unfortunately for herself, English Miriam chose this instant to a shrilly screamed protest.

"Trust him not, Hamdi! Trust not his tongue—beware of him! Listen not to his words, for he will trick—"

"Silence that she-devil!" roared Hamdi Bey furiously. "Gag her.

His men fell upon Miriam, wrapped a cloth about her mouth, bound her hands and feet, dropped her on the sand. Hamdi Bey turned again to Solomon.

"These witnesses may be disposed of quickly," he said, with a glance at Sargent, who remained seated. "The others do not understand our words. Speak! It is a question of money?"

"No, sir, it ain't," returned Solomon, who had dragged the stub of a pencil to light and was writing something in the notebook.

"What!" cried the Turk, with a black scowl. "Do you mean—"

"It ain't a question o' money at all, sir, as the old gent said when 'e 'ired a new 'ousemaid." Solomon emitted a wheezy chuckle. "First, sir, tell me one thing! Was it your men as killed them 'ere Arabs what left Damascus with me?"

Hamdi Bey was puzzled. He made slow response.

"My brother's men, at my orders. Why?"

"I'm just a-getting these 'ere accounts all shipshape, sir—there we be." Solomon put away his pencil with a complacent air. "All down to date, just like that—except maybe a matter o' two or three murders that ain't been reported yet. 'Owsomever, we ain't interested in further details, as the old gent said when 'e buried 'is third. If you'll be so good as to cast your eye on this 'ere, sir, I'll be werry much obliged."

While he spoke, Solomon had thumbed over the pages of his notebook. Now, holding it open, he extended it.

Hamdi Bey, hand on revolver, accepted the notebook and took a backward step. For an instant he watched John Solomon, as though anticipating some trick; he was both reassured and puzzled by the calm air of the cockney, who struck a match, held it to his pipe, and awaited the issue.

The Turk transferred his attention to the notebook.

A slight start escaped him; then, as he read, a singular change came into his face. The heavy, powerful features were overspread by a slight pallor that became a ghastly livid hue; this, in turn, was followed by a rush of blood that suffused the man's face in a deep flush.

Hamdi turned a page and read on. A pulse on his temple began to throb terribly; his eyes dilated suddenly—suddenly a violent oath burst from his lips and he dashed the little notebook to the sand stamping on it furiously.

"Who in the name of Eblis are you?" he cried out, glaring at Solomon. "What does this mean, that writing—"

"Just what it says, sir," returned the cockney with placid calm.

"The devil himself is in you! God has nothing to do with this affair."

"Beggin' your pardon, sir, that 'ere is a werry great mistake," said Solomon earnestly.

Hamdi snatched out his revolver, his face contorted with passion.

"You Nazarene dog!" he shouted. "Who told you these things about me? Who dared tell you those things—"

Solomon emitted a wheezy chuckle.

"Why, sir, if I were you I wouldn't go a-losin' of me temper! It don't pay, I says. Providence is a werry mysterious thing, and there ain't an accountin' for what it does, sir. Them 'ere is me accounts, and I 'opes as you finds 'em all correct—'cause why, if they ain't, then I'm werry much mistook in me judgments."

With a violent effort, Hamdi Bey regained control of himself. He put up his weapon, and regarded Solomon with what was meant to be insolent contempt. In reality, some dread emotion was written in his face; whatever the words he had read in that little red book, they seemed to have reached into his very heart and soul.

"You think that your God will save you!" he sneered. "Very well. Allah upon you! In three minutes you die."

"In three minutes," rejoined Solomon, quite expressionless, "you'll be in 'ell, sir. And werry 'ot I 'ope you find it!"

The Turk stared at him, thunderstruck by the calm pronouncement. The ten soldiers grouped around, their interest concentrated on what was passing, although they understood little or nothing of it, stared from their leader to Solomon and back again.

So absorbed were they all that when Solomon moved a pace to one side and knocked out his pipe, not even his two guards moved.

"You are a madman!" said Hamdi Bey, slowly.

To Sargent, sitting there motionless, but with muscles tensed, it was evident that John Solomon was still sparring for time. But why? The end was bound to come quickly. He had been ready to spring at Hamdi when the revolver flashed out—for Sargent was minded to go down fighting rather than be tortured by the Turks.

"No, sir, beggin' you pardon," returned Solomon. "It ain't me as is mad—it's you! You come to this 'ere place to meet a messenger of the Senussiyeh! You wanted werry bad to keep the meetin' secret, but 'ere you be, and only ten men with you! And you know werry well, indeed, that if the Arabs dreamed as 'ow you were 'ere, they'd wipe you out, just like that! There ain't a tribe in a 'undred miles o' this place that don't 'ate you! But 'ere you be, just like that!"

Hamdi Bey swaggered, and managed a thin laugh.

"Exactly—and here you be also," he mimicked. "You have a minute left, Nazarene, pray hard for a miracle from your god. Pray, indeed!" He turned and beckoned two of his men. "Your carbines! When I give you the word, shoot this fat infidel through the head."

"A miracle?" repeated Solomon, speaking now in Arbi that all might understand.

He turned his eyes upon the sand and held out his hand. Lower, and lower he stooped, while all watched him intently, wondering at his posture. Then, swiftly, he plunged his pudgy hand into the sand. For a moment he remained thus, motionless—then whipped out the revolver he had taken from English Miriam.

There was a gasp from every throat; the thing seemed a miracle in every truth. One man close was not impressed. As the revolver was flung up, Hamdi Bey threw himself forward to intervene.

Sargent launched himself.

He struck bodily against the Turk, drove home his fist, sent Hamdi staggering, and followed up with his advantage. Twice again he landed heavy blows, before the soldiers piled upon him and dragged him down. Through the turmoil he heard Solomon's voice.

"Dang it! Now you've gone and done it and no mistake!"

Then Sargent realized his frightful error, realized that in another instant Hamdi Bey would have been shot, except for his intervention. It took the heart out of him and he struggled no more. He had ruined John Solomon's last desperate play. He lay quiet and let himself be fast bound, and dragged again to his feet.

Solomon had been swiftly overpowered and was being bound likewise. Hamdi Bey, wiping blood from his face, groped for his revolver, but it had fallen from the open holster. He shouted at his men.

"Shoot them—shoot the dogs!"

The men about Solomon and the American fell back. The others lifted their carbines. From Hamdi Bey broke a savage laugh.

"Now die, Suleiman!" he cried.

"Suleiman dies not!" rang out another voice, hard and powerful.

Hamdi Bey whirled around and stood like a man paralyzed. From his men broke a low cry, a gasp of fear; they froze in their tracks.

At the corner of the remaining segment of wall was standing an Arab, who, to judge from his attire, from the princely fillet about his haik and the gorgeous sword at his waist, was a sheik or emir. His bearded features were grave and stately. At sight of this man, whose appearance seemed nothing short of black magic, a terrible cry burst from the staring Hamdi Bey.

"Ibn Rashid!"

That cry intensified the terror of his men.

"He who moves, dies!" cried out the Arab. "Look about you, Osmanli, and move not!"

The Turks glanced about and trembled. Movement appeared around them, along the crest of the mud wall, among the heaps of mounded sand. Men were there, wild tribesmen of the desert, men who hated the Turks with a deadly and ferocious enmity.

"Bind Hamdi Bey, release these two men, take to your horses—and go free."

Full well these Turks knew they were cornered, outnumbered, surrounded, and in their hearts was frightful panic. That apparent miracle of Solomon's had shaken them completely. They did not pause to reflect that the emir and his men had stolen up while they themselves were intent upon the scene inside the ancient walls; they surged forward in a frantic haste to obey and save their lives.

A curse on his lips, Hamdi Bey swooped forward to retrieve his revolver, but that moment of petrified astonishment had undone him. Two of his own men plunged upon him, others aided, and presently he was dragged to his feet. Others of the Turks hastened to release the two bound men. The figure of English Miriam was disregarded.

Ibn Rashid looked at the Turks. "Go!" he said. "Leave your rifles."

They hurriedly flung down their arms and broke for their waiting horses, while from the encircling Arabs cackled jeers and jests to hasten their flight. The stately emir turned to Solomon and gave him the marhaba or sign of greeting.

"Peace be with you, Suleiman," he said. These words, rarely given to any non-Moslem, signified much. Solomon responded with the usual formula, then broke into English.

"And upon you, peace. Werry 'appy I am to see you, too! I'd

begun to think as 'ow you wasn't going to show up. This 'ere, sir, is me werry good friend, Nur-ed-Din ibn Saleh, the Egyptian."

The emir gave Sargent a keen, piercing glance, and smiled slightly.

"I have heard of this Egyptian merchant. Allah further his aims, since he is your friend! I have kept the appointment. All that I have is yours, Suleiman. What do you wish of me?"

Solomon placidly brought out his clay pipe and began to whittle tobacco into it. As for Sargent, he gazed in little eagerness at this ruler of the Nejd, who had ridden across Northern Arabia to keep an appointment here with John Solomon. Gradually, and not for the first time, there was in upon him a realization of the tremendous ability of the little Cockney—the ability to see ahead, to plan future events, to make them subservient to his will.

"If you'll take a look at the document in the tunic of Hamdi Bey," said Solomon in Arbi, "you'll see why I have had you come to this place."

Ibn Rashid strode up to Hamdi. For a moment the two men stood eye to eye, and in the ashen face of the Turk there was ghastly dread; the bearded face of the emir was implacable and stern. Between these men lay something that had not yet come to light.

Then the Arab thrust his hand into the tunic of Hamdi Bey and brought to light the letter from the Senussiyeh. He paused and glanced through it. His face changed; he thrust the rolled vellum into his breast and looked at the Turk.

"Hamdi Bey!" His voice rolled across the sand. "Three months ago you slew by vile treachery two men of the tribe Chammar, who were my kinsmen. From them you took a woman of the tribe El Goursan who was destined to my harem, and made of her a thing of shame. Is this not true?"

The figure of the Turk quivered slightly. Then he drew a deep breath.

"O son of a bearded father," he returned with cool scorn, "it is true. Allah be my witness, I have made a scorn of the name of Rashid!"

"Spoken like a man," said the lordly emir, not without a flicker of justification. "And for those words you shall die as a man, instead of by the cross I had sworn would hold you!" He swept up his arm, threw an order at his men. "Four of you take this man out to the desert beyond the trees and slay him with your rifles."

Four Arabs swooped down from the high mounds of sand, laid hold upon the Turk and were gone with him. The emir turned to Solomon.

"Suleiman, I dare not linger here an hour, even to break bread with you. For this letter I give you thanks; once again I am in your debt. Do you come with me to Nejd?"

Solomon removed his pipe and slowly shook his head.

"No. Leave us six camels, if you can spare them, and four men. We go to Port Said."

"It shall be done. The camels are being brought up—we brought six swift runners as you requested of the best Chammar brand. We ourselves have horses." Ibn Rashid made a swift gesture toward the recumbent, gagged figure of English Miriam, and into the eyes of the woman came a sudden terrible fear. "Who is this?"

"My prisoner," responded Solomon calmly.

"We must go at once, and so must you, before those Turks send pursuit. Farewell and Allah bless thee."

"And cover thee with protection," rejoined Solomon. His hand touched that of the Arab—then the latter strode away.

Across the sand rolled the volleyed crack of rifles.

Sargent stood as in a dream. He had one swift glimpse of Arabs mounting, caught sight of Ibn Rashid waving a hand to them, then men and beasts were gone along some way that dropped them almost instantly from sigh below the desert level. He was standing close with Solomon in the hot sunlight.

The little cockney knocked out his pipe.

"That's what I calls a werry good job," he stated. "And it

came near being a werry bad job indeed, just like that! Them 'ere camels will be up in no time, Mr. Sargent, and we'll get your loads aboard and be off. We ain't got no time to lose, as the old gent said when 'e lost 'is third."

Crossing the sand Solomon stooped over English Miriam and loosened her gag and the bonds that tied her wrists and ankles. He stood looking down her as she sat up.

"And now, miss—what?"

The woman shrugged—a hopeless, dreary gesture of finality.

"Nothing," she said in English. "I'm done for. Go on and kill me, or leave me to the Turks, as you like."

Solomon emitted a wheezy sigh.

"Miss, you ain't been an' lived up to your reputation. You've fallen down 'ard. I'm werry sorry for you, but I'm a-goin' to kill English Miriam—it fair 'as to be done, miss! You're took your chances, and you pays the shot, as the old gent said—"

"I've failed. Go on." The woman looked up, a miserable futility stamped on her features. "I deserve all you can do."

"Werry good—then English Miriam is dead, just like that!" said Solomon cheerfully. "Now, miss, if so be as you'd like to go to Port Said with us, mebbe I could use you. I'm establishin' a big orphanage up the coast a bit, for Armenian children. Seein' as 'ow you speaks the language of these parts, you could be mortal useful, if you want the chance to get away from them 'ere Senussiyeh an' turn over a new leaf. Speak up werry quick, miss! 'Cause why, them 'ere camels are roamin' and we're a-goin' away from 'ere in a 'urry."

The woman's eyes widened in slow, numbed comprehension.

"You—you mean it?" she fairly gasped.

"Yes, miss."

"Oh—God bless you!" Her features worked; suddenly, she plunged forward at his feet, dry sobs shaking her body, a flood of incoherent words pouring from her lips. Solomon turned and gestured toward the American.

"Me and Mr. Sargent is a-goin' to roust them camels," he said. "We'll be back in no time, miss, so you be ready."

They left her there, stretched on the sand, convulsed with sobs, and walked toward what had been the entrance of the walled space. There Sargent saw a file of camels coming rapidly over the horizon. He touched Solomon's arm.

"You're really giving her a chance. Aren't you risking a lot?"

"Charity don't consider no risks, as the Good Book says," and Solomon chuckled wheezily. "A werry good job it is as she didn't know you was a Christian, Mr. Sargent. 'Owsomever all's well that ends well, as the old gent said when 'e buried 'is second. Dang it, I wish I 'ad a shave."

And John Solomon reflectively fingered his stubby chin.

ABOUT THE AUTHOR

H. BEDFORD-JONES is a Canadian by birth, but not by profession, having removed to the United States at the age of one year. For over twenty years he has been more or less profitably engaged in writing and traveling. As he has seldom resided in one place longer than a year or so and is a person of retiring habits, he is somewhat a man of mystery; more than once he has suffered from unscrupulous gentlemen who impersonated him—one of whom murdered a wife and was subsequently shot by the police, luckily after losing his alias.

The real Bedford-Jones is an elderly man, whose gray hair and precise attire give him rather the appearance of a retired foreign diplomat. His hobby is stamp collecting, and his collection of Japan is said to be one of the finest in existence. At present writing he is en route to Morocco, and when this appears in print he will probably be somewhere on the Mojave Desert in company with Erle Stanley Gardner.

Questioned as to the main facts in his life, he declared there was only one main fact, but it was not for publication; that his life had been uneventful except for numerous financial losses, and that his only adventures lay in evading adventurers. In his younger years he was something of an athlete, but the encroachments of age preclude any active pursuits except that of motoring. He is usually to be found poring over his stamps, working at his typewriter, or laboring in his California rose garden, which is one of the sights of Cathedral Cañon, near Palm Springs.